ACIDULOUS

FOR NOT EVEN BLOOD, IS THICKER THAN ACID

ESTEVAN AYON

AYON PUBLISHING

Copyright © [2026] by [Estevan Ayon]

All rights reserved.

No portion of this book may be reproduced in any form without written permission from the publisher or author, except as permitted by U.S. copyright law.

TO MY BROTHER

Your life was cut short, but your spirit lives within your family.

CONTENTS

CHAPTER 1

Fairy Tales Have No Happy Endings

I met Henry when my sorority pranked his fraternity. He asked me out while wiping green slime from his curly brown hair, and I loved that he had a sense of humor—so I said yes. It didn't take long for us to fall for each other, and before we knew it, four years had passed. We got engaged and moved in together. Pretty fairytale type of thing, right?

In a way yes, yet we weren't perfect. Like any couple we had our arguments, but we had one rule. After any bickerment we had to tell each other a stupid joke. It always worked and we'd be nothing but smiles after any feud. That was why I truly believed that we would last forever. I mean those who laugh together stay together, right? Wrong!

Exactly one year ago, a part of me died—a piece of my soul I know I'll never get back. Even now, when I close my eyes, I'm pulled back to that hot summer day that changed everything. It started so simply, so insignificantly... the day I forgot my *Quiche Lorraine* for the back-to-school staff orientation.

I had just pulled up to the school when I noticed that I didn't have the quiche. Luckily, I had left an hour earlier to set up for the party, so wasting no time, I hopped onto the freeway and began the thirty minute commute back home. I recall being a little aggravated as I drove back home, but I figured that a well fed staff will be happier than a staff with decorations.

Like always, my humor eased my frustration, and I even laughed a little. Sadly, that was the last time I would ever laugh, because of the cruel joke life itself was about to play on me. Oh, how I wish I could erase that vivid day from my life because the moment I pulled into the neighborhood, I knew something was wrong.

I immediately noticed that Henry's green *Mustang* was parked in the driveway. How odd, I thought. Maybe he had also forgotten something at home? Wouldn't that have been ironic? I remember smiling at the idea as I stepped inside.

"Henry?" I called out. "Where are you?" I checked the living room and kitchen. He wasn't there. As I walked down the hallway, I heard soft R&B music playing. Our bedroom door was shut.

It hurts me to my core to even think back on what happened next. There I was, hitting "record" on my live feed, thinking I would catch my adorable fiancé dancing to his music. I wanted to capture his cuteness for the world...but that is not what happened.

As soon as I opened the bedroom door, my heart shattered. Even now, the memory makes me feel sick. What I saw scarred me for life. My sister, Jazmine, was in my bed— with my fiancé, and all my friends and family were witnessing it on my live stream.

I lost my mind. I threw up on the floor, and still, they didn't notice me. So I left. I ran out of the house and dove into my car. I drove to a nearby park, where I cried—really cried—for over an hour. It wasn't until I got a phone call from work that I finally understood what had just happened.

As clearly as if it were yesterday, I remember reaching for my phone, but I couldn't even answer it. Notifications flooded my screen.

Bing. Bing. Bing. Bing, Bing, Bing!

They wouldn't stop. My eyes scanned the messages: *This can't be real. Oh my God. Her sister? Poor her. Her life is over.*

That was when the severity of my new reality truly hit me. It wasn't just that people had seen my live feed—my Instagram had saved the video to my profile... for everyone to see. A wave of panic crashed over me.

I vaguely remember my hands being drenched in sweat as I tried to delete the post, but before I could, more messages started pouring in, messages that still haunt me to this day.

That's what you get for treating Jazmine like a baby. What did you expect? You may have degrees, but that doesn't take away your stupidity.

I was crushed to see those types of remarks offending me for something that wasn't my fault so I rushed to delete the video, but it was in vain. It had been viewed over four hundred times. Still I removed it, but the damage was done.

Looking back at that moment, it was the exact time that I went from a well respected person to the person people felt sorry for. I was no longer Lucianna, the hard working woman who took care of her eight year old sister Jazmine at the tender age of sixteen, when her parents died. Oh no, that was far gone.

I was now the naïve woman who had never disciplined her younger sister for any of her wrongdoings. Apparently, Jazmine had quite the reputation. I would have never known if it hadn't been for all the people who later reached out to see how I was "doing."

They claimed to be "supporting me," when in reality all they did was speak negatively about Jazmine, and about my naïveté.

Oh, she was always jealous of you. She slept with two married men. How could you not see this coming? Were you blind?

I knew the people who came with gossip didn't have the best intentions, but in a strange way, I'm grateful for them. They helped me understand one thing: My heart had broken because of what Henry did, but my soul was shattered because of Jazmine. I had always believed we shared a bond that ran deeper than blood...but I had been so stupidly wrong.

Now, a year later, I see everything clearly—the red flags I missed, or chose to ignore. She was envious of me. Growing up, she always saw herself as the ugly duckling. That's how others saw her too, or at least, that's what she believed. But to me, she was always beautiful in her own way. She just never saw it.

She simply viewed herself as the tiny girl with alopecia. She was born with alopecia and never had a single hair on her body, but to me that didn't take away from her beauty. If anything, it made her other features stand out. Like her eyes. Deep, dark emerald eyes that, in certain light, looked almost pitch black.

They glue you right into her round shaped face, and her tiny lips that are so cute and shaped like Betty Boop's. Her skin is absolutely a beautiful shade of deep brown and it is flawless. It always looks like it is glowing. Truthfully, when she would come home as a teen crying how all the boys thought she was ugly I never understood why, but now I do.

I was viewing Jazmine through the loving eyes of a sister, almost a mother figure. That wasn't the case for her classmates. See Jazmine didn't start wearing a "real" wig till she was about eighteen years old because we didn't have the money to afford one. Thus, throughout her high school life she was that "weird, short bald girl."

In retrospect I should have done more to support how she felt during those times, but I couldn't understand because I truly saw her as beautiful.

I thought the other students were just jealous of her. Especially when they created that nasty fake profile of her online calling her every name in the book, *bald bitch, no boobs, skinny twig, no ass, brown girl.*

I thought it was envy. I remember telling her, "Oh they are just mad that they don't have your unique beauty." Jazmine did not buy my words, and did not want to go back to school until the girls were gone.

"I'll never go back to school unless they are removed!" That scared me. I didn't want her to drop out of high school, so I asked my best friend Francisco, who was studying cybersecurity at the time, to discover exactly who the culprits were.

He did. It was a group of four girls. They all got expelled thanks to me threatening to sue the school. However, they claimed that Jazmine deserved it because she had given a blow job to one of the girl's boyfriends in the school restroom. I didn't believe it for a second, but now I know it was the truth.

She is not a good person, and I feel so stupid for always trying to see the best in her. Even after catching Jazmine with Henry, I still gave her the benefit of the doubt. In my mind, I convinced myself Henry had somehow tricked her—maybe even groomed her from a young age.

All of those thoughts ran through my head, and it wasn't until later that day that I realized none of it was true. I was at my best friend Francisco's house when she showed up—unexpected and uninvited. I wasn't going to speak to her, but I wanted to save our relationship, so I caved and agreed. Even though my gut told me not to.

I should have listened, because what she told me destroyed any hope of decency I still believed she had. My stomach still turns when I think about that moment. "You jealous, manipulative bitch." "Why did you post that online?" "Everyone thinks it was my fault." "Some of my friends aren't even talking to me anymore." "How could you!" "I hate you!"

I was left stunned and didn't know how to react. Thankfully my best buddy knew what to do. He got right in the middle of us and stood up for me. He told her off to the point where she was crying.

He told her, *I am not going to stand down any longer! You have mistreated Lucianna since the day I met you ten years ago! You are nothing but a jealous brat! You have always been jealous that people turn their heads twice to look at her. You are envious that she is prettier and more successful than you!*

It irks you that she is only 34, yet she is already the principal of a school! On top of that you probably hate that she is beautiful and you are nothing but a fraud. Look at you. You've had a boob job, a bbl and a nose job! Lucianna has had nothing of the sort.

She naturally has an hourglass figure, and has no need for any enhancements, and another thing. I will be that person and tell you straight up to your face that you will never have her long dark hair! Your wigs will not replicate that. Plus her skin glows better than yours!

At that point I was crying too. I couldn't stand to hear anymore fighting, so I rushed back inside to Francisco's apartment, but before I reached the door Jazmine had the audacity to call me out.

"Aren't you going to defend me from your faggot friend?" That was the last straw. I walked up to her and punched her straight in the mouth. She dropped, stunned, her wig slipping to the side.

"You'll pay for this, Lucianna!" "Oh—and by the way... I've been sleeping with Henry for over six months." With that, she left.

And that brings me to the present. Exactly three hundred and sixty-five days have passed since I last saw Jazmine and Henry. A lot has happened in those twelve months. I never went back home. I sold my part of the house that I shared with Henry to the bank, and I got an apartment.

I relocated fifty miles away, and I took a job as a high school literacy coach. Sure it was not the same pay as being the principal of a school, but it still paid more than being a teacher. Without the added stress of both jobs.

Which is what I needed. Less stress, and more time to build the shattered pieces of my soul that were still scattered around me. Not even a trip around the sun has healed me, but I have gained some optimism during this time. I've learned that it was not my fault that I was stabbed in the back.

It is all Jazmine's and Henry's fault. But their actions don't define who I am—and I'm grateful I finally understand that. See, for the first six months after it happened, I hated myself. I saw myself as a failure. I couldn't even look at my reflection. I felt like a monster who didn't deserve to be loved. But not anymore.

Now I saw myself clearly again. I was a beautiful woman. My brown skin was radiant. My long black hair was thick and full . My big hazel eyes were soft and dreamy. My natural red lips looked painted on, and my body was full in all the right places. Gosh dang it, I was me again!

As I took it all in, a small smile formed on my face, followed by a quiet sense of renewed hope. I was smiling—something that had become rare after everything I had been through. For nearly ten months, I had turned to stone.

I had become a bitter person who did not give two shits about anyone else. But that bitterness only did more damage to me. I was hurting myself more and more by being that way, and if it wasn't for Francisco, I might have never realized it.

It took my best friend sitting me down, and having an intervention with me to make me see that if I didn't change my attitude, I could lose him too. That was the epiphany that I needed to understand that I was not this "new person" who was always mad. I was a cheerful gal.

The truth is, I am kind by nature. It may have taken me an entire year to realize that, but now I understand. I can't live my life hating others because in doing so, I was only poisoning myself. And that's why I decided to read the letter. A letter that Jazmine had sent.

I wasn't sure how, but she found out where I worked and emailed me a letter. Instead of deleting it, I read it.

Dear Lucianna,

It has been a year since I last saw you sister. I really miss you, and I feel awful for what I did, and what I put you through. I really do miss you sister, and if I could take back everything that I did I would. If I could turn back time and do it all over again I would. I should have told you when I started falling for Henry. At last, I can't turn back time, but I can try to be a better person. I want to meet you sister. I want to tell you something in person before you hear it from the grapevine. Can we please meet somewhere? I am free this coming Saturday at 5p.m. Would that work for you?

Your sister,

Jazmine.

That was the letter that she emailed me one week ago. I know I should have talked to you before I responded, Francisco, but my emotions got the best of me and I wrote, "See you there." This is why I have to see her.

You don't have to go see her. She doesn't deserve you, Lucianna. Francisco, you know better than anyone that in order for me to fully heal I have to settle things with her. With Henry it is a lost cause, but Jazmine is my sister.

We only have each other. Plus my mother promised us to always be in each other's lives. Maybe this is a sign from my mom? A second chance to restart from zero?

Look, babe, I love you. I'm your number one supporter, but as your best friend, I have to call you out. This all sounds like bullshit. And I need you to know that I think it is total bullshit. I also wish you had told me the moment you got that email, not the day of the meeting.

That said... I'm here for you. Whatever you decide, just know I've got your back, okay? Francisco glared at me, his expression intense. His rosy lips were pressed tightly together, and his dark eyebrows nearly touched. He was serious. He wasn't the type to wrinkle his face unless he meant it.

Guilt settled in my chest. I hated putting all of this on him. Especially when he had been nothing but supportive through everything. If I'm being honest, his support showed me something I hadn't fully realized before. He was my family now. The brother I never had.

You mean the world to me, okay? I nodded my big bobble head and walked toward him. I wrapped my arms around his thin frame, so easily that my hands met at his back. I squeezed until he couldn't take it anymore, and just for laughs, I lifted him off the ground.

It must have looked ridiculous—him at 6'2, and me at 5'6. *Hey, you're going to crush me!* He laughed, looking down at me, his rounded brown eyes lighting up. *I'll agree to this, but only if I can drop you off at her place. I don't want her to know what kind of car you drive, just in case things go south, okay?*

Deal, but enough about me now. How was your date yesterday? *Shoot me now. All he wanted to do was talk about himself. He didn't even ask me a single question. I mean is it so hard to say, "and you?"*

Don't give it a second thought! You deserve better, and never settle for less than what you need. *Exactly, and the same goes to you, babe. Now, how about I make both of us a nice Cesar Salad, and if you still want to go to Jazmine's place after lunch I can drop you off. How does that sound?* I think that sounds like a good idea, but I get to wash the dishes, okay? *Deal.*

We spent the next hour eating and laughing together, and then it was time to make the nearly-hour drive back to the town where it had all happened. My body suddenly felt stiff, but I had to do this.

With weak knees I followed Francisco out the front door. *Are you sure you want to do this?* Yes. I faked a smile for him, but there was no fooling him. He just nodded, and put his hand on my shoulder as we got into his car.

My heart was beating like crazy the entire ride. I had not been back to that town since my heart was torn from my chest. Even to get my things. I had hired movers to do all of that for me.

I just couldn't bear going back, and even now as I see the exit sign to my old town I still feel a tad nauseous. *Exit 76 one mile away,* I turned involuntarily when the sign came up, and that caught Francisco's attention. *Lucianna, we can turn back right now if that is what you want?*

No, Francisco. I need to do this. This is more than just seeing my sister. It's about confronting the pain I've carried all this time. And more than that, I want to let go of the fear of what others might say about me. I want to be free of it all... so I can finally live my life in a healthy way. *Understood,* he said softly. *Well... here we go.*

He reached over and gently took my hand. It was comforting. A moment later, he exited the freeway and turned onto the familiar, bumpy road. We stopped at the sign, then made a left. The gas stations lining the street filled my view as we drove past them, heading deeper into a place I hadn't seen in a year.

Another stop sign. Another turn, and then Francisco turned right onto a street I knew all too well. The houses stretch out on either side of us. After a couple of seconds, we slowed again, then made one final left into the neighborhood where my sister was living. Our old family home.

We both owned that home, but I moved out of that house when I got engaged to Henry. My sister has lived there all her life, and I didn't mind it because she needed the stability. She has never been able to keep a job, and I never wanted for her to stress about where she was going to live.

That said, the taxes on it cost me about 5 thousand dollars a year. This would be the first year that I would not pay for them so hopefully she had money saved because if she did not then I would sell my part of the house to the bank.

That's the smile I want to see. I felt my face get hot. Francisco was looking at me with a big smile. He must have thought I was happy to be pulling up to my childhood home, but that wasn't the case.

I had a smile on my face because part of me wanted my sister to lose the house. She didn't deserve to live there freely. If it wasn't for me that house would have been lost when my parents died.

I worked two jobs and went to school full time to keep us in that home, but alas I am not here to fight. If I want to make amends with my sister, and properly heal I need to start thinking more positively. Think happy thoughts Lucianna.

I took a deep breath, and I visualised myself calmly on the beach. Immediately I began to feel at ease, and in perfect time because Francisco had just parked his car on the side of the street. It was time. I was right outside my home, my sister's house.

Everything looked exactly the same. I don't know why that surprised me. For some reason I thought she would have changed up the place, but no. Everything looked identical to when I last saw it. It was as if no time had passed.

The metal crusty looking fence surrounding the house was still losing its color. The house still had weeds outside of it. The dead cherry tree still had not been removed. The Christmas lights were still hung up even though

It was August. The cracked front window had yet to be replaced and the garage still had the dent from where Jazmine crashed her car into it while she was texting.

Are you ready? Francisco broke me out of my trance and I nodded my head yes. I took in a couple of more deep breaths and I unbuckled my seatbelt. *I will wait for you outside, okay?* No, I don't know how long I will be here for. Just got to the mall. I don't want you melting in the hot sun while you wait for me.

You sure? Yeah, and here is my *Starbucks* gift card. Buy yourself whatever you want. *Well a Quad Espresso in a Venti cup it is.* I"ll text you when I am ready to be picked up okay? *Got it, babe, and remember I am here for you.*

I know you are. I hugged Francisco, then slowly opened the car door and stepped out. He gave me a small wave before driving off. I was alone now. But I wasn't scared. As a matter of fact I felt brave.

It takes courage to face your fears and I was doing just that, so without further ado let's get this party started. I quietly opened the squealing fence, and I made my way up the driveway. I then weaved my way through all the weeds that had grown from the yard and I reached the front door.

I knocked three times since the ringer that was working perfectly just a year ago was hanging by a thread. *Knock, knock, knock.* "I'm coming." My body tensed up as my sister's hoarse deep voice filled my ear drums. Be brave, Lucianna. I reassured myself as the creaking wooden door opened.

"Lucianna!" "Sister!" "I am so happy that you came." I stared dumbfounded at Jazmine. She smiled at me. Her shiny veneers slightly blinded me. She had a luscious blond wig on and brightly painted eyebrows. Her makeup looked nice, and professionally done. I was confused.

Why had she dressed up to see me? She never cared to impress me before. "Come in." She said again, but this time she stepped out of the doorway. Ah, my answer soon came to me. She was celebrating.

She had a giant baby bump. The baby bump was almost as big as her. It looked like an iceberg ready to ram me as Jazmine reached over to hug me.

I gently moved to the side. Just because I came to see her did not mean that I did not have boundaries set. She took the hint and said, "Let's go to your old room and talk." I nodded and followed her inside.

As I walked through the door I noticed that she was not alone. Drinking champagne were her two best friends. Two ladies that I absolutely despised. They were the most judgemental people I had ever met. Back in the day I never understood why Jazmine was friends with them, but now I did.

However, they were the least of my concerns. Sitting right across from them and staring right at me with a stupid grin on his face was my ex, Henry. He was dressed in a suit and tie. His curly brown hair was combed to the side.

Hello, Lucianna. He silently said. My blood rushed to my face and I felt lightheaded. I immediately looked away, and continued to my room. It was apparent that this was some sort of baby shower, maybe even an engagement announcement? Everyone was dressed too nicely.

My head started spinning in circles. Why did I come back here? Should I leave? A million thoughts crossed my mind at that very second.

CHAPTER 2

The Wedding Announcement

I should have left—I know I should have. But I wanted to make some kind of peace with my sister. After all, she was the only direct blood I had left, and that meant something to me. Still, I hated that she hadn't met me alone, in private.

Well, Lucianna, I thought, she's pregnant by your ex. That made sense. They were forever tied together, so I understood why Henry was there, but her best friends? There was no need for them!

I started to feel agitated by Jazmine for being inconsiderate, but then it hit me, maybe they showed up unannounced? Was this a surprise baby shower or something? I mean they are all dressed so nicely.

Ah, it had to be that. That assumption made me feel better, and with a calmer mind I sat down on my old sunken bed. The same twin bed that I slept on for so many years. The wooden frame had chipped away drastically since I last used it, yet it was still comforting.

It reminded me of when my mom used to read to me before going to bed, and when my dad would come tuck me in after work. I'd stay up waiting for him, and then I would fake sleep when he came to tuck me in. "Lucianna?" Huh? I turned around surprised. I was so in my thoughts that I had almost forgotten what I was here for. "Are you feeling okay?"

Yeah, sorry. "I was just thinking about mom and dad. "I think of them every day that I am here, and that is why I really want for us to be okay." "I don't know how to start, so I'll just say what is on my mind." "Is that okay?" Wait. Let me close the door. I don't want Henry or your friends hearing our conversation.

Jazmine's eye slightly twitched. That had annoyed her, but she bit her tongue. As much as I hate to admit this, it brought me a bit of happiness to see my sister annoyed. I smiled and shut the door.

Okay, go ahead, Jazmine. "I'm sorry for betraying you." "I am sorry for embarrassing you." "I am sorry for TAKING your man." My stomach knotted up. She had emphasized the word "taking" by slightly raising her voice. Before I could react she continued.

"You are my sister." "I have missed you, and I love you." "I wish I had not fallen in love with Henry." "I really hate that, but what can I do?" "Please forgive me, Lucianna." I observed every single movement of her body as she stared at me. Her tiny lips quivered. Her eyes were locked on me. Even her left leg was shaking. She was nervous.

I could feel that she was genuinely sorry about what she did, but there was also a hint of arrogance and pride. She was not crying. Her voice had not cracked as she asked for forgiveness. It was clear that she was proud of having Henry to herself, and she wasn't sorry about that. That said, it was also apparent that she did not want to lose me. What to do?

I looked at her without saying a word for almost a minute, and then I came to a conclusion. I did not want to lose my sister. What was done was done. I would forgive her, but she wasn't going to be in my life like she was before. Things would have to change!

Never again, would I give her another cent. The days of seeing her daily were gone. The times of hearing her vent about her problems were in the past. If she wanted for us to have a relationship again then it had to be symbiotic. No more parasitism from her. I won't let her leech on to me again. "Sister, are you going to say something?"

Jazmine. I lowered my voice to almost a whisper. I forgive you. I love you too, but we can't return to how things were before. I am still healing, and in pain. "I understand." Just know that I will be with you in all the important moments.

We may only see each other a few times a year, but I will be there when you need me most. "I hope I can be there when you need me most too." Now both of her legs were shaking. With a trembling hand, I gently reached and touched her belly. When are you due? "I am due in two months." Congratulations. I said just as I felt a small kick coming from her belly. It made me smile brightly. At least something positive was coming out of this hell.

Do you know if it is a boy or a girl? "No, but today is my gender reveal-baby shower so I'll know soon." Is that why everyone is outside in the living room? "Yeah, I wanted you to be a part of this moment with me." "You really are special to me Lucianna." She looked at me with watery eyes.

I could sense her sincerity this time as she spoke, and I was thankful for it. Still, I was really ticked off that she indeed knew about the "gender reveal party" and still scheduled a meeting with me anyway—knowing damn well her friends would be there. But oh well. It didn't matter anymore.

What mattered was that my sister seemed genuinely sorry, and thankful that I was here. That was enough. Tears began to swell in my eyes. I tried to hold them back, but they spilled down my cheeks.

"I am so happy you are here, Lucianna," she said. "This special day would have meant shit if you weren't here." I smiled at my sister. "There's one more thing I need to tell you." Yeah? What is it? "I'm getting married in two weeks."

Married? The word hit me like a sledgehammer to the face. Time seemed to stand still. Just a year ago, I was supposed to be the one marrying him—the man my little sister was now about to marry. How could life be so cruel?

I did not know what to tell Jazmine, but it was too late to be mad at her. She had already betrayed me, and was pregnant by Henry. Plus I had already forgiven her for all of that. There was nothing that I could do to change the past, so I swallowed my pain once more and faked happiness for her.

I am ecstatic for you! "I knew you would be!" She was all smiles and she grabbed my hand and took me out of my room. "Okay, now where is the cake?" "I am ready to see what I will have!" She enthusiastically said as she guided me to the kitchen table. I pulled out a seat and sat down. At least she had the knowledge to know that I did not want to sit next to her friends or my trash of an ex.

"Here it is." I watched as she carefully took out a two tier cake that was frosted in almost a pitch black buttercream frosting. She carefully sat it down on the table in the living room, and then Henry came to her. He put his arm around her waist, and then looked back at me. This time I stared directly at him, and I smiled while holding up my middle finger to him. He quickly turned back around.

I felt proud of myself. For the past year all I wanted to do was flip him off, and show him that he was a piece of shit. I had finally done it, and automatically I felt a sense of relief flow through my body. I must have been smiling stupidly because Jazmine looked back at me and winked.

She probably thought I was having a blast being here. Oh if she knew what I had just done. Henry wouldn't tell her. I knew that for a fact. He always thought he was a "gentleman," psh. "Let's cut the cake!" Jazmine loudly said, interrupting my thoughts. *I am ready to record!* One of her obnoxious friends excitedly said. "Okay, here I go."

I stood up from my chair and came closer to the living room. I surprised myself. I was genuinely excited to see what Jazmine would be having. "Here goes." Jazmine slid the knife down the middle of the cake and pulled out a pink slice of cake.

Cries and cheers filled my ears. Henry and Jazmine kissed, and then her friends embraced her. It was sweet, and before I knew what I was doing I walked over and hugged her tightly.

Congratulations, make her an independent woman. "Just like her aunt." "Thank you for coming again." I smiled at Jazmine, but I had to go. I didn't want her thinking everything would go back to the way it was before because she was having a child.

Jazmine, it is time for me to go. "I understand, but before you do I have one last surprise." She dashed into the spare room, and I stepped back into the kitchen to wait. The room felt different now—too quiet, too still. That's when I felt Henry's eyes on me.

He didn't even have the balls to apologize. Coward. "Everyone, close your eyes," Jazmine called from behind the propped door. I turned and looked at her friends. Their eyes were closed—Henry's too. But I wasn't here to play along. I kept mine open... and saw the horror before anyone else did.

From the vanity mirror in the guest room I could see the monstrosity that Jazmine was committing. She was changing into my wedding dress! The dress that I had custom made for my special day. It was a large Cinderella style wedding dress, and she made it look like trash.

The train of the dress was long and dragged all the way past the floor. The bodice of the dress was very tight and it would not go fully over Jazmine's implanted chest. The puffy sleeves looked like they were suffocating Jazmine's large shoulders. The back of the crystal embroidered dress was only a quarter of the way zipped up because of her tummy.

This was too much. I had to get out of here, but I would not make a scene. I was beyond that. I would not give my selfish bitch of a sister the drama or attention that she was so desperately seeking. Instead while everyone still had their eyes closed, and before she had the chance to walk out, I left the house. I quietly closed the door behind me as I tasted the salt in my mouth.

My tears were coming down hard as I sped walked down the driveway. I had to get out before they noticed the reason as to why I left. I had to call Francisco. I pulled out my phone, and to my utter relief I didn't have to call him. He was waiting for me down the street. He saw me and started the car up.

I ran inside, and he didn't wait twice to drive off. We drove in silence for a good twenty minutes until we reached a small town which was the half-way point between my old town and my new one.

There Francisco exited the freeway and eventually pulled up to a *Denny's Diner.* My guilty pleasure. *What did she do to you, Lucianna?* He wiped a tear off my cheek. His hands felt smoother than mine. It made me smile.

There is that beautiful smile. Let's go inside and order something. Tell me everything that happened. I nodded and got out of the car. We entered the *Denny's* and were quickly seated. It was pretty empty. The dinner rush had yet to start. Good. I did not want to be around people.

Can I get you two started with something to drink? I"ll have a pink lemonade, *and you sir? I want a coke, light on the ice. I'll bring that out for you two.*

Mu'um, we are also ready to order. Francisco added before the waitress left. *What can I get you guys? Two Grand Slams, please.*

The waitress took our order and left. I told Francisco everything that had happened. He was so mad that laugh lines creased his Botox-filled face. I felt bad for stressing him out like that, but he was the only person I could talk to.

You need to cut her out of your life, right now. Change your email, your phone number—everything. She isn't your family anymore. I really want to, but I can't bring myself to do it. Francisco... I see so much of my parents in her.

You see your parents in her, but they are not her. You embodied what your parents were. I hate to tell you this, but she is not a good person. She has some serious issues, and she is using you to make herself feel better. That is diabolical. That is ruining your life.

You are getting out of her life until she seeks help. Buzz, buzz, buzz, my phone went off. I didn't even have to look at my phone to know who was texting me. I opened the message. *What did she text, babe?* Even Francisco knew.

I am so sad you didn't get to see my dress Lucianna, but my wedding is on August 1. I want you to be one of my maid of honors. Please tell me if you can, or at least come to my wedding. I know our lives won't be the same, but this is a special moment in my life and I want you to be there for me. Please let me know.

I am blocking her right now. Francisco took my phone from my hand. I didn't try to get it back. "Excuse me, I happened to overhear you two talking, and I think you shouldn't block your sister." I looked behind Francisco. A friendly looking young man was trying to get our attention.

"I kind of overheard your entire conversation without meaning to." "I'm sorry." Francisco turned around and raised an eyebrow at the guy. He was visibly annoyed, but he would let me decide how to react. It's okay. I told him with a warm smile.

The man nodded his head up and down, acknowledging that we were okay with hearing him out. He began to speak, but it was hard to pay attention to what he was saying because he kind of took my breath away.

I surprised myself. I wasn't one to get airheaded by someone's appearance, but this guy was super handsome. He had an incredibly chiseled jawline. His hair was as dark as a moonless night. His eyes were light brown, and he was pretty fit.

What was going on with me? I had not found anyone attractive in over a year. My face felt flush, and a wave of shyness flowed through me as his deep voice penetrated my ear drums.

"I don't want you guys to think I am some superstitious individual, but I think I was put in this specific spot to tell you to not lose your sister." *Uh huh.* Francisco groaned. "I am sure whatever she did to you is beyond terrible, but don't lose that strand that connects you two."

"Remember you don't have to like her to still love her." "You don't have to be friends, but just be there for the important moments in life." I stared at the man as he spoke. He looked innocent and kind. The freckles on his cheeks gave him a hint of childlike purity.

What makes you so knowledgeable on the subject matter? A visibly annoyed Francisco told him. "My brother died two years ago." "We were not on speaking terms, and I regret it every day of my life."

"We never could stand each other, but he reached out to me on his wedding day and I never responded back." "I wish I could turn back time." My stomach flipped upside down. This had to be some sort of sign to not completely cut my sister out.

"Anyway that is all I wanted to say." "I hope you two enjoy your meal." "Oh and one more thing, you are absolutely beautiful." With that he smiled and headed out the door. I was left dumbfounded, but Francisco knew exactly what to do.

Babe, I don't know what just happened, but you need to get that man's number! The entire time that he was talking, you were staring at him like a dog looking at a piece of meat! My cheeks burned. Francisco let out a giggle.

Go ask for his number or I'll ask for you. I can't do that Francisco! I haven't been with anyone since Henry. *And that fucker is getting married in two weeks! You know what, I am not wasting time.*

Francisco jumped out of the booth and rushed to the stranger. He was out the door before I could stop him. This couldn't be happening. I was sure that he would reject me. A young guy like him wouldn't want anything with a 34 year old like me.

He couldn't be older than 25! Ugh. *She is over there trying to sink into the booth.* Francisco laughed as he walked over with the man. "Hi, your friend told me you wanted my phone number?" "I am flattered, and I would love to give it to you."

"I am Jake by the way." I am Lucianna. I said while giving Francisco a look of murder. That made Jake laugh. "That is a beautiful name." "Mind adding your number on my phone?" He handed me his phone and I handed him mine. "Thank you, I'll text you this evening."

With that he left once more and I was left with a burning face, and a laughing Francisco. I am going to kill you! *Hey, I only did what is best for you, and look, you got a phone number from a young guy. You cougar, you!*

For some reason that instigated a laughing spell on me. Oh yeah, this cougar is ready to go on the prowl! *Everyone better be careful because Lucianna is back on the hunt, and she is a ten out of ten.* You are so silly Francisco. You are always making me feel like I am some sort of beauty queen.

Lucianna, look I know looks are not the only important thing in life, but babe you are extremely beautiful. To top it all off you are sweet, kind, intelligent and forgiving. You deserve to get back out there!

Francisco reached over and gently took my hand. It was soothing—enough to ease my jitters. I exhaled slowly. You're right, sweetie. I told him. I deserve to open myself back up, and Jake is correct too. *How?* I don't need to like my sister to still love her. *Oh.*

I don't want to have regrets if something happens to her, so I will attend her wedding. That said, I won't have a relationship with her, but I will be there for her when she has important moments in her life. However, I do not know if I want her to be in my life when I have special moments. I guess time will tell.

Like I told you before, whatever you decide I will support. Thank you sweetie, I told him as I took the last bite of my burger. *But what I won't support is how slow you eat!* He joked. I know, I know, but I am finished now. I gave him a little wink.

Shall we head out? Yes, let's go buddy. We headed out of *Denny's,* and Francisco dropped me back off at home. I was in my pj's before I knew it. I was glad to be home, and I also felt happy that today had happened.

At least for now I felt like there was less weight on my shoulders concerning Jazmine, and to put a cherry on top to my day, Jake, texted! *Hi, Lucianna. This is Jake. Do you want to play 20 questions to get to know each other?*

I felt butterflies in my tummy. Should I respond right away or wait a little? Hmmm. No, I needed to respond now. If I was going to start dating people again, I did not want to play any little teenage games. If the person takes a while to respond with no warning then they are not for me.

Well here goes nothing. *That sounds perfect Jake. I'll start the game. How old are you?* Message sent. The message bubbles started flashing immediately. He was on. That was a good sign. It meant that he was dedicating time to me. I appreciated that.

I am 26 years old. My birthday was last week actually. How old are you, and what is your favorite food? Okay, so he is eight years younger than me. That wasn't too bad. Plus, if he was mature then it shouldn't matter, I hoped.

My favorite food is tacos, but my favorite "to go" food is hamburgers. What do you do for work? Message sent. Once more the messaging bubbles appeared again. I would be lying if I said that didn't make me happy. I was feeling like a little schoolgirl.

I was sure I looked just as silly as one too, but who cares. I felt good and that is all that mattered. *Oh, I had a feeling you liked hamburgers.* Jake added a little wink emoji at the end of the message.

I almost dropped my phone from laughing so hard, but I composed myself and continued reading his message. *I have my own bakery. I opened it up last year. I specialize in famous desserts from around the world. What type of music do you like? Do you have a current favorite song?*

I don't know what I had imagined, but Jake owning a bakery was not it. That shocked me, but in a positive way. That was a sweet profession. I respected that, and it made me more curious to learn about him.

My favorite song right now is an old Spanish song from the late 80s called Asi Fue. My taste in music varies. I don't have a particular style. What about you? What is your current favorite song, and musical genre? I hit send, and lo and behold, five minutes of texting had become thirty.

Time was flying, but before I invested more time in talking to him, I needed to know what his intentions were. I was a tad nervous asking him, but as a grown woman I needed to know.

Jake, I know this is a forward question, but what exactly are you looking for? I will be up front and tell you that I haven't dated in over a year. I am not sure what I am looking for, but it is not a hookup. That much I can tell you. Sent. I set my phone down and took a deep breath.

CHAPTER 3

Butterflies

I felt kind of silly asking such a direct question, but at the end of the day, if I was going to start dating again, I wanted to feel like I was in the driver's seat. That desire didn't come from nowhere—it came from what Henry put me through. What he did really traumatized me. For crying out loud, I truly believed we were doing so well, but look how that ship sailed.

In retrospect, when I think back on us, I realize I may have mistaken comfort for something deeper. I assumed things were well simply because we were always laughing and having fun, but now I see that wasn't enough. I never asked Henry if he was truly happy.

I didn't think it was important because I felt a positive energy between us, but now I know. I have to ask the hard questions. Especially when times seem good. Even if it means being blunt. That said, it is not like I want to jump into a relationship right now. That is far from my mind. All I want to do is make sure that I am not someone's sex toy.

Bubbles typing. Before I would ever think of getting into someone's bed I would want to get to know them as a person. Don't worry we are on the same page. Also, I value your direct approach to this. It will lead to a lot of unnecessary headaches. Now that we have all that cleared, what was the last concert you went to?

Perfect answer mister, perfect answer. I was giddy. I was glad that we were on the same page, and it took a small pressure off my chest. Now I could go back to texting Jake without worrying about any drama.

Which in turn allowed me to really open up to him because I didn't see our texting as a pressure sort of thing, but more of a friend that could possibly become more. It was nice, and I am quite embarrassed to say this, but I fell asleep around 12 a.m. with my phone in my hand texting Jake.

I awoke the next day with a dead phone, and a smile on my face. I had agreed to have breakfast with him. Our breakfast date was set for 9:00 a.m. at the *Denny's* where we had met, and based on the amount of sunlight entering my room I had a good two hours to get ready. It couldn't be any later than 7:00 a.m.

Perfect. This would give me more than enough time to get my morning routine out of the way. I was thankful for that because if I don't follow my routine, my entire day feels thrown off. With that in mind, it was time to get out of bed, but first things first, I needed to charge my phone and text Francisco.

I wanted to make sure he knew where I was going, because you just never know these days. It's better to be safe than sorry.

With that settled, I plugged my phone into the charger by my bed and headed to the restroom. I turned the water to lukewarm and washed my face. This woke me up fully, and I examined myself. More specifically my face. I had noticed the first hint of fine lines under my eyes about three months ago.

It made me sad in a way, but also proud at the same time. Not everyone has the luxury of getting older. I know that first hand, but at the same time it is sad to see your youth fade right before your eyes.

It's okay, though. I will enjoy the process to its fullest, while at the same time taking care of myself and aging gracefully. That, unfortunately, is harder than it seems. Honestly, I've probably aged two years with all the drama I've been through this past year.

Sigh. I rubbed my face in pity—but no, I shouldn't be doing that. *Snap out of it, Lucianna.* Shaking the thought off, I grabbed my toothbrush and began to brush my teeth. This was probably my favorite part of my morning routine, because it made me feel clean instantly—which is always a good feeling.

With that done, I finished up in the bathroom and headed to the living room for my yoga session, and boy did I feel stiff today. Probably from sleeping slightly up, but graciously after a forty-minute yoga stretch I felt as limber as a feather.

With a relaxed body and a clear mind, it was time to text Jazmine back. I picked my phone up cautiously—I did not want to do this, but I didn't want to have regrets in life. I took a breath, trying to make peace with it. At least, after her wedding, I wouldn't have to see her for a good while. Besides, it's not like I would have to stay at the wedding long.

That said, I sure as hell wouldn't be her bridesmaid. I had made up my mind. Alright—now it was time to text her. *Thank you for the invitation. Please send me the wedding invite either here virtually, or to this address.* I gave her Francisco's address.

I didn't want her to have mine, and I was sure he wouldn't mind. *I am happy for you Jazmine, but unfortunately I won't be able to be your bride's maid. Don't worry I will still be there for you, on your big day. Sent.* I put my phone down. My hands were clammy from my nerves, but I felt good.

A pressure had been taken off my chest, and with that taken care of I opened my closet. Immediately the smell of lavender perfume from the freshener that I had in there hit my nostrils. It was a nice soothing smell that made me feel at ease every time that I stepped foot in my closet.

Ah, I breathed in a deep breath as I walked over to my dresses. Today was going to be a hot one, and I wanted to wear something light. *Hmm*, should I wear the fancy dress that I bought for a party that I never wore, or should I go for the plain and comfortable white dress that I usually wore for work?

Hmm, I pondered a bit, but then an idea entered my mind. If Jake did not like me at my normality then he wasn't worth it. Plain it is, and if he wanted to see me fancier than he had to earn that! *Haha*, I giggled to myself as I pulled out the polyester white dress.

Now, flats, or heels? Or what about neither? My black high top vans caught my eye. I grabbed them and headed to the large mirror that was by my door. There I put on the dress and shoes, and I examined myself. The dress fit snugged in all the right places. It also gave the illusion that my waist was smaller than what it was, and it complimented my hips very well.

Now how should I do my hair? In a ponytail or down? Definitely in a ponytail. That way I wouldn't have to comb it as much. I pulled my long black hair into a ponytail and smiled. All that was missing was a hint of my signature burgundy lipstick that helped my features pop out. I applied the color and my look was complete.

I felt pretty, but was it even worth going on the date with Jake? I mean he is twenty six years old. He could go out with someone his age. Should I cancel our breakfast together? I walked over to my bed and laid down to think.

I closed my eyes and everything that had happened to me the past year flashed before my eyes. I had gone through so much. I was not a quitter.

I was beautiful and kind. Plus I wasn't about to put my self worth in any man or anyone ever again.

At worst I would get a friend from this, so I am going to have breakfast with Jake. Feeling better I went to the kitchen and grabbed my keys, and I left the apartment. I walked to the elevator and into the car garage.

There I found my car and put the GPS on to the *Denny's. Twenty-four minutes from here.* Not too bad of a drive, but before I got going I needed to turn on the AC. It was only 8:25 in the morning, but I could already feel the heat of the day.

Oh summer, I love you, but I hate you. *Buzz, buzz, buzz.* I glanced over at my phone. Francisco was calling. I stuck an earbud in. *Hello, Lucianna, you be careful okay? Don't do anything that can put you in danger. Let me know if you two decide to go anywhere after breakfast, okay?*

I will Francisco, but don't worry I promise it is only breakfast. *Alright, well let me know how everything goes, and have fun babe.* I will, bye sweetie. Suddenly, I felt really lucky. Francisco might be the only person that I had in my life, but that was something. I was beyond grateful because not everyone has that.

I guess I truly was blessed. Sometimes it might not seem that way considering what I have gone through, but I am healthy and I am loved. I have to remember that more, but enough of that love dubby stuff. It was time to head out. Wasting no more time, I turned my music on, and I started my drive.

I got to the *Denny's* parking lot before I knew what I was doing. I guess time goes fast when you are karaoking at the top of your lungs to your favorite songs. *Ha.* I laughed to myself as I parked my car in the empty lot.

Emphasis on the word empty. There were only three cars there, yet I still ended up parking in two spaces/lines. Oh well, parking isn't my fortress. I mummered softly as I parked correctly, and in perfect timing because just as I turned my car off I spotted Jake coming out of the *Denny's.*

A nervous feeling transversed my body. My hands began to sweat, and my legs felt wobbly. Why was I this nervous? You know the answer to that Lucianna. This was my first "date" with someone new in years, and it did not help that Jake looked handsome as hell.

Even from twenty feet away I could see how attractive he was. He wore a black v-neck shirt that fit him tightly. His biceps bulged, and I could see a vein pop out. His wavy dark hair was combed to the side, and he wore golf shorts that showed his muscular legs. My heart began to flutter.

Whoah, was he too good for me? No, I have to be confident in myself. Relax Lucianna. I took some deep breaths and I opened my door. I slowly got out of the car, and before I could close the door Jake was right beside me. "May I close the door for you?" I felt my cheeks get red. It is not that I needed anyone to close or open a door for me, but it felt nice to be asked.

I appreciate you asking, but I got this. I smiled at him as he looked straight into my eyes. "You have such beautiful eyes." "Your eyelashes are so long!" My face felt hot. I wasn't expecting such a direct compliment.

I didn't know what to say, so I quickly said, "Thanks." He flashed a bright smile at me. I had to compliment him back. Uh, I like your outfit. You remind me of a golfer. "That was the look that I was going for." "I am glad I nailed it, ha." You most certainly did. He gave a sly wink. "Shall we go have some breakfast?" Yes, let's go.

We walked over to the *Denny's* entrance and this time I let him open the door for me. I hated grabbing public door knobs, but to Jake I said, "Thank you for that." He smiled at me as the hostess came over to greet us. *Party of two today?* "Yes." *Right this way. Is a table okay?* Can we have a booth instead? *Of course.* The hostess led us to a booth on the empty side of the restaurant.

Here are your menus. Your waiter will be with you shortly. I took the menu from the hostess, but I already knew what I wanted so I did not open it. "Looks like you know what you want." Oh, I definitely do. I always come to have dinner here with Francisco. "Perfect." "I know what I want too." Oh, and what is that?

"Definitely the Grand Slam." "With a cup of black coffee." A small grin appeared on my face. "Oh I see I have you smiling." "May I know why?" He flashed his perfect grin at me. My heart went up several beats as his little mustache curled above his lip. Which in turn made my legs shake a bit. Gosh, I hoped he didn't notice the nervous wreck that he made me. My stomach was filled with butterflies!

I really felt so foolish, but hey that's normal when you are on a first date, right? "Everything alright, Lucianna?" My cheeks burned. It had been a good ten seconds since he asked me what I was getting and here I was still looking at him without answering. Get a grip, Lucianna! I took a deep breath to calm my nerves, and then I answered him calmly.

I am getting the same thing as you, but instead of a coffee I will get an orange juice. "Well, aren't we two peas in a pod?" Once again he flashed his award winning smile at me, but this time I was ready for the butterflies.

Hopefully, if I was having them, then he was too. That thought made me feel better, and I quickly answered him. Hmm, I don't know about that yet. I playfully raised an eyebrow at him. This time it was his turn to blush. His cheeks got rosy, but he quickly played it off by calling the waiter over. Who took our order and brought us our drinks.

While we waited for our food we began to talk about everything. It turns out that Jake's father is from India. That explains his beautiful dark silky hair, and his mother is American. Which also explains his beautiful caramel skin. I also learned that Jake's bakery is in my old town, and it opened last year. Around the time that I left.

That is why I never saw it. "If you don't mind me asking, will you attend your sister's wedding after all?" The question caught me off guard, and made me uncomfortable. I shift my body to the side. Jake stared at me, and his face got bright red.

It was apparent that he knew he overstepped a boundary. "I am so sorry." "The last thing I want to do is talk about something that you don't want to talk about." "It's just that our date is going so well, and your vibe is amazing."

"I want to see more of you, and since the wedding is next week, from what I remember overhearing, sorry." "I just thought, why can't I be your date?" "I mean that is if you feel a connection to me." I glared at him intensely.

He looked so cute sitting in the booth. His big shoulders sunk down like a little kid who had just gotten in trouble. His left hand was shaking a bit. He was nervous. It brought a smile to my face.

Well how about we go out again tomorrow but for lunch. Let's say a picnic? If that goes well then we can see about the wedding. He nodded and we finished our food. "I had a nice time with you." As did I. "What park would you like to meet at tomorrow?"

I can go to the one by your bakery. It is a beautiful park, and there is a lot of shade. "Sounds perfect." "Let me go and wash my hands before we go." I nodded okay, and took out my phone.

Jazmine had texted back with a million heart eyes emojis and a virtual invitation to her wedding. It was not in a week, but 10 days. *COME JOIN US IN CELEBRATING OUR LOVE. THERE IS NO REQUIRED DRESS CODE. BRING AN EMPTY STOMACH AND YOUR DANCING SHOES.*

As much as I hated to admit it, the virtual invitation was cute. The lettering was in golden writing and the background was a dark purple with a picture of Henry and Jazmine kissing. In another life I would have been so happy for my sister, but right now I didn't feel anything. I wasn't mad or sad. Which I guess made me happy.

I just felt neutral. Her wedding simply felt like a chore that I had to attend, but maybe it would be better with a date, but I shouldn't get ahead of myself. I "liked" the wedding invitation so Jazmine could see that I acknowledged it, and then I sat my phone down. Which was perfect timing because Jake was walking back this way.

"Ready?" Yes, let me get in line to pay for my breakfast. "No need to." "I took care of it." Jake, you didn't have to do that. "I know I didn't, but I wanted to." I have to pay you back. I like things to be 50/50.

"No, please." "How about this, you bring lunch for our picnic tomorrow?" Alright. I smiled, and we left the restaurant. He walked me to my car, and with a trembling hand he reached out to hug me.

I felt my body fill with goosebumps. My legs felt like jelly, and when Jake looked down at me, my tummy went cold. He puckered his rosy red lips and kneeled his head down and to the side. He was coming in for a kiss.

My heart was racing, but I felt excited at the same time. I closed my eyes and his lips met mine. Sparks, fireworks, explosions were just the few things that I felt at that moment. It was wonderful, but after about ten seconds I pulled away from the kiss.

I did not want him to think that I was an easy meal, so I chose my next words carefully. Jake, I had fun today. I'll text you this evening. See you tomorrow. "Sounds good." He slowly walked back to his car. I opened my car door and sank to my seat. I was feeling a million things all at once, so I gathered myself together a bit and then I drove off.

I spent the next three hours on the phone with Francisco. We gushed about my date and the endless possibilities of what could happen in hypothetical situations. It was all so stupid, but I really loved it. This was a form of happiness that I had not felt in a while. The type of happiness that makes you forget your pain. A type of enjoyment that even blurs time and space.

Like how in the world was it already 6 p.m? My day had flown by in a flash. It was time to ground myself again! With that said, I grabbed my running clothes and I changed. I was in and out of the door within five minutes, and an hour later I had run my six miles.

When I got home I showered, and then I made myself a big dinner. Home-made enchiladas with extra cheese and tomato sauce. For my drink I had a nice coke. It was all heavenly, so with a full stomach I went to my suede couch and I laid down. It was time to watch a movie, but before that I had to respond to Jake's last message.

He had messaged me about two hours ago that he was finishing up his day at the bakery. I responded back with, *"How did it go today?" Bubbles typing.* Wow, he had seen my message already! Could he really be that into me?

I didn't know if that was a good thing, but it made me feel happy. *I am just locking up now. What are you up to?* He keeps his bakery open late. It was almost 9pm. *"I am about to start a movie."*

"Do ham sandwiches with lemonade sound good for tomorrow?" Bubbles typing. Anything you bring will be fantastic I am sure. I am heading home, so I wish you a goodnight for now. See you tomorrow Lucianna. Sleep with the angels. Heart emoji.

I was smiling at my phone like a stupid girl, but I loved every second of it. *"Goodnight, Jake." "See you tomorrow, and come hungry!"* I placed my phone down for the night, and instead of watching a movie I headed to my bed and began to read the horror book that I had bought a week before. It was a peaceful night and I eventually drifted off to sleep.

The next day when I woke up I did the same thing like I do every morning. My routine. I washed my face, and brushed my teeth. I made my bed and did my yoga. I then had a light breakfast. I had a microwavable bacon and egg burrito, and then I checked my phone. I had a good morning message from Francisco, and I was delighted to see that I also had one from Jake.

Good morning, beautiful. What a charmer he was. I could get used to that. *Good morning, Jake. I am excited for this afternoon. See you at 1.* I added a smiley emoji, and then I opened Francisco's message.

Tell me everything that happens babe! I will Francisco, and please send me a picture of the guy you are going on a date with tonight! All caught up with my messages, I headed to the grocery store because my fridge was nearly empty.

I was not big on cooking, but I could whip up a ham sandwich. I laughed to myself as I placed the loaf of potato bread next to the ham and tomatoes in my hand cart. All I needed now was the lemonade.

I grabbed the organic one, maybe Jake would think that I made it. If he asked I'd of course tell him that I bought it, but I wouldn't disclose that information willingly.

Once again I giggled to myself like an idiot and then I walked to the self checkout line. It was pretty empty. There were five machines and only myself and an older lady who looked like she was struggling to pay were there.

Ma'am do you need help? *Oh young lady,* she said in a soft startled voice. *Please, how can I pay with cash?* I excited out the card choice and selected the cash option and then I showed her where to feed the machine cash. There you go ma'am.

Anything else you would like help with? She looked at me intensely. Her wrinkled eyes got wide and she placed her hand on my shoulder. *You are *in danger. Someone is trying to hurt you. They are jealous of you. Please be aware of your surroundings.*

I pulled back from her grip. She shook her head, and said, *Thank you so much sweet young lady. You are an angel.* She grabbed her bag and walked away. I was left dumbfounded.

CHAPTER 4

Falling Down The Rabbit Hole

Quite frankly, I was spooked. My body was covered in goosebumps, and I suddenly felt dizzy with fear. Who was this lady? I tried to be rational, but as the room started to spin around me, I knew I was getting in over my head. This was not the place or time.

Relax, Lucianna. Breathe, I told myself. Obviously, the old lady was just a little out of her mind—yeah, that had to be it. It wasn't her fault, and I shouldn't think twice about it. Now, shake it off, Lucianna. I lightly tapped my cheeks, trying to come back to reality.

That helped a bit. The room stopped spinning, so I slowly walked back over to pay for my things. But... what if she wasn't out of her mind? No. Don't think that way, Lucianna. You've already suffered enough. Life can't be this cruel to you.

Yeah, that's right, I thought. I've served my dues. Feeling a tad more at ease, I hurried over to my car and drove off. On my way home, I blasted music to try to drown out my thoughts, but even that couldn't completely shake the hold of the woman's words in my mind.

She had clearly said I was in danger, and that people were jealous of me. Was she being serious? Was she suffering from some sort of episode? I mean, after she told me all these things, she acted like everything was normal.

Yeah, that had to be it. She must be suffering from some sort of cognitive problem. No need to freak myself out. Besides, I didn't have time to. It was almost 11:30 a.m. *Crap!* I was going to be late, and with that realization I slowly started to forget my encounter with the older woman.

Good, because I had more important things to worry about, like making these sandwiches that weren't going to make themselves. With that in mind, I rushed into my kitchen and prepped the food. I then carefully placed everything in my picnic basket. I made sure to put the lemonade jug at the bottom so it wouldn't squish the sandwiches.

Now that all of that was taken care of, all I needed to do was change. Luckily, I knew exactly what to wear. A while back, I had bought a cute white tank top and a beautiful purple skirt with shorts sewn into it. The skirt was classy but sexy at the same time. It went down to my knees, but it was tight enough to show the shape of my hips and butt.

To top it off, I had a newer pair of white Nikes that I was dying to wear again. Needless to say, it was time to change. I put my outfit on and looked in the mirror. I felt confident. I had been doing ab workouts since last year, and even though I didn't have a six pack, I did have visible abs. That's why I wanted to wear my crop top. I liked what I saw.

I gave myself a flirty look in the mirror. There was nothing wrong with showing off what you worked hard for. Ha. I smiled and walked out of my room. I grabbed my picnic basket and headed out the door.

Before I knew it, I was halfway there. The traffic at this time was minimal, and I welcomed that, but what I didn't welcome were the old lady's warnings playing in the back of my mind. Ugh, go away. Think of positive things, Lucianna.

I tried to do just that, but I couldn't shake the thoughts. So instead, I decided to call Francisco. He always knew how to make me feel better.

Hey babe. Are you on your way to the picnic? Yeah, I am. I am excited. Surprisingly not too nervous. *You have no reason to be nervous. He wants you more than you want him, and that is how it should be.* As much as I hate to admit that, you are right.

I loved Henry more than he loved me, and he betrayed me. *Don't think about that creep right now babe.* I won't, but anyway, tell me how your date went. *He was a sweet guy, but he was looking more for fun than a serious relationship. I am tired of just fooling around with people. I want something serious, and when I told him that he was honest with me. He said he just wanted fun right now.*

I'm sorry about that, Francisco. You deserve the world. You know that right? *I guess.* His soft voice cracked lightly. It broke my heart a bit. He deserved so much more, and I had to let him know that.

Don't say I guess, sweetie. You are the sweetest guy I've ever met. You're a gem. Please don't ever forget that. I love you so much. *You say that I hype you up, Lucianna? You make my ego go through the roof.*

We both started laughing. I felt happy again, and the old lady's warning soon slipped my mind. Well, I have to go now, Francisco. I am about to pull up. I'll text you how everything goes.

Have fun, and be safe, babe. I hung up the phone and parked the car. Like before Jake was already there before me. I liked that. One of my pet peeves was when people were late. This was already extra points for him.

"Do you need help with your basket?" Thank you, but I got it. I yelled back at Jake as he walked over to greet me. "Are you sure you don't need help? I'm a tough girl. I flexed my biceps at him, and he smiled.

Which made me instantly blush. That and the fact that he was wearing a tight white tank top. His abs were poking out from underneath the shirt. *Woah*. I had to divert my eyes away.

I didn't want him to see me checking him out. "I'm glad you're here." As am I. Shall we eat? I asked as nonchalantly as I could, but inside my heart was racing. "Yes, I found the perfect spot for a picnic just 400 meters from my bakery." "Follow me." I followed Jake, and stared at his muscular legs as he walked.

He was really fit. It made me blush more. I had never gone on dates with anyone this in shape. I was usually the "in shape" one out of everyone that I had ever dated, but I should not get ahead of myself. I was not dating him, yet, so bring it down a notch Lucianna.

"You see the blanket by the duck pond?" I do. It is gorgeous, and there is shade. "Yeah, just be careful the grass is a tad moist from the morning." "They had the sprinklers on." I'll be okay. I winked at him, and just as I did that I almost slipped on the floor. Luckily Jake was fast. He grabbed me by the hand, and brought me against him.

His face was just millimeters from my face again, and this time it was me who kissed me. I did have to tiptoe since he was about 6'1 and wasn't expecting a kiss, but gosh once again I felt nothing but fireworks. Explosions filled my body, and it made me drop my picnic basket. I didn't mind. The food was safe and secure.

Which allowed me to fully lose myself in the moment, and, shy as I am to admit it, we kissed for over two minutes. I hadn't intended for it to last that long, but I got swept up in it. I only pulled away when I felt his hand drift lower, reaching for my butt.

That was a no for now. I had promised myself there would be no groping until at least the third date. Thankfully, Jake understood. Without a word, he simply slid his arm around my shoulders instead. The gesture was gentle... grounding. It made me feel safe.

"Are you ready to eat?" he asked as we settled onto the furry blanket he had brought. I am, and you mister? "Oh yes please." Okay, here's your sandwich, and lemonade. I hope you like it... it's the best meal I can make.

"Don't you worry." "I love cooking, and I wouldn't mind cooking for us." He jokingly smiled and bit into the sandwich. "Oh, wow!" "This is the best damn sandwich I have ever eaten." I burst out laughing, almost spilling my drink from my mouth. You are a charmer! "Oh I wouldn't say that."

Uh, huh. How about you tell me more about yourself? I feel like you know more about me than I do about you. "Hmm, well let's see." "I am left handed." "I'm scared of bats." "I love roller coasters." "I am a *Disney* kid at heart." "I like pretty girls who make delicious sandwiches."

I rolled my eyes at him. He gave me an innocent boy stare. It made me laugh again. "I'm glad my life amuses you." Oh go on. I gently shoved him to the side. "Hmm, what else." "Oh my last relationship ended when the person that I thought was the love of my life cheated on me."

His voice cracked a bit as he said that. I reached over and hugged him tightly. He really understood my pain. I felt a connection with him. Especially as I could feel his heart beating in my chest. I liked that.

"Mine if we lay down a bit?" Not at all. I laid on my back, and before I had time to adjust he placed his body over mine. He then leaned in for a kiss. His lips were moist on mine. I really enjoyed the feeling.

We kissed again for a while, but this time it was he who broke it off. "I want to give you my special dessert, but we have to go to my bakery." "Care to join me?" I nodded yes, and picked up my basket as he folded the picnic blanket. "It is right over here." I stared at the sky blue building that he was pointing at. *A Taste of Heaven.* What a cute name.

"My mom helped me think of it." "She has helped me a lot with the place." "Maybe she is in there now?" Suddenly my face got red. I did not want to meet a guy's mother who I barely even knew.

"Shall we go into my bakery?" Uh, how about you choose your favorite dessert and we can eat it on the way to the car. Jake grinned, and raised an eyebrow at me. He knew I was shy, so he stepped inside his bakery and came out with two slices of *pastel de tres leches.*

"I am not latino, but this is my favorite dessert in the world." Jake, great minds think alike because that's also my favorite dessert. "I'll make this for you whenever you want it." Oh is that so? If I am craving cake at 10 p.m. you'll jump out of bed and make it?

"Without hesitation." His answer made me happy, but I had to ground myself. I was not about to fall for someone just because they knew how to "smooth talk." *Hmm.* You are a charmer, aren't you? "Only to you."

"Look I am not here to toy with you or anyone." "I am genuine." His face grew stern. He reached down and grabbed my hand. His hand felt soft but firm at the same time. "I won't toy with you okay?"

My legs felt like jelly as he told me he wasn't here to play. I had heard those words before—from Henry. But this was Jake. *You have to trust again, Lucianna.* Okay... I would give him the benefit of the doubt. I slowly nodded, letting him know I understood, and then we walked hand in hand back to my car.

"I want to see you again tomorrow." "Can I?" My stomach filled with butterflies. This guy liked me, and I was crushing on him. That said, it surprised me how fast I said, "yes." I didn't even have to think twice about it. Hopefully this wouldn't come back and bite me in the ass.

"That makes me glad." "You want to meet at the cinema in your town tomorrow at lunch time and choose a movie together?" "We can have lunch after." That sounds great to me. "Whoopie." He flashed his bright smile at me as he reached down for a kiss. Our lips met and it was heaven all over again, but this time after 30 seconds it was me who pulled away. I had to keep him wanting more.

See you tomorrow, charmer. "See you, pretty lady." I got into my car and drove off. I don't even remember the drive home—let alone how I spent the rest of the day. One moment I was walking through my front door, and the next, I was lying in bed, feeling happy... and sleepy.

I closed my eyes, and time slipped away. Before I knew it, I was pulling up to the movie theater. Everything was happening quickly like it usually does when someone has a crush. It was a scary feeling, and the only thing that was clear was that I wanted to see him more and more.

Which was why I was grinning from ear to ear when he greeted me with roses at the movie theatre. It was the sweetest thing ever, and to put a cherry on top, while we watched a horror movie, we were hand in hand the entire film.

I was on cloud 9, and quite frankly, I didn't remember a single thing from the movie. All I knew was that we were now at a *Subway*, and he had me laughing so hard at his dumb dad jokes that soda was practically coming out of my nose.

"Why didn't the skeleton go to the party?" *Hmm,* I don't know, why? "Because he had noBODY to go with." That is so corny, but you are so cute! "Oh you think so?" Yes, I do. "Well, why don't you take a picture with this cute guy?" Just as long as you send the picture after. "Of course." He pulled his phone out and we took a selfie together.

In it we looked cute. His strong broad face mixed well with my round face. His light caramel skin meshed perfectly with my brown skin. We really looked good together. "Picture sent." Got it, and hey Jake I was thinking. "Yeah?"

You have asked me out every single time now. How about I return the favor. Would you like to go to my sister's wedding with me on Saturday the 15? "I would love that." Feeling emotional, I hugged him. He kissed me and held me tightly. I could feel the cashier stare at us.

I felt shy and stood up. "Does this mean I won't see you until the wedding?" I nodded my head yes. I didn't tell him this, but I needed time to soak up the three amazing days that we had.

"How will I survive almost an entire week without seeing you?" With this. I pulled out my phone. He started to laugh. "Fine, fine." "I just really want to see you every day." I was at a loss for words after he said that, and again without thinking I opened my big mouth.

Jake, you know I am not planning to stay long at the wedding. Maybe you can come and spend the night after? Did I really just say that outloud? I quickly got my answer. "I would love that." "Maybe then I will ask you something important too."

I was smiling like an idiot. He was going to ask me out. I couldn't contain my glee and hugged him again. *Buzz, buzz, buzz.* "Sorry, Lucianna, I have to take that." "I'm so sorry." "I forgot about our appointment, mom." "I'll be there in forty-five minutes."

"Lucianna, I forgot that my mom has a doctor's appointment." "I have to go back to the bakery, but I had such a blast with you." "I can't wait to see you this Saturday." "Text me when you are home, okay?" I nodded as he kissed me on the cheek.

He then ran to his car. Drive safely! I yelled at him. He turned around and gave me a scout's honor salute. It made me laugh, and I went back to my car and just sat there. There were a lot of things going on in my mind.

I mean for pete's sake, just a year ago I was crying every single day, and now I was smiling uncontrollably. I felt so happy, and as insane as this may sound, I had not thought about my sister or Henry the last few days.

I didn't think that was possible, but it was. Life was going well, and as much as I hate to admit this, it was because of Jake. Every time that I had been with him I felt like my true self. The old happy, Lucianna, but that wasn't all.

The more that I think about it, this was the first time in my dating life that I have ever truly felt like my authentic self with someone. From not feeling ashamed of saying my lame jokes to just knowing that I will get an active listening ear to my concerns.

I was lucky to have met Jake, but I shouldn't sell myself short! The more I think about it, I was already 100% happy with myself before Jake. If I hadn't been, then I wouldn't have been content even with him. That thought made me feel ecstatic.

The realization that my year of hell wasn't wasteful. I learned to love myself again. I learned who was important in my life, Francisco. I learned to forgive. That is why I forgave Jazmine, so thank you Universe for helping me come to this conclusion. I am a badass!

Okay, now with all that gushy things out of my way it was time to find a dress for my sister's wedding. Which was just a few days away! Thankfully, she said there was no dress code, so I knew exactly what I wanted to wear.

I had seen a red dress at the *Calvin Klein* store two weeks ago, and as luck might have it, the store is just across the street from the theater. It was too hot to walk there, so I put the car into gear and I slowly drove down to the store. It looked empty. Awesome. I got out of my vehicle and entered.

Welcome in. We have a 20% discount on everything over sixty dollars. Oh that is great.

I told the seller and headed straight to the back of the store where I had seen the dress just days ago, and yes there it was, right on the rack. My dress. I eagerly reached for it and headed straight into the fitting rooms.

Let me just make sure you fit well like last time. I removed my tank top and jeans, and I put the dress on. I couldn't help but smile. My hips looked plumped. My breasts were covered enough to give a modest, but sexy look. My butt looked perky. Fantastic. I am taking this.

Did you find everything you needed? Oh yes. *Awesome. Will it be cash or card?* Card please. *That will be 100 dollars, but 80 with the 20% discount. Would you like a bag?* Yes, I will. *Here you go. Have a nice day, ma'am.* You too. *Oh, and by the way your hair is absolutely gorgeous.* Aww thanks.

I smiled at the seller and headed back to my car. Once I got home I pulled my phone out and there was a message from Jake. *Got back safely. I will be at the bakery till 8pm. I miss you already, cutie.*

His message made me glow because he already had a nickname for me, "cutie." It took Henry almost a year for him to do that, and even at that, it was under my suggestion. What a fool I had been.

I, on the other hand, had given him countless cute names, but that was not a mistake that I would make with Jake. *I'm glad you're safe and sound, Jake. I'm home too. I am going to do some painting that I have been putting off in my spare room, and then I'll probably be lazy and watch movies. Heart emoji. Sent.*

I placed my phone on the table and went straight into the closet for my paint supplies. I had been meaning to paint the spare room for months now, but for some reason I just didn't think that I would be spending much time in this apartment.

That has changed now. I do feel good here, and this place has been my little shelter of healing. I don't want to leave, at least for now. So, I might as well make this place fully mine. Now let me get started!

I poured the dark blue paint in the tray, and I laid an old bed sheet over the carpet of the spare room. I taped the barrier that separated the carpet to the wall, and I grabbed a chair and taped the part of the ceiling that met the wall.

Then I got to work. The entire room was painted three times over by the time I was done, and I was satisfied. I was going for a relaxing vibe, and the dark blue made it feel like it was nighttime at the beach. Perfect, exactly what I wanted.

What I didn't want was to be covered in blue paint, and by the looks of it, that is exactly what I got. For some reason I had a smudge of paint plastered across my left cheek. My right arm was also coated in paint.

Ugh. I can never do anything right. I giggled to myself as I made my way over to the restroom. It really did feel nice to have normal thoughts again. *Ding dong, ding dong.* I jumped two feet into the air.

What was that? *Ding dong, ding dong.* The sound was coming from my front door. Could that be my door bell? In my year of being here I had not once heard the sound. It caught me by surprise, but who could be ringing? I was not expecting anyone.

My body tensed up, but still I tiptoed to the front door and I peaked through the peep hole. It was Francisco! I quickly opened the door for him. Francisco, why did you show up unannounced? Is something the matter?

As I asked him my questions I knew something was up. His hair looked messy. I could see his sweat dripping down his forehead. He had obviously rushed here, and his breathing was heavy.

I'm, I'm sorry, he said, trying to catch his breath. Come in, tell me what's wrong. My stomach was knotting up. I hated seeing my friend like this. I put my arm around him and brought him inside.

I shut the door behind us with my leg as I sat him down on my couch. Sit here, and let me get you some water. I ran to the kitchen, and I pulled the fridge open. I grabbed the bottle nearest to me, and I practically flew back to Francisco. Here you go, sweetie.

He took the bottle and drank a few sips. I brushed his dark hair out of his face, and at last I saw his breathing slow down. Okay, now tell me. *I'm sorry for coming unannounced, but I tried calling you, and you did not answer.*

I'm sorry, Francisco. I finally painted my spare room, and I had music on, so I didn't hear my phone go off. *I thought something bad had happened to you.* What, why? I stared at him, and his eyes filled with tears. Fuck. Something bad had happened. I just knew it.

CHAPTER 7

Who Am I Becoming?

I climbed out of bed, and I dragged myself to the restroom. I was still extremely sleepy, so I brushed my teeth to wake myself up. That didn't do the job, so I hopped into the shower. Once the cold water poured down my body I felt awake, and the realization of what today was truly hit.

The big wedding. Shivers went down my spine. Did I really want to go through this? Expose my little sister for who she truly was? Yes? No? I pondered for a moment as I dried myself off, but no answer came to me.

Feeling frustrated I walked over to the tiny window next to my shower, and I glared out to the radiant blue morning sky. The sun's beautiful rays struck my face and put me at ease. I soaked it all in, and I knew in my heart that there was no turning back on my decision.

Like I had told Francisco yesterday, this was the only way to release my anger and frustration. Plus, it was the only way to teach Jazmine, Henry and Jake that life has consequences, and boy did I know that.

I hadn't even executed my plan yet, but my hands were already shaking. The consequences of taking a stand. Which unfortunately meant I was already stressed to the max, but I had a solution for that. Yoga.

That was something that I would and could never skip, especially today. I needed to feel as stress free as possible, so all dried up and changed, I headed back to my room and put on my video work out.

I stretched extra long today, and after forty-five minutes I tiptoed back into the kitchen. It was only 8 a.m. at this point, but my stomach was already grumbling. I needed to eat something. I was craving food that wasn't processed. Freshly handmade tortillas and scrambled eggs came to mind.

Wasting no time I grabbed the flour and measured three cups of it. I added that to a bowl, and then I used two tablespoons of baking soda, half a cup of butter, and one cup of water. I mixed everything until it was incorporated into a nicely rounded dough.

While that rested I grabbed two eggs from the fridge. Next I tossed them into a greased up pan. I then scrambled the eggs together, and for some additional protein, I pulled out a can of spam. I thinly sliced up the spam into small pieces and cooked them next to the eggs. I would need all the energy possible for today.

While the eggs cooked over a low flame, I cut two 3 inch ball size pieces of dough. I wrapped up the rest and put it in the fridge because I only wanted two tortillas. Once I did that I rolled them out with an empty glass bottle from my cabinet and I cooked them over a griddle. With everything finished I sat down and ate.

It was fantastic, and I felt genuinely better. *Buzz, buzz, buzz.* I picked up my phone. *Hey, babe, I hope you slept well.* I did. How about you? *I slept okayish. How are you feeling?* My morning started off rocky, but after a nice cold shower, and homemade tortillas I now feel better. *Hey you made tortillas and didn't invite me?* Don't worry, I saved enough dough to cook some for you. *Ha, you better.*

Babe, is the plan still a go? Definitely. *Okay just making sure. I am going to finish up some work that I have, but I will be waiting for you at the venue at the allotted time. Okay?* Thank you sweetie. *Please text me if anything, okay? I will rush right to you.* Don't worry Francisco, I will. Bye my brother. *Bye my sister. Love you.* Me too.

I put my phone down, and smiled. I felt safe having Francisco on my side, but what to do now? I had the entire day to waste before the wedding? Hmm. The remaining *Final Destination* movies it was.

I walked over to my living room, and I flopped onto the couch. I turned my TV and put on the fifth movie, but before I could hit play I texted Jake. I had to ensure he didn't suspect anything.

Good morning Jake, today is the big day. I am so nervous, but excited to see you. How are you today? I stared at my phone for a minute, and then he opened the messages. He started typing. My heart began to race again, but this time it wasn't from happiness, it was from anger. *Good morning cutie. I can't wait to see how beautiful you are today. Don't tell your sister, but I am sure you will steal the show. Is everything okay for 5 still?*

I rolled my eyes as I texted him. *Yes, that is perfect. I'll message you when I leave the house. I have to get ready if I am going to look my best.* I put my phone down and hit play. I spent the next four hours just enjoying two good horror movies, but at last it was 2 p.m. I had to get ready, but the first thing I needed to do was clean my apartment.

One thing about me was that whenever I felt sad or mad having a dirty apartment made things so much worse. Something about clutter just made me feel shitter. Ironically the one "good" thing about suffering so much for the past year was that my apartment was always spotless.

Not a funny joke Lucianna. I muttered to myself as I began to clean the kitchen. Which wasn't too messy, but there was a sink filled with dirty dishes that I had to wash. I started with those, and then I dried them off and put them away. Next I swept the entire floor, and I oiled my wooden table. It smelled like fresh pine.

A scent that reminded me of my mom. Following that I scrubbed the counters off, and soon after I was done with the kitchen. The living room was next on my list, but honestly all I had to do was rearrange the cushions on the couch. It was still clean. I hardly ever used my living room.

Okay now it was time to tidy up my bedroom. Thankfully that too was not too disorganized. All I had to do was put some clothes away, and that is exactly what I did. I hung up some dresses, a few pairs of pants and some shirts. Done and done.

If things didn't go my way today at least I would come home to a clean living space. That made me happy, but now it was time to get ready. I had a little over an hour and a half. I would need all the time because I truly did want to look my best.

I hated admitting this even to myself, but I wanted to secretly outshine my own sister on her wedding day. I knew in my heart that it was terrible to even think that, let alone want that. However, it was what I felt in my heart.

Plus, I secretly knew that if I looked my better than her it would also show Henry that he left someone more conventionally attractive for Jazmine. Which would hurt his pride. He was always "proud" of having the "finer" things in life. Again, I hated thinking that way, but my mind was filled with sadness and rage. Also, concerning Jake he would see that I wasn't broken by him, if I dressed to impress.

Instantly I felt awful once more feeling this way, but I shoved the thought out of my mind and began to brush my hair. I combed it in sections since my hair was so long. I brushed the top part first and made my way down till I reached my flanks. I repeated that process till it was as straight as silk.

Once finished with that, I headed to my restroom and started on my makeup. Normally, I wore light makeup. A red lip and foundation, nothing more, and nothing less. This time however I applied black eyeshadow. I curled my long eyelashes, and I put on a dark silky red lip. Lastly, I added my foundation and a glossy toner. Done and done.

I looked at myself in the mirror. I barely recognized who was staring back at me. I looked like a dolled up version of myself. It made me smile. It was rare for me to put this much effort into getting ready.

The last time I had gotten ready like this was two years ago when I got promoted at my job. That was a fun time. I was not fighting nerves then like I was now, but I had to stop thinking negatively. It was time to change, but not with the outfit that I had bought at *Guess.*

That outfit would not work now because I had bought it when I thought my sister really had changed. The outfit that I had chosen to wear now was to upstage Jazmine. Again, I hated to be doing that, but it was something that I had to do!

I carefully pulled out the large black sealed packaging that was hung in the far end of my closet. This bag contained a fancy dress that I only wore once before. It was the dress that I used for my promotion banquet when I had become a principal. It was perfectly elegant. It was classy, but with a hint of seductiveness.

It was a silky black velvety dress that was custom made for me by my mom's best friend who was a seamstress. The dress had no sleeves, and it had a v-neck that was cut down up to the breast to reveal enough but to keep it modest. There were shimmering crystals around the waist and hip area that perfectly displayed my body.

However, what made this dress exceptionally beautiful was that it also had a turtle neck kind of thing going on. This helped enhance the beauty of my face, well according to my seamstress. On top of this the dress came with black fishnet gloves that gave it a princess feel.

It was also long and reached up to my ankle, and it was figure hugging. It was the perfect dress, and what made it even more special was that Henry and Jazmine never saw me wear it in person.

Henry had a project that he had to travel out of state for that evening of my promotion, and Jazmine had made up some excuse as to why she couldn't attend my promotion banquet. Figures, anyway it didn't matter. What mattered was that I could wear it for her wedding.

I was certain that this gown would have all eyes on me. Like on the day of my banquet. I relished that idea. I would be the center of attention as I enter the reception. All eyes would be on me instead of my sister. A small smile appeared on my face, and I felt instant regret.

What was happening to me? Why was I so happy to destroy my sister's wedding? My stomach dropped at the realization that I had gotten evil due to all the pain that was thrown my way. Was I a bad person?

I closed my eyes and thought about that. My mind raced back at all the sacrifices that I had done for Jazmine and Henry, and then I got my answer. I was not evil. If anything I was too nice, and anyone in my position would probably have done much worse. I just hated the fact that I was happy to be causing pain.

I didn't want to be like this, and I hoped that once this wedding was over all these feelings would go away, and if they didn't then I would go to therapy. Yeah, that's what I would do. Another grin appeared on my face, and with that I began to change.

Surprisingly, the skin tight dress was easy to put on this time. When I originally wore it two years ago it was a challenge, but I guess I had lost weight since then. It made sense. This past year I had not eaten like I was supposed to.

Oh well, at least I would be able to walk with it easier. My legs had more room to move, and even my shoulders felt more spacious as I slept the top part of my dress over them. The only downfall was that it wasn't as tight on my waist like I wanted it to be, but I guess that didn't really matter.

I still had an hourglass figure, and that was what mattered right now because that would get people's attention. *Vain, vain, vain.* I know. Nevertheless, I could confidently say that I never felt better than anyone based on my appearance.

Even though my entire life others have always complimented my looks and body. I never saw anything special about that. For me what was special was a person's heart, and I can proudly say that I still feel the same way. That epiphany made me happy. My old self was still in my heart. I just had to find her, and I would get her after today. But before then I had to put the final touches to my outfit.

All I needed to finish my look were my red heels. That would give my outfit the pop that it needed. I went back into my closet and pulled out my 3 inch heels, and I put them on. Almost done, all I had to do now was to have a final look in front of my mirror to see if I looked nice.

I walked back into the restroom and stared at myself in the mirror. On the outside I looked beautiful, but my eyes looked lost. There was still some shine to them, but not the same glow. If Jazmine truly loved me she would notice that something was wrong. I secretly prayed she would notice, but enough of that. It was time to go.

I left my apartment, and I closed the door behind me. I then made my way over to my car. Within one minute, I was on my way to Jake's bakery. It was show time.

CHAPTER 5

Another Betrayal

Tell me sweetie. Whatever it is, we will get through it together. He slowly nodded and grabbed my hand. *I found out something awful today. I thought you had hurt yourself because you had also figured out what was happening. That is why I rushed over here.* Tears left his eyes and dropped to the floor. I was confused, but still, I listened to what he had to say.

Jake is not who you think he is. My stomach turned to knots. What do you mean Francisco? *I will start from the beginning so you can understand everything.* Still confused I stared blankly at him as he took my other hand and sat us down on the couch. He was trembling.

This morning I had a spur of the moment breakfast date with some random man. Okay, and how did that go? What does it have to do with Jake? My voice was cracking. *Babe, please let me just finish.* Alright. *The date was going well, and midway through it we started talking about our travels.*

He told me he had recently been to the Grand Canyon, so I asked him to show me pictures. As he scrolled through them, everything felt normal—until he stopped on one. The moment I saw it, I almost lost it right then and there. What... Why?

By that point, my legs were shaking uncontrollably. I could feel irritation creeping in—I was getting annoyed with Francisco for taking so long to explain what he had come to say—but deep down, I knew he had a reason.

Jake was in the photo. Jake as in my Jake? *Yes.* I thought about that for a second, but I didn't see an issue. Hmm, why is that such a bad thing, Francisco? He only lives 30 minutes from here. He is bound to know many people from the area.

Babe, please listen. Francisco was getting on my nerves. I wanted him to get to the point, but I knew that he was telling the entire story for my benefit so I let him speak. Go on, please.

There were five people in total in that photo. All of them were guys. Which gave me a bad feeling. Why? *I suspected that they were all gay.* My body froze upon hearing that. Francisco stared at me, and asked if I was okay. I quietly whispered, "go on."

You know I am the last person to be stereotypical, but all the men, including Jake, were wearing tight tank tops with small shorts. I had to know what was going on, so I asked him. Are all the men in that photo gay? *My date laughed and said, 'oh you better believe it.'*

My head started to spin. My vision got blurry. This couldn't be. Surely it had to be a guy that looked like Jake. It just couldn't be. Francisco, are you 100% sure that was Jake? *At first I wasn't, so I asked him who everyone was on that trip, and when I heard the name, Jake there was no denying it.*

All my body was trembling now. I was nauseous from what I had heard, yet surprisingly I was not sad. In fact I was the opposite of sad, I was furious. I was starting to really like that mother fucker, but you know what? Fuck that. I was not going to let my world shatter over someone who was dealing with an orientation crisis.

I now had more respect for myself, and I knew my worth. Francisco, *yeah, babe?* Thank you for being a great friend and always being upfront with me. You are the only person that I can count on, and I won't lie, I am disappointed.

However, I am not sad. Thankfully, I did not reach that point of no return with him just yet. Francisco stared up at me, but he did not look happy with my speech. There had to be more. He was still holding back information. Just tell me everything, please!

He lowered his head and said, "okay." *I was so mad that I ended our date. I did not want to associate myself with someone whose friend goes off tricking people. He is "guilty" by association, but don't worry I made up an excuse that I had an emergency come up.*

Immediately I felt awful. It was so like Francisco to put my needs above his. Ugh. Why did you do this? He could have been someone special for you, Francisco. *No, I don't want to hear anything. You come first before any guy, and besides he is guilty by association like I said.* I didn't say anything to that. He was right, so I let him continue telling me what he needed to tell me.

When I got home I started to stalk my date and surely enough I found the picture that he had shown me with Jake. I carefully looked into Francisco's eyes, and even though he looked away I knew without him even telling me, that he had gained access to their accounts, or very useful information somehow.

See Francisco works in software, and sometimes dabbles into hacking. *Based on how you're looking at me, you know what I did.* I nodded my head slowly. *I input Jake's face in a program that I created that is kind of like*

Google Finder but more advanced. What did you find? I felt my heart beat a little faster.

Francisco came closer to me and hugged me tightly. It was almost uncomfortable, but I didn't pull away. I knew I would need it. What did you find? Please tell me. *He is almost like a ghost.*

Even if you type his name online he does not show up. He probably pays a service to keep his online presence nonexistent. Is that a good thing or bad thing, Francisco? My heart was beating like a jackhammer now. *Lucianna, I'm scared to tell you.* Why?

I don't want you to lose who you are again once I tell you, babe. Please know that I am here for you, and I will always be here for you. You are stronger than anyone I know. Just spit it out please. I can't take this suspense anymore.

Francisco's left leg started to shake. *Like I said he is almost like a ghost, but my face finder software found him in one other place.* Where? *I found Jake on one of your sister's bridesmaid's Instagram accounts.*

The world stopped spinning once again. I could hear my own blood flowing through my veins. I could hear the small spider that was on the wall spinning a new web. My stomach felt heavy. Suddenly, my hands started to shake uncontrollably, but Francisco grabbed my left hand and put it on his heart. He was trying to ground me.

I would never show you this, but I know you are stronger than those mother fuckers! Francisco had tears running down his cheeks as he pulled his phone out and showed the picture. That bloody picture will always live in my mind like a battle scar. In it Jazmine was giving Jake a side hug. He had his hand on her head. They were at some sort of pool party with a few other people. Henry was there as well.

He was wearing the bathing suit that I had given him a month before I found him and my sister having sex. I couldn't believe what I was seeing, but it was right in front of my face. I couldn't handle this. *Black.*

It all went dark. This was too much for my mind and heart to handle. *Lucianna, please wake up. I am getting scared.* I twitched my wet eyes open. Francisco was looking down on me. His face was red and puffy. He was crying.

Where am I? I moaned softly. *You are on my thighs.* Why is my face wet? *Babe, you were crying while you were knocked out. You fainted.* Francisco gently said. Which triggered everything to come back to me again like whip lash.

Jazmine and Jake knew each other, and that meant one thing. They had somehow orchestrated my "meeting" with Jake. THIS COULDN'T BE TRUE, BUT I KNEW IT WAS! FRANCISCO!

WHY IS SHE DOING THIS TO ME? IT IS ONE THING TO FALL IN LOVE WITH SOMEONE ELSE'S PARTNER, BUT A WHOLE OTHER THING TO PURPOSELY HURT SOMEONE. ESPECIALLY WHEN THAT SOMEONE IS THEIR OWN SISTER!

I was shouting at the top of my lungs. My mind was spinning in circles. WHY? WHY, DID SHE DO THIS TO ME? WHAT DID I DO TO DESERVE THIS? I HAVE ALWAYS DONE EVERYTHING TO MAKE HER FEEL LOVED AND SPECIAL. WHY DOES SHE HATE ME?

Francisco stared at me with Bambi-watery eyes, and pulled me comfortably towards him. He began to caress my hair. *Babe, I think I know why.* WHY? *I stalked Jazmine's and Henry's individual instagrams and I learned quite a bit of how they have been doing over this past year. The first couple of months they individually liked posts pretraining to things like, love not being something that should be punished, etc.*

Probably to justify what they did to you, but in the last two months or so Henry has liked two very crucial posts. One of them said, 'When you still think about her.' The other one said, 'If I could turn back time.' I think that might have sent your sister over the edge. You know how jealous she can be. But to that level? *Yes.*

Remember how she ripped my charger up when she thought we were talking too much, and wanted more time with you? Yeah, but she was 12 then. *It doesn't matter sweetie. She still ripped my charger because she wanted you for herself.* I thought about that for a moment. I had thought the gesture was cute at the time. I figured she loved me so much that she only wanted me to be with her, but now I see how toxic the entire situation had been.

Suddenly I felt guilty. I had to apologize to my best friend. Francisco, I am sorry for not punishing her for ripping your charger. I looked shamelessly at him. He smiled. *Hey you bought me a new one, and made her apologize babe, but that's in the past.* Yeah, in the past when she used to love me, and not hate my guts.

Lucianna, I don't think she hates you. As strange as this sounds, I do believe that she still loves you. In a sick and twisted way. Francisco made sure to emphasize the twisted part. It made me want to defend Lucianna, but I knew my best friend had no ill intention towards me, so I bit my tongue and let him speak. *About three months ago she liked a post that said, 'If you have a sister, never let her go.'* THEN WHY THE FUCK IS SHE DOING THIS TO ME?

Why did she hire her friend to play this dirty trick on me? *She is jealous of you. She may love you, but her jealousy triumphs over the love she has for you. Also, please forgive me for saying this, but she is just a bad person. She is evil. She doesn't have remorse. I am not a psychologist, but she is a narcissist that wants everything for herself.*

Each word that Francisco spat out were like slaps to my face. I didn't want to believe it, but there was no denying it now. My baby sister who I raised like my own daughter turned out to be a monster, and there was no one to blame but me.

It was all my fault. I was always too nice to her. I defended her when she didn't need to be defended, and now she is a grown ass adult who thinks she deserves everything in the world. *Don't make that face!*

I know you are blaming yourself, but it is not your fault! You raised her to the best of your abilities. You were still a kid yourself. You didn't have to raise her, but you stepped up to the plate and did it anyway. She wasn't a baby either. She knew how much you were doing for her, and she's 100% to blame for who she is as a person.

I slightly nodded my head to Francisco's words. He was partially right. She wasn't a baby when our parents died, and I guess she always had those jealous, narcissistic tendencies, but mom and dad must have nipped them in the butt when they saw them. That is where I went wrong, not punishing her when she deserved it. *Stop now.* My best friend broke my train of thought and pulled me in for a hug.

Don't blame yourself, babe. You can't change the past, but you can decide how you move forward from this. I don't want you to lose you for another year. It will break my heart. My body froze upon hearing him say that.

I had been so broken last year, that I had not seen how much I had hurt Francisco for not being myself. I would not do that to him again. *I'm always going to be here for you, okay?*

I know, and even though all of this just tears my heart, I don't have enough tears to cry for an entire year again. Plus, I don't want to go through all of that again. *You don't have to, Lucianna. She doesn't know where you live, nor does Jake.*

Cut them off, and forget about them. They are not worth your time and effort. Francisco wiped his tears away as he looked at me. He hugged me tighter. I welcomed the hug, but it wasn't going to be enough to help me move forward. In order to do that I had to take action in my own hands now. I couldn't just sit around and accept this being done to me. Not this time.

No more lying around! The days of having me as a punching bag were over, and with epiphany, I stood up and looked my best friend right in the eyes. He looked perplexed, but I smiled to ease his nerves. *Are you feeling better, babe?* No, but I will with your help. *What do you mean?*

Francisco, my sister crossed a line that I did not know existed, let alone think was possible to cross. She made a fool of me, and what Jake did was beyond evil. *Yeah, and that is why you have to forget them. They are not worth it. Quit all communication with them. I will be there every step of the way.*

I stared blankly back at my best friend's empathic face. He meant well, but his advice was wrong. I couldn't cut Jazmine out of my life just yet. I may not have punished her enough as a child, but I would teach her a lesson that she would never forget as an adult. *Babe, I know you—what are you planning?*

I met his gaze, steady now. Francisco, I need your help with getting revenge on Jazmine, Henry, and Jake. That is the only way I can move on with my life. *But babe,* not buts! I know that I will always feel lonely, bitter, heartbroken, and ashamed if I do not teach these fuckers a lesson.

Francisco's mouth opened slightly, but then he shook his head in agreement. *If that is what you want, I will do everything that I can to help you, Lucianna. But, as your best friend I need to be real with you.*

I don't think it's the best choice for your heart. That said, quite frankly you are right. They deserve to be taught a listen. Plus we have the upper hand over them. They do not know that we know. They will pay for what they did to you.

Francisco was smiling from ear to ear now because he loved getting justice, and I was certain this would help heal him too. When he found out what Jazmine and Henry did to me he wanted to hack their social media accounts and post what they had done to me for all their friends to see.

It had taken all my willpower to stop him. I almost wished I hadn't, but now we would both get the payback we deserved. *Do you already know what you will do to them?* Yes, I already know exactly how I will retaliate, but I will share that information with you tomorrow. Right now, what I need is to unwind. I need a mental break. *I understand, babe. Shall I go?* No, please.

Can you spend the night with me? *You don't have to ask twice.* Relief washed over me at his answer, and the rest of the afternoon became a blur once more. All I remember is watching a movie with him before heading off to take a much-needed shower.

Once there, I shamelessly cried and cried. As much as I hated to admit it, losing my sister all over again pained me deeply. Oh, how I wished my mom and dad were still here. Life would have been so different if they had never died. I was certain my sister and I would have shared the closest bond possible, but no. They were gone, and I had to raise her... and look where that got us.

Estranged. And me, crying in the shower. Ugh. I let out a slow sigh, forcing myself to regain composure. Once I had, I turned off the water, dried myself, and slipped into my underwear before putting on a large shirt.

Feeling better, I stepped back into the kitchen, a familiar smell filled the air. Sopes—one of my favorite Mexican foods. *Welcome back, babe. I hope you're hungry.* A smiley Francisco handed me a Sope which was a hand made fried bread topped with ground beef meat, and with a tomato sauce creaming all over the lettuce, beans and avocados. Pure heaven on earth.

My nostrils were in heaven. *Are you ready to pig out?* Yes, sweetie. You shouldn't have done all of this for me! *Nonsense, now sit down and eat!* I sat on the stool by the island table. Francisco handed me my plate and I bit in.

Immediately the taste of soft bread and grease hit my tongue. It was blissful and I took some more bites and tasted the perfectly cooked meat. My taste buds were crying from joy. Unfortunately, my stomach did not feel the same.

As soon as my first bite of food entered my stomach I lost my appetite. My stomach got knotted up, and I could not eat anymore. Francisco noticed immediately. *Knots in your stomach?* Yes. I am so sorry. I am hungry, but the anxiety of all of this won't let me eat such a perfectly good meal.

Don't worry, babe. Have it tomorrow, and go off to bed. I am here if you need anything okay? I nodded my head and went to my room. Once there, I went to my drawer and pulled out a sleeping pill. The last one that I had taken was months ago, but I knew that I would be needing it tonight. I placed the bitter pill in my tongue and swallowed it with the help of some water.

Hopefully this would help me sleep through the night, and with that I turned my lights off and headed to bed. Thankfully, I fell asleep pretty fast, but I woke up at 5 in the morning with sweat all over my back and tears covering my face. I had a nightmare. A nightmare where my sister hated me for being me. A night mare that was my reality.

I didn't go back to sleep after that. Instead I spent the next two hours critiquing every part of my face and body in the mirror. My hips were too large for my thin frame. My arms were so skinny that I could barely see any muscle on them.

My waist looked bigger than when I was in my 20s, and the visible crow's feet on my face were taking the beauty from my face. *Ugh,* why am I so ugly? I yelled to myself. Maybe if I had different sized lips, or different shaped eyes people wouldn't be coming in and out of my life like a revolving door?

CHAPTER 6

Revenge Is A Dish Best Served Cold

You are everything in this world, but ugly. Ah! I yelped as Francisco's soft-spoken voice caught me off guard, causing me to stumble toward the mirror that I'd been staring into. Before I could lose my balance he pulled me back toward him.

I am not letting you do this to yourself again. Come with me, and we can have breakfast. Afterward, I want to hear the idea you have for revenge. Let's put that big beautiful brain to use in a positive way.

I didn't respond. Instead, I quietly followed him back into my kitchen. I was embarrassed to even acknowledge that I had spent my early morning critiquing every part of my body and face.

Something that I had gotten way too comfortable with this past year. All thanks to my sister, Henry and now Jake. Ugh, just the thought of his name made my skin crawl. He probably thought I was the biggest fool. Falling for a guy that wasn't even attracted to women. I could only imagine how disgusted he must have felt by kissing me.

Every time his lips touched mine must have been agonizing for him. Why did he do it? Was it all just a cruel game—something my sister had put him up to? The thought alone made my stomach twist. It was wrong. Inhumane. And the more I let it sink in, the more my sadness hardened into something sharper.

Anger, an uncontrollable fury that had me huffing under my breath by the time I sat on the kitchen table. My chest felt tight, but then I saw it—a bowl of *Chocolate Coco Pebbles* waiting for me. The sight alone softened the edges of my frustration.

It was such a small, silly thing, yet it grounded me instantly. It was Francisco's doing. He knew exactly what to do to make me feel better. See, this cereal had always been my favorite as a kid, and somehow, he had gone out of his way to bring a piece of that comfort back to me.

A smile filled my face. *That is the beautiful smile that I like to see. Now enjoy.* Thank you, sweetie. I grabbed my spoon, and this time I ate slowly, and was thankfully able to keep everything down. I was calmed by the time I finished.

Now, tell me your plan. I am all ears, babe. Well, last night I wanted them all to suffer a lot, but after a night's rest I thought of a simple yet effective way of giving them all (specifically Jazmine) a small taste of their own medicine. *Tell me.* Are you able to hack the systems of the town hall where the wedding will be?

You mean the sound systems, tvs etc? Yeah, that was what I meant. *That is child's play, Lucianna. Don't offend me.* Francisco slightly shoved me to the side. We both started laughing. Laughter was exactly what my body and soul needed because after that laugh it was much easier to tell him what kind of revenge I had in my mind. *What else, babe?*

My plan is simple. I want a video of myself playing on every TV/screen in that hall explaining to everyone who the real Jazmine is, and everything that she has done to me. This video will of course expose Henry as well. I paused and waited for my best friend's input.

You are right. It is simple and yet effective. I like it, but what about Jake? For Jake I want to hang flyers with a QR code near his bakery to show his customers who they are supporting. When the customers scan the code they will watch a small clip explaining what he did to me.

I love everything about this, Lucianna. It is enough revenge to show them that you are not a pushover. Thanks sweetie. *When do you want to record the videos?* Now since the wedding is tomorrow. *Okay, you want me to record you, or will you do it on your own?*

Buzz, buzz, buzz. Someone was calling my phone. I jumped up and ran over to it. It was Jake. Shit! Francisco, I haven't responded back to him since yesterday. What do I tell him so he doesn't suspect? *Uh, tell him that my boyfriend cheated on me, and that you had to comfort me!* Are you sure that will work? I lifted my eyebrow in doubt.

Trust me, he'll believe it. He is one of the girls. I tried to keep the smile from appearing, but Francisco had a way of making everything better. Ha. I will do that. I guess he was one of the "girls," and that thought brought me some comfort.

Jake knew how tough life could be since gay men also suffer in society, unlike straight guys. At the bare minimum he knew some pain. *Buzz, buzz, buzz. He must be very 'worried' about you, Lucianna.* Oh, I'm sure he is. I rolled my eyes and answered the phone.

Hello? *Lucianna! I was so worried about you. You have not answered any of my texts since yesterday.* He was breathing hard on the other side. Oh give the man a golden globe for his "acting skills." I thought as I got ready to use mine.

I'm so sorry, Jake. I said with my voice quavering. Francisco, my best friend, had an absolutely horrible day yesterday. He found out that his boyfriend was cheating on him. I went straight to his house and accidently left my phone at home.

Jake's huffing and puffing soothed a bit. Right on cue. *Is he okay? Do you want me to go over and bring you guys some lunch?* Ha, I'll never give you the satisfaction of knowing where I live you jerk.

Oh, you are the sweetest thing in the world, Jake. That is okay. I brought Francisco back to my place. I am going to cook him his favorite foods, and that means we can text like normal since I have my phone with me. I missed you a lot yesterday. You know that? I bit my lip as I said that.

I have never been a good liar, and if Jake was here he would have seen it written all over my face. *Okay, cutie. Text me once you can. I can't wait to see you tomorrow. Shall we meet tomorrow at my bakery?* Yeah, does 5 p.m. work? *You got it.* I can't wait for tomorrow. Oh, and don't forget after the wedding we can come unwind at my place. *I wouldn't have it any other way.*

I hung up the call and slowly kneeled to the floor. I felt queasy. This was too much for me, but I knew deep down in my heart that if I didn't beat them at their own game I would never forgive myself. My newly freshly wounds would never heal. On top of that my egocentric maniac sister, who I foolishly still loved, would never learn a true lesson.

I owed it to my parents to try to put her on the right path, and being punished was the only way I saw fit. Uhh! I wailed in my dreary. *Lucianna, babe what is it? Are you having second doubts? Remember, you don't have to do anything you don't want to do, okay?*

Oh Francisco my sweet friend. I looked at him as he looked down at me. His eyes were filled with tears. It broke my heart to see my best friend like this. I couldn't let him see me down on my knees, so with all the strength I could muster I got up.

I took a deep breath and went over and hugged him. Sweetie, this is something I must do. Please wait for me here. I will go to the restroom and record my "expose video now." *Are you absolutely sure?*

Yes, you know that I need to do this for my soul, *and to punish Jazmine, right?* I felt my cheeks get red, but I nodded yes. There was no lying to my best friend. Okay *babe. I'll be here.* Perfect, once I am finished I'll come back out and I will send you the videos so you can do what you need to do with them. *Got it.*

Once more I walked out of my living room, and I entered the spare restroom in the middle of the hallway. I never used that restroom so it was completely empty. Nothing but white walls. This was a perfect place to record, so without any hesitation whatsoever I propped my phone by the counter of the sink and I turned my camera's timer on.

I fixed my long black hair a bit, and then I moved my palm over the phone's camera sensor. The video was starting in, 3, 2, 1. *Hi everyone, this is Lucianna. For those of you who don't know me, I am Jazmine's older sister. In a way I am also like a mother to her as I raised her when our parents died.* My voice was getting high pitched so I took a deep breath and I wiped the tears from my eyes, and then I continued.

I love my sister with all my heart, and I also see her as a daughter in a way. I paused for a second to remove the newly formed tears again, and I recommenced. *Today is Jazmine's wedding, and I am happy for her. Truly I am, but I am also heartbroken.*

Unfortunately, I am recording this video with all the pain in my heart. My sister who I loved like a daughter destroyed my life. Henry, her new husband used to be my fiance. We were supposed to get married, but then I caught Henry, and Jazmine having sex in my bed. Yep you heard right.

It shattered my world, and I decided to move out from this town and start my life anew. It was a difficult year not speaking to my sister, but eventually she reached out to me, and I forgave her. I even decided to attend her wedding. I mean she is my only living family member, so why not try to reconcile? Especially since she is with child.

Well, that is what I tried to do. Forgive and move on with caution. Woefully, Jazmine had other plans. Apparently she was mad that Henry had been liking some posts on his instagram regarding feeling regret about leaving me. That sent Jazmine over the top once more.

She has always been a conveying jealous mean girl, and what did she do? She hired her friend to "date and trick me." Yes you heard me right. The man right next to me at this very moment. Go on ahead and find him. Yep, that guy with the big mysterious eyes is actually one of Jazmine's best friends.

He is just as bad as she is. He did his part in making me fall for him, but thankfully I did not do such a thing. However, I will admit that he was passionate and a good kisser, but you want to know what is so sad in all of this?

Even as I enjoyed our cuddles and kisses, he was probably vomiting in his mind. Why? Oh, because he is a gay man, and of course there is nothing wrong with that, but what he did is beyond forgiveness. Once more I wiped the tears from my eyes and continued to speak.

Anyway, I wont take anymore of your time Jazmine. I genuinely don't wish you any harm. Just know the only reason I did this was for you. I want you to be a better person, and hopefully by feeling some of the pain that you have made me feel, you will change.

Your daughter needs a healthy momma. I believe in your ability to change. Don't forget the sweet little girl you used to be. Bye forever. Oh, and before I leave fuck you Henry, and fuck you Jake.

I waved my hand over the camera and the recording stopped. I then opened the *Google Photos* account that Francisco and I shared, and I uploaded the video. There he would be able to access it and do what he needed to do with it.

As for the flyers to hang around Jake's bakery I quickly emailed Francisco the fonts that I wanted him to use. The flyer would be simple. Just a picture of Jake with the warning, *Don't Support This Person Who Preys On The Love of The Innocent*. Done and done. I was certain that Francisco would make everything look perfect. I didn't even have to text him to start. I could see that he had already downloaded my message.

Great. Now that everything was done on my end I had time to overthink. Gosh, I hated doing all of this. It was not healthy, but what choice did I have? Mom, dad, what would you guys do in this situation? I closed my eyes and lied down on the fresh restroom tiles. I tried to clear my mind and just relax.

I thought long and hard on that tile floor for what seemed like hours, and it wasn't until I got a text from Francisco confirming that everything was a go on his end did I come back into my reality. With caution I rose from the floor and looked at myself in the large wooden framed mirror.

Staring back at me was a thirty-four year old woman. A woman who had been brought to her knees, but was now standing. There was no backing down anymore. I knew in my heart that I was doing the right thing for me, by standing up for myself.

Even if it hurt my sister. She wouldn't die. It would teach her a lesson in the long run, and plus it would also teach Henry and Jake a thing or too. Yep. I nodded to myself. I was not the victim. I was now the survivor. The time of being a Debbie downer was over. It was time to go back to Francisco.

Cautiously I left the restroom and walked down the hallway. Immediately I could smell pizza, but not just any pizza. It was *Papa Johns*. Ugh, that is my favorite pizza Francisco! *Ha, I was going to start cooking, and then figured I would rather order in.* I'm happy you did. Do you want me to whip up a salad? *Already taken care of.*

How in the world did you do everything so fast? I looked at him perplexed. *Babe, you were in the restroom for 3.5 hours.* Oh, so I hadn't just imagined that? *Nope, but it's okay. You needed your space, but come over and eat now.*

I ran to the kitchen table and sat down. The smell of grease triggered a hunger that I didn't know I had. Immediately I opened the pizza box. It was a 10 slice meat lover's pizza. My favorite. I eagerly grabbed a slice and placed it on my plate, but before I could take a bite Francisco came up to me.

Everything is ready with the video. Are you 100% sure this is what you want to do? I did not even flinch and quickly nodded my head. *Okay then. I will pick you up right as the video is finished playing at the wedding. No ifs and or buts, okay?* I wouldn't have it any other way. *Great, now dig in!* You don't have to tell me twice!

I picked up a slice of pizza and took a bite. Crunchy, greasy, meaty, cheesy—it was everything I needed. It smelled like pure garlicky heaven, and before I knew it, I had devoured three slices and washed them down with a large cup of ice-cold water.

I was so full I could barely move, and honestly, I didn't mind. It gave my mind something else to focus on, pulling me out of my thoughts for a while. Which was much needed, and to top things off once I cleared the table, I noticed Francisco had already set up the first *Final Destination* movie in the living room—one of my favorite horror franchises.

I'm telling you, if I ever get a vision that something bad will happen on a flight you better listen to me. I'll be right behind you getting off the plane! Oh, and I never want to see you drive behind a truck with logs! That is off the table! We both started to laugh like kids. It was a nice moment. Nothing but talking pure nonsense, and I loved every second of it.

My best friend was doing his best to distract my mind and I truly loved him for it. Huh, that made me think of something interesting. I might have lost my sister, but you know what? I really had gained a brother.

A brother who was stronger than anyone I ever met. For crying out loud Francisco's entire family stopped speaking to him because he was gay, yet he still managed to smile everyday. He was strong, and I had to let him know. Sweetie? *Yeah?* You are my family now. You are my brother, and you are my motivation.

Whoah. His mouth opened slightly. Is everything okay? *Yeah, babe, but that means the world to me. You are my sister too, and I love you.* He reached out and hugged me. Needless to say we both balled our eyes out after.

It was extremely therapeutic, and following our crying session we had a deep conversation where I learned even more about Francisco. Sadly his father would beat him any time that he didn't act "manly" enough. It broke my heart.

I hated him every day of my life up until I was 17. When I turned 17 I socked him in the mouth and walked away from it all. I felt euphoric and free, and now I don't hate my father or family. I honestly pity them.

You let the ball of anger out that was also hurting you. *Exactly, but it could have been worse. I know of people who let their anger consume them. I don't want that to happen to you sweetie.* It won't, but just like you did, I need to let this darkness out of my body. I need to be free from the hate that I feel towards Jake, Henry and Jazmine. Once this is out I know for a fact that I will be set free. *I will be here every step of the way.*

With that deep conversation out of the way we watched four of the *Final Destination* movies. It ended up being a terrific day, and Francisco went home around 9 p.m. I called it a night soon after, and thankfully I didn't need a pill to sleep.

I drifted to dream land before my head even touched the pillow. Sadly, I did not get a restful night's sleep. All through the night I was awakened by horrid dreams of Jazmine, Henry and Jake taunting me. By 7 a.m, I had enough and decided it was time to get up.

There was no point in having more nightmares when today was going to be the biggest one of them all, and this one was real. Today was "the big wedding," and the only way to end this nightmare was to start it.

CHAPTER 8

The Big Day Is Here

The entire thirty or some so minute drive to Jake's bakery I was a nervous mess. Was I going to slip up and tell him that I knew he was a lying sack of dog poop? What if he already knew that I knew?

Ideas swirled in my mind as I thought about every possible scenario where things could go south. Several times I contemplated driving back home, but when I pulled up to the parking lot near Jake's bakery I surprised myself on how collectively calm I had gotten.

My heart was no longer racing. My left leg wasn't twitching anymore because deep down I knew that if I didn't show Jazmine, Henry and Jake that I wasn't some rag doll that couldn't be pushed around then I would never forgive myself.

Plus, I would never be able to live with myself because my soul would never heal if I didn't get the justice that I needed. With that realization, I put the car into park and turned it off. I quickly dried the sweat from my hands and fixed my hair.

A glimmer of hope formed on my face as I applied some lipstick, and that gave me enough confidence to get me out of the car and greet Jake as he walked over to me. He was smiling from ear to ear. I was pleased to discover that I did not feel angry or sad upon seeing him.

All I felt was pity. He no longer looked like a handsome masculine man to me. He looked like a pathetic little boy. A little boy who was so immature that he got his confidence from tearing down women.

"Lucianna, you look stunning." "You literally left me breathless." He came in for a kiss. My body tensed up, but I responded as naturally as I could. I locked my lips into his. Nothing. I felt absolutely nothing for this lost child.

That made me grateful. "You just look wonderful." Hey, you don't look shabby yourself. He smiled at my fake compliment as we reached his car. He then opened the door for me. "Your chariot awaits." Fake, all fake.

Thank you, Jake. You are such a gentleman. My soul hurt from lying, but I smiled and got into his car. "I have to say, I am afraid all eyes will be on you instead of your sister." Huh? Did he know my plan? No, he didn't. He was just complimenting me.

Relax, Lucianna, breathe. Oh, no way. This is Jazmine's day. I am so proud of her, and I am so glad that we are on speaking terms again. I was doing my best to play along with him. He was falling for it.

"Aren't we lucky that they are getting married at the town hall?" "That is only a 10 minute drive away." Good because I cannot imagine sitting down any longer with this dress, "or in this suit." We both laughed, but not for the same reason. He was laughing at my joke, while I was laughing at his stupidity.

Just keep on driving, you coward. I silently thought as he wrapped his gross hands around my fingers. "Isn't it cool that we don't have to bring presents anymore thanks to online registries?" His pointless questions were agitating me, but I responded anyway.

Hmm, I kind of miss bringing presents though. It was always fun to shop for someone. "Yeah, I guess you do have a point, but at least we don't have to carry the present around, right?" You are right about that. "Yeah, but you know what?" What?

"I missed you these last two days." I'll give Jake something, he was a charmer. That was why he had fooled me so quickly, but now that I knew better, the entire ten minutes that he talked till we reached the town hall were an absolute torture. All I wanted to do was slap him across the face. Which honestly surprised me because I was not a violent person.

"We are here, cutie." I looked around the parking lot. There were probably around 60 cars there. Damn. It was definitely a wedding. "Are you feeling okay, Lucianna?" I turned around to face Jake. He had a "concerned" look on his face. Yeah, I am okay. I am just very timid. I haven't seen most of these people since I was dating Henry. "Don't worry, I am here for you, and with you."

Damn the guy could act. If I didn't know any better I would have really believed that he cared for me. He then leaned over his seat and softly kissed me on my cheek. My mind was strong, but my body at that moment was weak. I felt a wave of satisfaction flow through me.

Instantly I felt like a hypocrite, but then I remembered that I was only human. "Ready to go in?" I am. He parked the car and I opened my door. There was a nice warm breeze that brought me back to reality. I had to get into character now, and play the role of the supporting, naive sister.

I was sure that those who knew what had happened between Henry, Jazmine and I would think I was the dumbest person in the world for being here, but who cares what they thought. I was here to heal. "Can I hold your hand inside?"

I thought about that for a moment. Did I want people thinking I was with Jake? Hmm, who gives two hells. I could not care less what others thought. Plus, if I did not hold Jake's hand then the entire plan could fall apart. That would be a big no no, so I intertwined my fingers into his hands. "Let's go."

My heart started beating like a jackhammer. As we walked across the parking lot I could hear people cheering from excitement. In another life I would have been so happy for my sister. All I ever wanted was for her to have the world.

It sucked that things turned out like this. *Invitation please.* A security officer by the door asked us for our invitations. It was customary in this wedding hall. I pulled out my phone and showed him. *Have fun you two.* He opened the door for us, and we entered the lobby.

It was decorated just like I had imagined. Jazmine always wanted a purple and gold wedding. There were freshly cut lavender flowers hanging from the ceiling. The smell was impeccable.

Right in the middle of the lobby there was a gold-colored table, and on the table were four vases of purple-colored roses. My eyes were immediately drawn to them. "It is very pretty, isn't it?"

Yes, it really is. "Look at that giant beautiful portrait of them hanging over the table." I picked my head up and looked at where Jake was pointing. It was a beautiful picture. It almost made me teary eyed. My sister looked genuinely happy. She and Henry were dressed in gold, and were hand in hand at the beach. It looked like Pismo beach to me. It was sweet.

For a brief second I felt proud and happy for them, but that soon faded as I reached a tall purple table that had the black crystal embroidered guest book. The guest book that I had purchased for my wedding. My fingers trembled from disgust as I opened the black book that still had L&H carved out in the side.

Lucianna and Henry. How sick of them to be using this book! My hands began to shake uncontrollably. I was close to ripping the pages from the book, but as I read the names of the over 80 people who had already signed my body eased up.

I couldn't forget why I was here, so I took another deep breath and calmed myself as I recognized some of the names on the list. A few were distant cousins, and a few were common friends that we once shared, but the rest were strangers to me. Good, that would make exposing them that much easier.

"They're starting to serve the food." Jake broke my concentration and I quickly wrote my name. I added a winky face next to my name. Finished. Will you sign? "Nah, it's okay cutie." "Any particular area you want to sit in?"

Can we sit next to the exit on that far left corner? "Whatever you want, cutie." "Are you ready to go in?" Give me a second please. I calmly combed my hair with my hands, and I took two deep breaths. Everything will be okay, Lucianna. You can do this.

I'm ready. Jake grabbed my hand once more and we entered the reception hall. Almost immediately I noticed my sister. She was all smiles. She had a long blond wig on. It was styled in waves, and she had a beautiful crown with a small veil over it.

Her make up was gorgeous. She had a medium red lip on that really helped her thin lips look fuller. She had gold-colored eye shadow that brought out her small eyes. The only thing that I didn't like was she was wearing a foundation that was too light for her.

That said, she looked stunning. On top of that she was glowing. Her big belly looked super cute in my wedding dress that she had tailored. Funny enough her baby belly gave the illusion that she had a nicer body than what she really did. It helped balance her lack of hips and big back. "I am assuming the pregnant lady in the wedding dress is your sister?" Jake joked.

Yes, that is her! Let's go say hi. I said a little too excitedly. "You're adorable." "Let's go." I let Jake lead the way, and as he dragged me along I felt his hand begin to sweat. He was nervous. I wondered if he felt bad for what he was doing to me, or maybe he was just nervous that his scheme would get exposed? I'll never know.

"Lucianna!" "You are here, and oh my gosh who is this?" Jazmine stared at me with joy in her face. If anyone looked at us at that moment they would have thought she was the happiest sister in the world. She ran up and hugged me, and then introduced herself to Jake. "I don't know about you just yet, but I am excited to hear about you."

"Welcome to my wedding." For a brief second Jake's eye twitched, but he quickly composed himself. "Thank you, and congratulations everything looks beautiful, and so do you." I carefully watched Jazmine interact with Jake.

She kept pressing her lips together as she spoke. I could barely contain my anger because ever since she was a child whenever she would be doing something she wasn't supposed to be doing she would press her lips together. She thought she was fooling me. I could have screamed the truth right in her face right then and there, but instead I bit my tongue.

I complimented her on her appearance and the hall. In all honesty that wasn't hard because I was being truthful. She looked gorgeous and so did the venue. Jazmine always had an eye for fashion and design. I always wished that she would have pursued that as a career, but she never had any drive.

It used to upset me that she never pursued her talents. For crying out loud she had this everyday hall looking like a palace. There were gold color chains hanging from the ceiling. There were thousands of purple and gold balloons floating in all directions. To top things off the tables were arranged in a beautiful swirl of both colors.

Also, the center pieces on the tables were just magical. I don't know how she did it, but there was a candle at the bottom of a vase surrounded by water and petals. "Your sister must have spent a fortune on the decorations!"

I looked straight at Jake as he spoke to me. I had been so caught up in the decorations that I had not noticed him dragging me to the table by the exit. I was glad that I had been caught up in my own little world because as we sat down he told me that everyone had been looking at me.

"Cutie you look so stunning that everyone is looking at you!" "I don't mind the woman staring at you, but those men looking at you from head to toe are making me mad and jealous!" His nose slightly flared as he spoke to me, and his face was red.

Either his acting was quite good, or there was something more to this now? Was he into me? I mean I guess he could always be bi, or he was jealous that people weren't staring at him? Who knows? It wasn't my problem.

"You really are special." "Take a look around you." "People just gravitate towards your beauty and peace that you bring." I turned to the side and saw two little girls staring at me. They were smiling at me. It brought me a sense of warmth, but when I turned to the other side I saw an older woman and man looking at me with a sense of disgust.

They were judging my decision to wear a black dress. I felt it in my bones. If they knew the reason they wouldn't have judged, but it made me laugh. In one corner I had admiration but on the other corner I had hate.

"Can we take a picture together?" Once again, Jake interrupted my trance. He looked so happy to be with me, and now he was asking for a picture? Gosh if he wasn't lying about not knowing my sister I would have really thought that he was into me.

He is not into you Lucianna. Stay focused. This is what evil people do. They manipulate and use others. I reassured myself and took a picture with Jake. "This might just be my new background picture." Uh huh I thought to myself. "I am going to grab us some drinks." "What would you like?"

A nice cold water bottle will be fine. I smiled at him, and he happily left me. Finally I was alone, but before I could even gather my thoughts someone started walking toward me. At first I could not tell who they were because their makeup and hair was distorting my perception of them, but as soon as they spoke I knew who it was. It was my ex-mother-in -law, Christina.

I had not seen this lady in over a year. Ironically, I used to be quite close to her. She was nice, and a good person. "Lucianna, I am shocked to see you here." Her voice was low and stern. Not at all cheerful and beaming like I remembered it. "You have some nerve showing your face around here."

Wait, what? I have some nerve coming here? What do you mean? I said angrily. My breathing got heavier as I stared at Christina in confusion. "You left my boy for another man!" "Why are you here?" She shouted right at my face. Thankfully, we were at the back table so no one heard us. "Leave, now please."

I really couldn't believe what I was hearing. Christina thought I was the villain in all of this! I was painted out as the monster who destroyed an engagement. I could not handle this, and I could not handle the way that she started to shove me out the exit. Without thinking twice I grabbed her hand and looked directly into her eyes.

Your son was a no good bitch who cheated on me with my sister. If you choose to believe that stupid lie that either he or Jazmine told you then you are an idiot. Lastly, I am not leaving.

I was invited by my sister who I have forgiven to attend her wedding. You have no say in this, Christina. Quite frankly it makes me sad that you believed that lie about me. You know damn well how much I loved Henry.

She didn't say a single thing as I told her the truth. She simply stared at me with her cold blue eyes, so I let her arm go. Which was a big mistake because as soon as I let her arm go she formed a fist and tried to swing at me, but it was to no avail.

Jake came out of nowhere and grabbed her arm. "Why don't you have a seat now ma'am, and leave my lady alone?" Christina turned angrily at Jake, but did not say a word. She simply walked away.

I collapsed into my seat. I was not expecting that. I really thought everyone knew the truth about what Jazmine and Henry did. I guess that wasn't the case. Some people really believed that I was the villain here. I didn't know what to think, but now more than ever I was glad that the truth would come to light. "Are you okay?"

"Who was that lady?" "Why was she trying to hurt you?" She was my ex-mother-in-law. "Oh." Yep. Apparently my sister, or Henry lied to her that I was the villain in all of this. I guess it is my fault that my sister was fucking him in my bedroom.

"Do you want to go outside for a bit?" No, I feel better already. Of course I was lying, but I did not want to miss a second of this wedding. Even if it meant being harassed by someone else.

"Well in that case here is your water bottled." I grabbed the cold bottle from his hands, and I drank a few sips. The water helped me relax a bit, and for the next few minutes I lost myself in people watching.

There were several people dancing in the middle of the hall to *Temperature* by Sean Paul. My sister was running around greeting people, and thankfully no one was giving me any grief. Quite the contrary, the little area where I was still empty. I was not sure how Christina had even spotted me.

Anyway it didn't matter. "Do you want to dance, cutie?" Before I could answer Jake pulled me up and to his side. *Stick With You* by the PCD was playing and the lights went dark. No one would notice me, which is what I wanted at this point, so I agreed. Ultimately, I would rather be dancing than anxiously waiting for the moment that the truth would come to light.

"I am not the best dancer, but for you I'll try." He put his big hands on my hips as we danced to the beat of the melancholic song. I closed my eyes for a brief moment and allowed myself to imagine how things could have been if Jake wasn't playing a trick on me. Things could have been so nice, but unlike this song I would not be sticking with him forever. "Thank you for dancing with me."

We started to walk back to our seat when I spotted Henry, and he spotted me. I hastily turned my head to the side, but he came toward me. "Lucianna, can I talk to you for a minute?" Jake looked at me to see what I wanted to do. I nodded my head and he left me with Henry.

CHAPTER 9

A Stroke

"Lucianna," what? I said with a stern voice. "Uh, you know." He began to stutter. It irritated me to my core. Now he was afraid to talk to me? Just tell me what you want to tell me already so I can get back to my date. I groaned at him angrily, but in my heart I was also a nervous mess. This was the first real conversation that I had had with Henry since everything happened.

"Lucianna, that man does not deserve you." "He is not a good person." I am sure that any man, and including the man that I am with right now is a much better person than you. You have no right in telling me who is a good person and who isn't because you are a terrible individual, Henry. His jaw opened. He wasn't used to me speaking this way." "I, I am sorry." It is too late for apologies that you don't mean.

For crying out loud you didn't even have the balls to tell your own mother what you did. Do you know that she tried to hit me today? "What, really?" "I am so sorry, and I am truly and genuinely so sorry for what I did to you."

"If I could turn back time I would, but what is done is done." "I won't try to convince you otherwise, but just know this, I still care greatly about you." "Even more than I could ever care for Jazmine." "If it wasn't for the child that I am about to have with your sister I wouldn't be marrying her."

Everything he was saying was going in one ear and out the other. It was all a lie. I now knew that he only cared about himself. He was nothing but a coward, and a loser. "Don't trust, Jake, please." At the very least he had a small percent of decency trying to warn me about Jake. However, I played his warning off. I simply smiled at him, and wished him a good marriage with Jazmine.

I turned my head and walked away, but then he yelled. "Jake is using you!" "He is one of Jazmine's friends." "He isn't even straight!" "They planned this all together to make you feel like a fool." There it was.

Everything that I knew was confirmed, but gosh hearing it said out loud in person really hurt me. What in the world did I do to deserve this hate from my "loved" ones? I began to feel hopeless again as Henry rushed back to me. "Leave this place and forget about Jazmine."

He looked at him with pitiful eyes. That made my blood boil. He of all people felt pity for me? I felt pity for him! I wanted to slap him across his ugly face, but instead I simply looked him straight in the eye and said, "If that is the case, why didn't you do anything to stop it?"

You said you love me, but you stayed with Jazmine, and you allowed her to plan this fake relationship with Jake, right? What kind of a person are you? "Lucianna, I only stayed with her because I was mad that you left and blocked me, and then when I found out she was pregnant I had no other choice." "I couldn't leave her alone."

I hope you have a great marriage with my sister. Don't worry, after today neither of you will ever see me again. I left Henry aside, but I could not leave my tears aside. They started to fall down my cheeks. A worried looking Jake ran to me.

"What's wrong, cutie?" "What did he tell you?" Yeah, wouldn't you like to know. I thought silently. He was just telling me that he is sorry for ruining my life and being a coward. We made amends, but it still makes me emotional. Jake's large eyebrows lowered, and his jaw relaxed.

He came in and gave me a hug. I smiled at him as I brushed my tears away. I wanted him to keep thinking that his plan had not been foiled yet. "They are serving the food now." "Let's go take a seat." I nodded my head, and followed Jake.

He caressed my hair and gave me a warm smile. He was a fraud, but the time for my vendetta was near. Once the food was served the couple's dance would start, and then I would expose these three demons. I eagerly went back to my seat, and in perfect timing because as I sat down the servers came and brought us our food.

Even with all the emotions going on in my body I could not help but admire the plate. It was a plate of *Birria with frijoles, pasta salad, orange rice and tortillas.* The traditional Mexican party food. It smelled heavenly. *Here you to you two.* I took my plate and Jake took his.

"I love latino food!" "You guys have the best cuisine. I smiled and grabbed a spoonful of orange rice. I brought it right up to my nose and smelled it. It smelled heavenly. A mixture of onions, salt and some chicken spice was what made this rice amazing.

Sadly, my stomach was all knots, so I only took a few bites. Jake on the other hand was so busy inhaling his food that he did not notice when all the lights went back on, and the music went off. It was time.

ATTENTION LADIES AND GENTLEMEN, WELCOME TO THE WEDDING OF HENRY & JAZMINE VANDERWAAL. I HOPE ALL OF YOU ARE ENJOYING YOUR DINNER. I ASK FOR

THOSE OF YOU ON THE DANCE FLOOR TO PLEASE TAKE A SEAT. ANYONE IN THE LOBBY PLEASE COME OVER AND TAKE A SEAT. OUR BEAUTIFUL COUPLE WILL HAVE THEIR FIRST DANCE AS A MARRIED UNIT. I'LL GIVE YOU TWO MINUTES TO GET SEATED.

A two minute timer started. "I'm excited to see your sister dance." "Do you know what song they will be dancing to?" She did not tell me, but I think I know what song. "What song?" Ha, you are a little curious guy, aren't you? I winked at Jake as I tried to maintain my composure.

We were only seconds away from my video playing. Francisco had insured that it would play right as all eyes were on the "happy" couple, so during their "first dance as a married unit." My revenge was near.

My body tensed up. My palms were sweating, but I held my ground and prepared myself. I slowly moved my chair out from underneath the table, so I could easily leave through the door that was just next to me once the video was over.

Five, four, three and here they are! Jazmine and Henry walked into the hall. They were hand in hand. Jazmine was smiling from ear to ear, but Henry looked flustered. Jazmine did not seem to notice, or at least didn't care.

She was all teeth and gums as she gave the cue to the DJ to play the song, but instead of music playing, and a video of their relationship being shown on the projector, I came on.

My voice was booming all over the hall. My face was being projected on the white empty wall that was supposed to be for them. Two mini TVs in each corner also played my video.

The room grew loud. People started to take out their phones and record. Jazmine began to shout to turn the tvs off. They immediately went off, but she could not turn off the projector. That was connected directly into the ceiling and to turn it off meant getting a ladder.

"Lu, lu, lu." Jake tried to speak, but started to stutter. I looked directly at him and smiled. Jake, you tricked me. I was falling for you, but thankfully I got wind of your plan before it was too late. You are an evil guy, and your revenge is coming to you at this very moment. "What, what, do you mean?" You took the remaining kindness in my heart, Jake.

"GIVE ME THE MICROPHONE!" Jazmine's deep voice was loud enough to be heard over the gasps of the people and even my own video, yet she still ran over and took the microphone from the dj's hand. "YOU JEALOUS BITCH!" She ran directly at me.

I stood up to face her. I was not scared of her. I wanted her to come and confront me. Maybe then she would understand the pain she caused me. "WHY DID YOU RUIN MY WEDDING?" How stupid did you think I'd be to not figure out the disgusting plan that you and Jake laid for me?

Why did you want to hurt me more? You already destroyed my life! I yelled at her with fury. Her lips quivered with anger and she tried to slap me but I grabbed her arm in mid air. Don't you dare try to hit me! She pulled her arm back with fury, and lost her balance. She fell right on her butt. AH! AH! IT HURTS! "LUCIANNA PUSHED ME!" "MY BABY!" "SHE WANTS TO KILL MY BABY!"

"HELP ME!" "MY STOMACH HURTS!" Before I could react a group of people rushed to Jazmine's side. Like always she had become the victim. I couldn't stay here anymore. I headed straight for the exit, but then a security guard grabbed my arm. He pulled me so hard toward him that I thought my arm would come out of its socket. Watch what you are doing! I yelled in frustration, but he ignored me.

"Wait!" An annoyed Jazmine yelped. "Let me ask my sister something before you remove her." The guard nodded his head. Jazmine *clicked and clacked* her way to me. She adjusted her wig, and then spoke.

"Why did you try to ruin my wedding?" "You had your time with Henry, but cheated on him!" "It is too late for you now!" Shut the fuck up you crazy bitch! You are the one who slept with him on my bed! Tell the truth Henry! I dogged him as I shocked myself with the vocabulary that came out of my mouth.

Like the coward he was, he lowered his eyes and turned to the side. "You see everyone." "She is lying." It is you who is lying. In a move of pure hatred I tore her wig from her head. Her face got dark red, and some guests started to laugh, but like the thugs they were, her bridesmaids came to her rescue.

The three musketeers came in and formed a circle around me. One of them yanked the wig from my hand before I knew what was going on, and the other two tried pushing me to the floor, but they weren't any match for me.

I was filled with adrenaline at this point, and I managed to kick one in the stomach before the security guard reacted. He dragged me across the hall with everyone staring in disbelief. My eyes hurt as the flash from the phones blinded me.

I am detaining you until the police arrive! I didn't do anything! *You pushed the bride!* No I did not, and you can check the surveillance video! He abruptly stopped his walk to ponder on what I said; which gave me enough time to call Francisco. *Hello Francisco*, meet me at the front of the hall now! *Got it!*

Now sir, can you please let go of my arm? *Sorry, ma'am, but I am well within my rights as a security guard to detain you until the police come and figure this entire thing out.* His brows were wrinkled tightly. He was being serious.

He really thought I had harmed my sister. My sister who once again had played the damsel in distress. Enough was enough. I was not going to sit around and do nothing, so with all my might I brought my left foot up and kicked the security guard right in his private area.

He fell straight to the ground. Unfortunately, taking me down with him. We landed with a thump to the floor which caused people to rush into the hall. *Don't let that lunatic escape.* A woman yelled. *Stop that bitch from leaving!* A man screamed.

Huh? I couldn't believe my ears. People were pouring into the hall now. *Why did you do that to the bride, you jealous whore?* The crowd of people formed a circle around me now. I felt something wet hit my face. Either someone threw water at me, or they spat on me. I couldn't believe it. What was going on?

I tried to stand up, but the groaning security guard pulled me down toward him once more. This time I hit my chin on the marble floor. The pain was electrifying. "Let her go now!" I turned my head to the left and saw a red faced Jake running in. He jumped at the guard and ripped his grip from my fragile purple arm. He pushed the people aside. Why did he save me? I had no time to think. This was my time to escape!

Wasting no time I rushed out of the hall, and jumped down the four steps leading to the parking lot. I could see Francisco in the distance sitting in the driver's seat. His eyes widened as he looked at the commotion that was going on. Start the car! I yelled at the top of my lungs. In a blink of an eye I was in his car and we were driving 70 mph in a 30 mph zone. I was breathing heavily.

Sweat had drenched all over my black dress. Tears filled my face, and a giant purple bruise was covering almost 50% of my arm. Warm blood dripped down from my chin. What the hell was going on with my life?

Why did I even want to seek revenge? Look where that got me! Crying and beaten up. *Lucianna, what in the world happened?* Francisco, I should have never done this! Look at me! I was nearly killed back there! She hangs out with monsters who are just like her!

She made it seem like I pushed her to the floor. She made it seem like I hurt her. The stupid security guard bruised my arm, look! I was dragged, and heckled across the hall. Am I some sort of animal?

Stop right now! You are not an animal. Jazmine and everyone who hurt you are animals. You are a kind soul, and we will get through this! I heard every word that Francisco told me, but I was in another world.

Had I really dragged out of a wedding hall like I was some sort of vermin? How could people be so cruel? I could hear Francisco speaking to me, but all I could focus on were flashbacks of being encircled by the crowd of people throwing things at me.

It was too much. I began to cry like a little five year old who fell from their bike. I even lost my air a couple of times. *Enough is enough. I am pulling over.* Francisco stopped his car and embraced me in his arms.

I am sorry, babe. I am here with you. Let your feelings out. He was speaking so fast. I couldn't understand anything, but even if I had, all I could hear were the profanities that were yelled at me. I felt numb and dead inside, but still I wanted to hug my best friend back.

I tried to move my arms up, but they felt like heavy bags of cement. What was going on? This wasn't normal. I tried to speak, but my chest felt heavy. Kind of like if there was an anchor on top of it. I tried to move my mouth once more, but it was like it was stitched together. It wouldn't open.

Something was happening to me, and Francisco couldn't see it because he had his head on mine. Oh no. Fear swept through my body as I felt one of my eyes begin to droop. Was I having a stroke?

I don't want to die, God. Please help me. I could feel the right side of my face getting wet, but not the left. That was the confirmation that I needed. I was having a stroke, and I couldn't yell for help!

It couldn't end like this. I desperately gasped for air. It was getting hard to breathe. Move, Lucianna, do something! I yelled at myself internally. Don't let your life end like this, ridicule and in defeat. Something in those words gave me the motivation and power to move my head a tad, and that is all that I needed.

With all my physical and mental strength combined at that moment I managed to slightly bang my head on Frarncisco's head. It got his attention. He pulled away from the hug and looked at me. *Lucianna, what was that for? Oh my goodness!* I heard a series of screams coming from Francisco, but at this point I was simply confused. The next thing I knew I was on my back.

Please, we are at 60 Boulevard Saint-Germain. Thank you! Lucianna, stay with me please. I don't want to lose you. You are needed in this world. Your light shines brighter than anyone that I know. At this point I could barely see. My eyes had filled with tears, blinding me almost completely.

I was scared beyond my witts, but then a familiar sound… *Weeooo, Weeoo, Weeoo,* the sound of an ambulance filled my ears. They were here, and in no time I was being inspected. Bright white lights penetrated my eyes. I managed to blink, and they were excited about that. *She has control of her eyes! We got to inject her with Alteplase now! Here you go! Okay, I have administered it to her. Let's go to the hospital now!*

CHAPTER 10

Will I Ever Be Okay?

My eyes slowly flickered open. It was bright. My room wasn't this bright. Where was I? I tried to lift myself from my bed, but I couldn't get my body to fully move. Only my fingers and toes seemed to be reacting.

What in the world was going on? I tried to think back on what had happened, and suddenly my body got ice cold. I recollected what had occured. The wedding, and the aftermath that left me feeling like I was about to have a stroke! Wait, did I have a stroke? Was I in the hospital? No this couldn't be the case! I had to be dreaming!

For goodness sake, who has a stroke at the tender age of thirty-four? Someone who has lived a tough life, that's who, Lucianna. Fear filled my insides. I had to wake up from this fever dream, but why couldn't I move? You had a stroke, Lucianna. A stroke that must have been caused by the immense stress that Jazmine, Henry and Jake put you through.

Oh no, please God. Don't let it be the case. I turned my eyes side to side to try to wake up, but it was useless. I was still stuck in my bright hell that was my nightmare. No! Get up, Lucianna! I cried out loud.

Bing, bing, bing, bing, a rapid and loud ringing filled my ears. Almost immediately I noticed someone rushing to my side. *She is up, but why is her heart rate through the roof? I think she must be realizing what has happened to her. You are right. Let me go ahead and add a sedative to relax her, and then we can explain what is going on with her. Sounds like a plan.*

There were two distinct voices talking. Even in my confused state I knew they were either nurses or doctors. Their presence helped me relax a bit, or maybe it was the sedative that they had given me?

Hello, Lucianna, I am Dr. Nguyen. I am here with nurse Jimenez. We just gave you something to help relax you. Don't worry it will not put you to sleep. I know you might feel confused and scared, but rest assured you are in great hands and out of any danger.

Dr. Nguyen was talking to me like I was a baby, and quite frankly I appreciated it. Her voice was soothing and easy on my ears. *Lucianna, what you had was a mini stroke. You are out of danger, and luckily you were brought and administered medication just in time. You should make a full recovery within the next 24 to 48 hours. We will keep you here until then.*

The doctor's words must have worked like a self-fulfilling prophecy because as soon as she had spoken them, I was able to move my hands and head again! *Ah! I see you're able to move your head again. That makes me happy.* This time I was able to look the doctor and the nurse directly in the eyes. They were both smiling down on me.

I will be back here to discharge you tomorrow if you continue to heal like you are now. In the meantime nurse Jimenez is here with you for the night. Have a nice evening. I tried to say thank you, but I did not have control of my mouth yet. *Don't strain yourself, get some rest. Your sister is in the lobby waiting to see you. Hopefully that will help. Anyway I must get going.*

I really did my best to try and scream, but my mouth was still shut tight. I moved my hands and neck back and forth but nurse Jimenez took that as a sign of happiness. *You must be happy that your sister is here.*

We called her right away when we saw that she was your emergency contact. My emergency contact? Damnit. That was right. I had not updated my insurance information in over five years. *Let me go and get here. I'll be right back.*

I felt a whiff of air hit my face as the nurse left the room. I probably had a minute tops before she came in here with Jazmine. *Sigh.* She was going to see me at my lowest, but I would not give her the pleasure of acknowledging her presence. I would fake sleep, so with that I shut my eyes and turned my head to the left of the door.

This would prevent my sister from directly seeing my face since I was now right up against the monitor. Good. *She is right over here. I'll give you a few minutes to be with her, but visits are finished in ten minutes, okay?*

"Thank you, I'll be right out." "I just want to make sure she is okay." *Click, clack, click, clack,* her heels went as she approached my bed. "Lucianna, it's me, Jazmine." Her voice was soft and echoey. "Are you awake, hermana?" She lightly touched my shoulder. My body reacted by delivering a dose of goosebumps all over it. Hopefully she did not notice that.

Squeerch, the bed went as she sat on it. "I hate seeing you like this." "I never wanted anything bad to actually happen to you." "You know I am horrible at apologies, but Lucianna I had to get back at you."

"You almost ruined my life and reputation by your accidental recording of me having sex with Henry." "I had to get back at you." "I didn't want to do it, but life is about getting even with those who wronged you."

"Even if you love them with all your heart." Was she being serious right now? "The easiest way I saw to get back at you was through Jake." My heart began to beat faster and faster the more she spoke. My sister was genuinely out of her mind. There was no way in hell that she ever acted like this when we lived together!

"I want us to be sisters again." "I love you, Lucianna, and don't even worry about my wedding." "Karma got you right back." "I mean for crying out loud you got a mini stroke, we are more than even!"

The more she spoke the more I became aware that I really didn't know my little sister anymore. Who was this woman? "Gosh, I miss you so much." "I know you are asleep right now, but don't worry I am recording this entire conversation so I can show it to you in the future." "I just want us to go back to what we were, when we lived together." I felt her hand comb my hair. I almost flinched but held it together.

"Sister, believe it or not I always looked up to you." "You are strong and independent." "You are beautiful and fearless." "Your simple presence in any room commands attention." "I really like that about you, and I want my daughter to have that as well." "That is why I need you back in my life."

I hated myself at that moment because I could feel my eyes swelling with tears. How could I be so stupid and be willing to forgive everything she did to me from one silly speech? I knew the answer.

If there was one thing Jazmine knew how to do, it was how to make you believe what she wanted you to believe. She was like an abusive spouse who knew exactly what to say to keep you in the relationship. Sadly for her, I would not fall for her tricks and manipulations.

"I don't have much time here, but I want to quickly try to explain what led me to Henry." "It wasn't what I wanted." "Believe me sister." "It wasn't." Then what was it? I thought in my mind as I tried to keep the squeals that come from crying in.

"All I can tell you for now is that it was natural." "You wanted to advance your career, and you left him home alone with no attention." "I felt bad for him, and started to cook and clean for him, and we just ended up falling in love!" "I swear it was never on purpose." If she was trying to make me feel better it did not work. I wanted to shake her and say, "YOU DO NOT DO THAT TO FAMILY," but instead I continued to fake sleep.

There was a long pause, but then she spoke again. "Well, I got to go sister." "I hope that next time we meet you will be holding my baby girl." "Love you, Lucianna." *Click, clack, click, clack,* the sound of her heels leaving the room eased my body as she left my room. That said, I did not move for about 2 minutes to insure that she was gone, and when I was certain I slowly stood back up on my bed and thought profoundly.

My sister was wicked. She was evil, but I still truly loved her. I wanted the best for her, but now more than ever I knew deep down that I would never be in her life again. Yes, she said that she loved me, but now the truth was clear. Jazmine only loved Jazmine.

That was a depressing realization, and *ugh,* my head felt like it would explode just thinking of her. I had to stop. Reminiscing of her was not good for me. In fact, it made me physically ill. No more doing that Lucianna. It was time to put myself first. The rest would fall into place.

I took a deep breath and let out all the negative energy that I held inside, and without wanting to, I drifted off to snooze land. When I awoke there was a different nurse taking my vitals. I must have slept that entire night because I could see the sun shining through the blinds. Good, I needed it.

Good morning, I told the nurse. *Wow! You look so much better. Look, you are talking and even holding your own body up!* I'm talking? Oh my gosh, yes! I am talking again! I yelled with joy. The nurse smiled. *Now take it easy. We don't want you too excited. Let me go and call the doctor to come look at you.* Of course! I stupidly said.

I could feel myself smiling from ear to ear because I could finally speak to Francisco! He was probably worried sick about me. *Knock, knock,* I turned my head to face a smiling Dr. Nguyen.

I am so happy that you are recovering wonderfully. May I hear your heart? Please. The doctor walked over to me and heard my heart and lungs. She felt my body around, and stretched my legs. I was able to lift my left leg fully, but my right leg was still stiff, but I had full control of my arms now.

What's the verdict doctor? *You are healing up nicely. However, I want you to stay one more day here. Also, I will prescribe you anti-stress medication for a month.* I'm sorry doctor, but I don't want to become addicted to medication.

A smile formed in Dr. Nguyen's face. *That is a common misconception, honey. These pills are nonaddictive. You will be fine, okay?* Are you sure? *Of course. This medication does not cause dependence.* Alright, I quietly whispered. I'll trust you.

Good. Plus, don't worry, our psychiatrist will come speak to you later in the afternoon. I want you to be well informed. That brought a smile to my face because at least I would have a doctor who actually specializes in stress and anxiety telling me about the medicine.

I will come check on you before I leave for the day. Your lovely nurse here will take care of you. It is breakfast time, so I want you to eat all your food, even if it doesn't taste too yummy, okay? You got it doctor. She nodded and left.

Lucianna, do you mind if I finish taking your vitals? I want to make sure they stay stabilized the entire day. That way you can go home tomorrow. Of course, but nurse, what is your name again? *Jayme.*

Nurse Jayme, I have a few questions that I didn't ask the doctor since she seemed to be in a rush. Nurse Jayme looked at me, and winked. *Lucianna, even if the doctor seems rushed you can ask any question that you may have.*

Your time with any doctor is your time with that doctor, or any health care professional for that matter. They are getting paid for their job.

Don't be afraid to use your voice, and advocate for your own health. I felt my cheeks get red after her speech, but I thanked her for the advice. *No problem. When we are on the clock with a patient it is our duty to give that patient our full attention.* Thank you nurse Jayme. *You are welcome. I'll come check up on you in 2 hours. Your breakfast should be coming soon.*

With that she left, and I went straight for the phone on the right side of the bed. It was a cord phone. I had not seen one of these in ages. It made me nostalgic. My parents had one of these phones when I was a kid. Oh how times were simpler then. A time where phones were only phones and not super machines that controlled our daily lives.

Anyway, I digress, I clicked on the physical buttons. It felt oddly satisfying punching in a number instead of tapping it on a screen. *Bring, bring, bring,* the phone rang and I waited. I hoped that he would be up. It couldn't be earlier than 7 a.m, and Francisco didn't start work till 8 a.m, meaning he didn't wake up till 7:50. *Hello? Is this the hospital? Is Lucianna okay?*

The tremble in his voice made me want to cry. He was so nervous for me. Francisco, it's me. *Oh thank God! I was so worried about you. They did not let me go see you because I am not blood related!*

I know sweetie, and I will make you my emergency contact in my insurance and remove my wicked sister. She had the audacity of coming to see me. *That bitch. I hate her!* Ouch, my ear, Francisco. *Ugh, sorry Lucianna. I just hate her, but enough about her for now. How are you? What happened?*

Unfortunately, I did have a mini stroke. *Oh my gosh. I am heading up there right now!* Yes, please. I really do need you here. *Let me just message my manager that I will be two hours late for work.* Okay, sweetie.

I'll be waiting for you here. I slammed the phone down, and in perfect timing because one of the staff members was bringing my food in. *Hello, breakfast is here.* The staff member walked over to my bed and pulled out a tray from the side of the bed. Thank you so much, I told him.

If you need anything else just dial 03 on the phone. I will be back up in half an hour to get your tray. Thank you, again. He smiled and left the room. I gently scooted my way up to a fully seated position, and I surprised myself how easily I did it. Thank God my body was rapidly healing.

I was even feeling hungry, so I peeled the plastic wrap over the plate and I instantly got a smell of plastic. My plate contained eggs that had no taste. There were slices of apples, and I hated apples. The only thing that looked and tasted decent was the brownie. However, I ate everything that was before me.

I wanted to get strong, so I gobbled everything up. I actually ate it fast which left me with some free time before Francisco would arrive. He lived about 40 minutes from the hospital, so I had about 30 minutes to myself. Which meant it was time to research what had happened to me, and how I could prevent another stroke from ever occurring again.

Within a few minutes of my research it was apparent that my stroke was caused by my stress because my family had no history of strokes. I wasn't overweight. I did not have diabetes. In fact I did not have any of the physical conditions that lead to strokes. The main thing I had in my life was stress which apparently can lead to high blood pressure, and trigger for a stroke.

Fuck, I had been stressed for well over a year. I had to manage that better because I wanted to live a long healthy life. The first step in doing that was getting a therapist. Thankfully, that wouldn't be too hard. Francisco had gotten me a therapist when all of this went down, but I only saw her once and gave up.

I wasn't in the correct head space for that, but I mean when are you when you need therapy right? *Knock, knock, is the queen of the hospital here?*

Francisco! You are here! I excitedly yelled. *Is the queen proper, in there?* Oh shut up! Come in, please. I need to see your face! Francisco came in with a bouquet of purple roses. *I brought this for you.*

Gosh, you are the sweetest thing ever! You can place them on that table over there. *I am so glad to see that you are you again, Lucianna. You really scared me yesterday.* His voice cracked, and his eyes watered as he talked to me.

Never leave me, okay? You are the only person in this world that cares about me, and if you were not in it, I don't know. I just don't know. I tasted salt in my mouth. I didn't even realize that I was crying, but seeing my best friend cry just brought me to tears.

Promise me, you'll never let Jazmine, Henry, Jake or anyone else ever get you like this again. Promise me that you are putting them behind forever! I stared at him as tears rolled down his cheeks. His lips were quivering, and he was breathing heavily.

That was it. Seeing Francisco so distraught helped me realize that Jazmine was not my sister, but someone who I simply shared parents with. The only family member that I had was my best friend, Francisco.

CHAPTER 11

The Decision To Move

Francisco, I promise you, that I will do my best to leave Jazmine behind. You are the only family member that I have now, sweetie. We may not share blood, but our bond is beyond unbreakable. *That is what I wanted to hear.*

Leave that trash behind. Don't worry about revenge anymore, and you will surely shine once again like you are starting to already. What do you mean? He looked down at my legs. I hadn't realized but my legs were dangling over the bed. I had moved them!

Oh my goodness. I brought my once stiff legs close to my body, and then I stood up in excitement. I was me again! This was amazing! Joy took over my body, and I decided to jump up and down, but I stumbled on the way down.

Francisco tried to rush over to prevent me from falling on the floor, but he was a little late. I still manage to bang my elbow on the cold tile floor. My knee scraped the side of the bed, and the weight of my body brought down the health monitor machine. Which in turn caused a loud beeping sound to fill the room.

Lucianna, babe, are you okay? I felt Francisco lift me up, but I was coming in and out of consciousness. I had forgotten that the doctor had said that my blood pressure was a tad low. Fuck. I hoped that I had not screwed myself over. The last thing that I wanted was to spend more days at the hospital.

"Just place her a tad elevated and she will be fine." I heard nurse Jayme's voice loud and clear as Francisco elevated my body onto the bed. *She was so excited that she could move her legs again that she began to jump up and down, and then stumbled to the floor.*

The rest was like a domino effect. "I can imagine." "The important thing is for her to not accelerate herself right now because she can have a reaction like she just did." *Understood.* Francisco sounded embarrassed, but then nurse Jayme reassured him. "On the brightside, she is obviously better." "More than likely she will be released tomorrow, and she will make a full recovery." "I am sure about it."

Nurse Jayme walked over to me, and smiled. I felt my cheeks get red as she injected something into my IV drip. "I put a relaxing sedative in your IV." "Now, why don't we let her get some rest, and you can come back to visit her around 4?"

I think that sounds like a plan. I'll be back soon Lucianna, rest well, babe. I tried to respond to Francisco, but before I could form any words my eyes closed, and I drifted off to dreamland.

I woke once more to the sound of a new nurse taking my vitals. "You're up." "Good." "How do you feel?" I still feel so sleepy. What time is it? "It is a quarter after 4." Oh gosh. I slept for over 5 hours! "Don't sweat it." "Your body needs rest, and by the looks of it you are almost in tip top shape." I hope so. I am kind of tired of being in this bed. Is there a way that I can go walk somewhere?

"Of course." "The hospital has a lovely garden." "Let me go grab you a pair of walking shoes." "Size please." 7 and a half. "Got it." The nurse left with a smile on his face. Meanwhile I stretched my arms and legs. I was feeling more at ease, and as soon as the nurse came back I put my shoes on and I was on my way to the garden.

The nurse held my hand for the first couple of minutes of my walk, but as soon as he noticed that I was strong to be on my own, he let me do my thing. While he sat down on one of the ceramic garden benches and watched me from afar. I was happy that he gave me that private space because it allowed me to think on my own.

Francisco was right. It was time to move on. Not only did I need to leave Jazmine, Henry and now Jake behind, but also my old life. It was time to start fresh. Which meant that I would have to resign from my job, and sell everything that I owned.

I didn't want anything from my past following me to my future, so that meant another thing. I had to move, and this time I needed to move far away. The only issue with that was Francisco. I could, and would not leave my friend.

I had to convince him to come with me, and I was sure that I could. Afterall, he worked online so he could live anywhere, but where? Hmmm... Maybe we could go to Asia for a year? I had enough savings to do so, and to not dive into all my earnings I could possibly even teach English there?

Who knows? The possibilities are endless. "It is nice to see you smile." Huh? *Oh sorry, I didn't mean to scare you. I just said it is nice to see you so smiley. It makes me happy when patients are content.*

I stared at the nurse intensely. It dawned on me that I had not paid much attention to him since I woke up. However, upon closer inspection he looked quite familiar. I had to ask him if I knew him from somewhere. Have I met you before? The nurse stood up from his bench and towered over me. He was quite tall, at least six foot three. He flashed his white smile at me. *Yes, I went to Union Middle School with Jazmine.* I stared at him blankly. I still did not recognize him. Plus, Jazmine was eight years younger than me. How the hell would I even know him?

I can tell you don't remember me. Maybe it was my growth spirit? He laughed quietly. *Maybe you will remember the time you picked up Jazmine from volleyball practice and got her in trouble for making fun of the fat short kid. You know the one who was crying as Jazmine and her friends laughed at him?* Instantly I remembered.

Jazmine was in 7th grade and she and a group of girls she wanted to impress were meticulously picking on a sweet boy. They were calling her every name of the book. From hog to cow, to shrimp. I remember being so mad that I yelled at her in front of everyone.

It was one of the only times that I ever yelled at her. I told her, "Don't you ever make fun of someone when you yourself aren't perfect." "Especially when you are trying to impress kids who probably laugh at you behind your back." I even forced her to apologize to the boy.

She was made for days, but I had stood my ground that time, and I had not allowed her to manipulate me that time. She eventually changed her tune with me. She knew bullying was something that I did not tolerate.

After that she hid whenever she bullied someone I suppose because she would get in trouble for that from time to time. However, since I trusted her word, and I never saw her do it again I believed her when she said that the bullying was directed at her first.

Gosh I was such an idiot. *Do you remember me?* He asked again. His voice sounded so tender asking if I remembered him, and I don't know why it brought so much peace to my heart. I wondered if it was because his voice was masculine but soft at the same time, kind of like Shawn Mendes's voice?

It's okay if you don't. Oh, but I do remember you, but boy you have had such a growth spurt! His cheeks got bright red when I said that. It made me laugh. He even turned his head to the side. He was timid. He looked like a big-ole muscular kid.

Don't be shy. I am glad you are doing well. I mean look at you. You are handsome, smart and I can tell that you are a good person. *It took me a while to realize who you were, but once I saw your last name, I knew it was you.*

Why, my last name? *Your last name is Ceja. When Jazmine would bully me "I tried to say well at least my last name isn't eyebrow in Spanish."* I don't know why, but that made both of us start laughing uncontrollably.

It felt amazing to have a laughing attack. My stomach cramped as I tried to get control of myself, and my eyes were watering, but gosh it felt amazing. The last time I had one of those was years ago.

Shall we go back inside? I don't want to keep you out too long. I nodded my head, and started to follow the nurse, but then I stopped. What's your name? *My name is Benson.* I extended my arm out and shook his hand. It is a pleasure to meet you, nurse Benson.

The pleasure is all mine. I just wish it wasn't at the hospital, but hey you are almost good as new! No, I should say better than before! I like that. Better than before. That is going to be my motto.

I smiled at that thought, and followed Benson back into the room. He helped me back into bed, and I was grateful for it because my body felt sore. *I'll come back in two hours to check on your vitals, okay?* Sounds perfect.

He soon left, and I turned on the TV on the wall. Thankfully it was a smart TV, so I clicked on Youtube and I started to watch a documentary on lions. It was interesting, and for that brief moment I was at peace.

I did not even remember that I was in a hospital until Benson came back. *I have some fantastic news for you. The doctor has cleared for your release at 8 a.m. tomorrow.* Will she come back to check on me one last time? *If you want to speak to her she will be more than willing to, but she has seen all your vital reports and your progress sheets that I, and the other nurses have filled out for you.*

You are back on the road to recovery. She just wants you to follow up as soon as you can with your primary care provider. The idea of not seeing the doctor again did not sit well with me, but I did not want to waste her time. I knew that she had more important patients to see.

Thankfully, Benson saw the look on my face and had the doctor in my room within ten minutes. "I am glad you are doing so well, Lucianna." "Like, I told Benson I want you to follow up with your primary care doctor so you two can come up with a treatment plan to never have this occur again." "The anxiety medication that I have given you is good for a month, but after then your doctor must prescribe it, okay?"

Thank you doctor for seeing me one last time. "No need to thank me dear." "I'll go ahead and leave you with nurse Benson." With that the doctor left and I was alone with Benson. He took my vitals once more, but this time he took his sweet time in doing so.

It was strange. He wasn't really making eye contact with me, and when he did his cheeks twitched. I felt like he wanted to tell me something. I had to know what it was.

Nurse, Benson, *yes?* Please tell me what you want to tell me. Whether bad or good, I will learn how to control my reaction. Not knowing, or people feeling pity over me will make me stress more, so tell me okay?

Benson crunched his lips up and nodded slowly. *Lucianna, this is off the records as your nurse, okay?* Of course. *There is a video circulating social media where a video of you appears during Jazmine's main dance.* Yeah, go on. *Well the video ends with you being chased out of the wedding hall.*

Benson paused for a minute to watch my reaction. I appreciated it. I took a deep breath and let it out. My body didn't feel stressed or anxious. Which did not surprise me because honestly, I knew this was going to be on social media, so I guess I didn't care.

Are you okay? Yes, of course. Do you have anything more to tell me? He nodded his head, and continued. *Most of the comments are people defending you. A lot of people are writing their horror stories that they had with Jazmine, and the good times that they had with you. I just wanted to let you know that people did not forget the type of person you are.*

My stomach filled with butterflies. The fact that the general public was supporting me made me feel happy because at the wedding I was treated like a piranha. I really thought that was how the world would see me, but that wasn't the case in reality.

The truth of the matter was that the people at the wedding that treated me horribly were the exception. They were the minority who just all happened to be at the wedding since they were all vile like Jazmine. *You really are respected and appreciated.*

I felt myself grinning at Benson's praise. *I am quite content that this news cheered you up. I wish I could stay and talk some more. Sadly, I have to go for the day, but off the clock and strictly as friends can I ask for your phone number?*

I would be lying if I said I was surprised that Benson asked for my number. I had caught him several times staring at me a few times in a more than friendly manner. It was sweet, and he was a good guy, but I was in no mood to be talking to anyone.

Besides I was leaving the city, and quite possibly even the country with Francisco. Benson, I wish I had met you a month ago, but right now I am in no space to be talking to anyone. In fact, I am moving.

I don't mind, Lucianna. I just think that you are a cool person. I would love to have you as a friend. He was smooth. I will give him that. I guess there was no harm in giving my number to him since I wouldn't even be seeing him. Besides, my number would be changed too.

Alright, give me your phone. He handed me his phone and I added my contact information. He was smiling from ear to ear. He then hugged me. It was heart-warming seeing him so giddy. It made me content when others were joyful.

I promise I'll only text once in a blue moon to see if you are okay. I gave him a little wink. *Well, I will let you rest up. Bye, Lucianna.* He shyly waived. Bye Benson.

I watched him as he left my room. Hopefully one day he will find the girl that he is meant to be with. As for me it was time to sleep. I closed my eyes and went to bed.

That night I had a dream. It was peaceful. I was in an airplane, landing somewhere where they did not speak English. I do not remember the language that they were speaking, but when I woke up I felt happy, and my decision had been made.

I had to leave the US for at least a few months. It was time to restart my life. *Knock, knock, knock, May I come in?* Before he even had the chance to come in I jumped out of bed and met him right at the door.

Francisco! I am so ready to get out of here. I am glad you came. *You can always count on me, babe, and I am happy to see you back to your cheerful and healthy self, babe.* I hugged him tightly. *The receptionist told me that they would discharge you at 8, so in about 20 minutes.*

They called me last night to bring you some clothes to change into, and of course to pick you up. Great, and oh, sweetie? I said, slyly. *Yeah?* Francisco raised his eyebrow at me. He knew me like the back of his hand. *What's up?*

Not only am I ready to get out of here, but I am also geared up to get out of this town, state and country. *Oh is that so? All by yourself?* With you, of course. *Hmm. Are you sure about that?* Yeah, what do you say? Ready to move for the next couple of months?

Definitely! Let's get the hell out of here! We started jumping up and down in a circle. I felt like a little girl. *This will be good for the both of us.* Yes it will! *Our future starts now, but before that, go change!*

In a blur Francisco pushed me to the restroom and gave me a bag of clothes. I locked the door behind me and began changing. I was happy with the *Hello Kitty* pajamas that he had brought me. They were my favorite lounging around pjs that I owned, and when I put them on I felt as comfy as could be. Now it was just time to fix my hair a little.

I always valued looking decent regardless of where I was. Hospital or not, I had to get ready, so I splashed some cold water in my face, and looked at myself in the mirror. My face was plump and radiating. My muscles moved. The small frown lines that I had by my mouth deepened as I laughed. It made me so happy to see them move; which is ironic because I always hated these laugh lines.

Not anymore. Now, I loved them. It was a blessing to grow old, and it was a blessing to control my own body. I'll always remember that now, and with that I left the restroom and walked back into the room.

"Perfect timing, miss Lucianna." "I am here to check you out." A nurse was standing by the door. She took my vitals one more time, and then gave me the greenlight. I signed all the annoying insurance paperwork, and before I left the room I called my doctor and set up an appointment for the following week. I was set.

Shall we go? You don't have to tell me twice.

CHAPTER 12

Lucianna 2.0

I was in for a surprise when we got back to my apartment. Don't even ask me how, but somehow Francisco had known I wanted to leave—before I had even said a word. All my kitchenware, plates, cups, everything was boxed up. He had taken down all the mirrors and even wrapped up my couches. I stood there, stunned. My apartment looked like someone had just moved into it.

Surprise. How did you know I'd want to move? *We're two peas in a pod,* he said with a grin. *Plus, you didn't really have a choice. I was going to move you out of here one way or another.* Oh, were you now? *Yes. Babe, I would've taken you by force if I had to.*

I laughed and playfully pushed him toward the wrapped-up couch, but he slipped and landed on the floor instead. We both burst into hysterical laughter, because there was no way in hell he could have forced me out of my home if I didn't want to leave.

He was pretty thin, and we both knew I could probably take him. Which made his threat that much funnier. *You are so mean!* I held my stomach as he made an offended face. Francisco, this is the second laughing attack I have had in just two days!

That makes me so joyful. I had not laughed this way since before I got my master's degree. *Babe, it is only the beginning. You are a changed woman.* Yeah, you are right. I really am. I flourished at that realization as I walked into my room.

Wow you even cleaned my room! *You better know it. I want you to feel comfortable and relax, so go ahead and get into bed. You still should rest today.* I did not disagree and got into my soft cushioned bed.

Francisco got in right next to me, and we both laid side by side. I loved it. I felt so relaxed, and I know he could tell because he then handed me his phone. I took it, and there was a list of five countries on it. *I was thinking these five would be good destinations where we can go for 3 months, and maybe more if we like it?*

Canada, Mexico, France, Philippines and The Bahamas. *What do you think of the list?* Well, you certainly chose amazing places, but you know what? *What?* Even though I love all these countries that you chose, something about the Bahamas just stands out to me. I think that is where we should go.

I'm up for it. Let's do it. We can spend 3 months in paradise, and simply soak up the good sun. I like the sound of that. *Let's get "apartment hunting" then!* Francisco ran out of the room and came back with his laptop. He was all teeth all smiles when he came back running in.

His laptop was already open, and even before he came back to bed I could see that the *Airbnb* website was already open too. *It seems like it is a one to one ratio with the US. With both our incomes we should be able to book something pretty nice right by the beach.*

You know, after living alone for an entire year, I'm glad I will finally be living with someone again. *Why is that?* Don't get me wrong, there were times that I welcomed the quietness of living alone, but it is not for me. I need to be with someone, and I am glad for the next three months it will be with you, sweetie.

I reached over and gave Francisco a tight hug, and then we got straight into more searching. It was actually quite fun. We looked at an apartment that was right by *Cabbage beach on Paradise Island.* It looked perfect, but oh when you read the reviews they were horrid. *Anything below a 4.5 star we will not take.* Ditto.

Look at that house! It is bright pink, and the windows are white. I love it. *The price is perfect, but we wouldn't be on Paradise Island. We would be right in the capital island Nassau.* That shouldn't be a deal breaker, sweetie. At the end of the day we can easily walk by foot to *Paradise island.*

It is only across the bridge. *You have a point.* Plus the reviews on this house, or shall I say villa look great. *They do, don't they? Let's see who is renting it out.* Francisco clicked on the profile of the renter and it turns out he owns over 50 condo styled-houses, and they are in the same small community.

Oh, how fancy. They are all part of the same gated community, and it has a gym and two pools. I think I am sold. *Babe, we are going to the Bahamas!* A sense of joy and wonder flowed through me. I was as happy as could be, but then reality kind of sinked in.

What's wrong? Well, I have to call the school and let them know what is going on. I want to leave on good terms. That is a good idea, but don't be sad they will find someone. *You come first.* Francisco was right. It is hard to leave students behind but I came first. *In order to give the best of yourself you have to be happy, right?*

Definitely! With the help of Francisco's motivational speech I was back on cloud nine. *There is that smile. Okay, babe, I'll let you call the school and I'll go make us a quick late breakfast.* With that Francisco headed to the kitchen and I called my principal.

Bring, bring, bring, Hello? Hello principal Cunningham. This is Lucianna. *Oh hello, dear. How are you? Is everything okay?* No, I was hospitalized from a mini stroke that I had. *Heavens! Are you there now?* No, I was just released today. *Oh, I am so happy about that.*

Me too, but unfortunately, I will have to leave my job. The doctor thinks it is best that I do not get any stressors in my life for a while, and even though I love teaching it also causes stress. *Lucianna, your health comes first. If you can get a doctor's note maybe we can put you on medical leave and you can retain your job?*

Tears started to fill my eyes. Principal Cunningham was a good woman, but there was no way in hell that I wanted to stay in this town. *How does that sound dear?* Principal Cunningham, I truly appreciate the offer, but I am also moving from this town. There are many bad memories that I have experienced not just here, but in this state. *Oh.*

I'm so sorry. *Don't apologize. I understand. You have to live your life. I am saddened with your departure from our team, but I wish you the best of luck. Please do your best to stay healthy, and if you ever want to rejoin our team, please let me know.* I will.

Will HR send me all the paperwork I need to be let go of my job? *I am emailing them now, but please don't stress about that. We are still in summer. Take care Lucianna. You are a young and independent woman with so much to offer to the world. Don't forget that.* Your words mean a lot, Principal Cunningham. I quietly said through sobs, and then I ended the call.

It was a bittersweet moment. I really enjoyed working in my new district, but my mental and physical health came first. It was time to move on, and now the next thing that I had to do was decide what possessions I wanted to sell, keep or donate. *Hmmm.*

I scanned my room, but honestly I didn't want to deal with selling anything. Even the furniture that Francisco had wrapped up. It could be days or even weeks before anyone bought it. Forget that. I would donate everything, and start anew.

In fact, I didn't even want to deal with my wardrobe either. I would just take enough clothes to fit in my backpack and then buy everything new at the Bahamas. Yes, it may be three times the price, but I would not buy anything extravagant. Plus it was worth spending more money for my well being.

Now with my things settled we could easily leave to the Bahamas when we wanted because Francisco legit only had a bed and a couch in his apartment. That meant that after my doctor appointment next week we could leave straight to our new lives! No more Jake, no more Jazmine or Henry.

This time my life would truly change for the better, and I would heal. No more baggage holding me down. That's right, I repeated again while staring at my reflection on the only possession that I owned from my parents. A large wooden mirror that hung right by my bathroom. The wooden mirror that I would be leaving behind.

It was the first thing my parents had ever bought that cost them a good chunk of money, since they had it custom-made, but I couldn't take it with me. Jazmine's name was carved into the wood—her signature right beside it. My mom and dad's were there too, but they weren't tied to something material like this. They lived in my heart. I smiled at that thought and gave myself one last look in the mirror before taking it down.

My deep, dark eyes held a faint hint of life again, and it made my heart feel full. The girl who once dreamed of becoming the best version of herself was slowly coming back. Even my skin seemed to glow—golden brown and flawless. My cheeks looked rosy, and my lips looked moist.

I felt happy, but when I saw my body it looked at least five pounds underweight. It was obvious that the stress had affected my eating, but not to worry I would gain that weight back. Then the old Lucianna would be back, but wait, did I even want the old Lucianna back?

The Lucianna who always smiled and said yes? The one who had no backbone? I looked deeper into the mirror as I placed it down onto the floor. I searched for an answer, and then it came.

Goosebumps filled my body instantly. Without thinking twice I went to my restroom and pulled out a thin purple shaving trimmer that I used on my legs and bikini line. I don't know what possessed me next but I took that trimmer to my head and hit the on button.

It was all a blur while I did it, but I do recall the strands of my long-horse like tail falling to the bathroom floor. The next thing I remember vividly were the big black chunks of my hair that filled the floor. Then there was nothing on my head anymore.

I wasn't completely bald, but I had a buzz cut. Maybe only 3 millimeters of hair were left on my head, and quite frankly I felt liberated. I felt like a load had been taken off my shoulders, well I guess a load was taken off my head. I looked like a totally different person. I looked like a little boy with big dark eyes now, and big lips.

It made me giggle, but after that giggle a rush of regret washed through me. Fuck. What was I thinking? I looked like a boy now. Tears filled my eyes, and soon hit my cheeks. I had acted on impulse.

Something that I never did. I was always the type of person who calculated and thought about all the options before taking a risk. Hey! Wipe those tears away. I told myself. This is what I needed!

Life should be about planning things out, but also about being spontaneous from time to time. In all truthfulness, this was probably the first time in my life that I did the first thing that popped into my head without thinking.

Maybe it wasn't a good idea, but I took the risk anyway, and that made me happy. Besides, in the grand scheme of things it did not matter. My hair would grow back, and at least I had finally done something I'd been afraid of. For so long, my hair had been my identity. Maybe now, I could finally discover who I really was on a personal level, and not just on a superficial one.

That thought brought me a sense of peace. I cleaned up the strands scattered across the floor and tossed them into the trash. Here's to it growing back soon, I joked to myself as I walked into the kitchen, where the smell of chocolate chip pancakes and eggs was already filling the air.

Ah! Oh my gosh! Lucianna! Honey! Francisco stared at me with his mouth wide open. His hands were trembling as he sat the pan with eggs back down on the stove. He ran over to me and touched my head. *Why did you do this? Where is that beautiful mane?* Surprisingly, Francisco's reaction did not bother me one bit. It made me laugh. This was the exact reaction that I wanted.

I wanted to feel different, and now I did. Look, I know that I should have thought this through, but, *let me stop you there. You finally acted on impulse, and babe, I won't blame you for that. I applaud you, but let's not make this a new thing, ok?* Hahaha! You got it.

Don't worry I already cried, and had my regretful moment, but you know what? *What is it?* Hair grows back. Besides, now I can try different hairstyles. Which is something that I was always afraid to do.

Well you got a point. Francisco couldn't take his eyes from my head, so I playfully pushed him to the side. *Alright, alright I'll stop. Well for now.* He joked, and he went to get a plate for us.

I hope Ms. Baldie is hungry. You best believe it! I grabbed a piece of egg from the pan and tossed it to Francisco who started laughing uncontrollably as it hit him right on the cheek. That made me burst out laughing, and needless to say that breakfast was filled with so much joy.

I was on cloud nine—honestly, I stayed that way the entire week. By the time my doctor's appointment came around, Francisco and I had already emptied both of our apartments, which turned out to be perfect timing.

My doctor and I decided on the low dose of *Busprione* (10 mg). A non addictive drug that can help alleviate anxiety. He also recommended a really good psychologist who I could have video calls or regular calls with every two weeks.

I already had a 1 to 1 with her. She was great. She was nonjudgemental and very understanding. On top of that my doctor recommended that I take *Aspirin* every time I have a stressful day. That was just a preventive measure.

In three months he would see me again and assess if I could come off my medication. I thought it was a good idea, and now with all of that out of the way it was time to go to the Bahamas!

Francisco and I were ready. We donated all our belongings but a few articles of clothing, and we broke our leases. Sadly, both our apartment managers kept our deposits, but it was what it was! Life was too short to worry about things like that. Now it was time to worry about swimming, and relaxing, but first we had to get our tickets.

Which airline should we take? What are the options? *American, Alaska and Delta.* Any direct flights? *American and Alaska.* What is the difference between them? *Alaska leaves Los Angeles right at 11 a.m, and American leaves Los Angeles at 7:00 a.m.*

Francisco, well there is your answer! Let's book with *Alaska.* I rolled my eyes at him, and he giggled. *Hey, you work at a school! You are used to getting up early.* Yeah? That doesn't mean I like it!

True. Well, fill out your information. He handed me his laptop and I entered my personal details, and then he filled out his. Five minutes later we both had tickets leaving tomorrow for the Bahamas.

I'll go ahead and message the villa host about our arrival time. We won't be arriving till around 8 p.m, and I want to make sure he is okay with that. Sounds like a plan. Ah! I am so excited! *I am too, babe. There is nothing tying us down anywhere. We are two birds ready to fly.*

Ah! I let out another excited scream. I could barely contain my happiness. Francisco, I am so glad that we are doing this together. I want you to know that if you weren't here I would never have done this. *I feel the same, babe. I am beyond stoked.*

This will be life changing for both of us, but now we should probably go get some rest. And do any last minute packing. *Exactly. We have a long day of flying tomorrow.* I nodded my head and walked Francisco to his car, and then I waited for him to leave the apartment complex. When I could no longer see his vehicle I headed back up the stairs to my apartment.

This was the last time that I would ever go up these steps. I murmured to myself as I reached the halfway point to the third floor. I was giddy, but that soon went away when I noticed someone riding a bike in the parking lot.

How odd. The area where I lived was not a bikeable location, and this was the first time I had ever seen someone on a bike in my year living here. It spooked me, so I picked up my pace and rushed to my door. "Lucianna!"

"Please wait!" I almost fell to my knees. Chills filled my body, and the hair on the back of my neck stood up. That voice. That cowardly whinny voice.

"Please wait!" I almost fell to my knees. Chills filled my body, and the hair on the back of my neck stood up. That voice. That cowardly whinny voice.

CHAPTER 13

The Collision

"I need to talk to you, please." "Just give me five minutes." His voice cracked from yelling. It made my blood boil, but that wasn't good. I had no time for that. My health came first, so I sprinted up the stairs to avoid him. "Please listen to me." There's no way in hell! I yelled back as I reached my front door."

"Lucianna!" "Please." I could hear his pathetic sobbing as he continued yelling my name. I had to get inside my apartment, but his constant bombarding of my name caused me to drop my keys at the edge of my door.

This gave Henry more than enough time to reach me. He was pretty fast. "I just need to tell you something." Get your slimy hands off of me! He slowly removed his hand from my shoulder. Being around this scum made my pulse rise instantly. My head started to hurt, and my breathing got rapid. I had to calm down.

This was exactly how I had gotten a mini stroke to begin with. Control the situation Lucianna. You are in charge. Take this opportunity to say what you could not say before, and then leave him be. I told myself in between my deep breaths.

"Can you just give me 5 minutes?" "I promise you I will leave after that." No, I can't give you that much time, but before I go inside I will tell you, please leave me alone. You already ruined my life. You are a coward who only looks out for himself. I regret the day I met you.

With that I pushed him aside and picked up my keys. "Give me one second is all I am asking." I am giving you one more chance to go back down the stairs or I will call the police. His mouth opened slightly from the shock. He could see that I was serious. "Fine I will just blurt it out here in the open for anyone to hear!"

"Jazmine faked her pregnancy!" He nervously yelled. I don't know why that revelation made my brain stop for a few seconds, but it did. That must have given Henry a false sense of me being willing to hear him out because he continued speaking. "This is life showing me that I need to get you back Lucianna." "I am here to do anything and everything to get you back."

Just hearing those words come out of his mouth restarted my brain. I pushed by him and tried placing my key in the knob, but in a rush, and with my back turned he pounced on me. He grabbed my hand, and forcefully turned my head towards his and kissed me.

With all the strength that I could muster I tried shaking him off but he had me pinned by my door, so I did the one thing that I knew would free me. I kneed him right in the balls. He let out a squeal as he fell like a brick.

Don't you ever force yourself on me! You chose Jazmine, and now deal with it! My heart was going a million miles an hour now, and to make matters worse my keys had fallen over the stairs to the parking lot. I had to get them, so I quickly sprinted down the three flights of stairs.

Woefully, as I reached the last step to get into the parking lot, I felt a sharp pain on my ribs. Before I could react to it I was on the floor, and someone was slapping my face. "How dare you kiss my man!" "You slut!" "You whore!"

Her tone death voice penetrated my ear drums, but her yells gave me the adrenaline that I needed. Using both my feet I kicked her in the chest. Waiting no time for her to react I stood up and punched her right in the nose. She looked stunned. This was the first time that I had ever laid hands on her.

I savored the moment, and then I spoke. Don't you ever lay your hands on me again, Jazmine. It was your coward of a husband who forced himself on me, and I know that you know that! Leave me the fuck alone!

You are a curse to me. I don't want anything to do with you. Jazmine stood up, and just stared at me with her mouth wide open. Henry on the other hand was running to me. "I'm sorry for cheating on you, Lucianna." "I love you!"

I didn't even bother reacting. I couldn't stay there. I ran to my car and drove off without thinking twice, heading straight to Francisco's place. I needed to calm down—this wasn't good for me—so I just kept driving until I finally reached his neighborhood.

He lived on the wealthier side of a small town about twenty-five minutes away, his apartment complex tucked beside a beautiful park. I pulled in and parked there first, needing a moment to breathe. For about ten minutes, I let the fresh air steady me before finally driving over to his parking lot to meet him. *This is for you, sweetie.* He handed me a Hershey's chocolate bar—my favorite treat.

I slowly ate it. I then told him everything that had happened, and he did his best to hide his fury, but his face could not lie. It was red, and the vein on his temple popped out. I felt awful telling him all of this, but he was the only person that I had now.

I am going back to your place to get your bag. I don't want anything happening to you. You just stay here. They can't enter this park since it is in the gated community. I nodded my head, and let Francisco leave.

While he drove off I walked back to the park. I soaked up the cool summer air. I then laid on the grass, and tried to ease my mind. I did my breathing exercises, and I slowly played back what had just happened to me.

Henry had said that Jazmine was not pregnant, and it was true. When she attacked me her stomach was not there. I don't know how she had fooled everyone, but who cares how she did it. She was not my problem anymore.

Yeah, she was no longer my problem! A wave of ecstasy filled my body at that epiphany. I was free from my past. A small smirk formed on my face. *There is that smile that I like to see.* Francisco walked toward me with my bag.

Thank you so much for going over there. Did you turn off all the lights, and leave the key on the island? *I left it right where you told me.* Good, that way the property manager can easily find them. *Here is your bag sweetie.* I placed the bag on the floor. *Let's go back to my apartment so you can get all showered up?* Okay, but first let's do this. *Do what?*

I grabbed Fransico's hand, and I tugged him through the sprinklers that had just gone on. *Ah, you little devil!* Embrace it, sweetie! Our lives are changing tomorrow. We are leaving all the negative behind! It is time to celebrate! That got him going. He began to do cartwheels all across the field, and I joined him. It was beyond liberating, and it was exactly what my soul needed.

I don't know how long we ran across that field, but it was dark by the time we stopped. *Let's take a picture to always remember this moment.* I'm sure we look ugly as hell, but that will make the picture perfect. *I'm turning the flash on so keep your eyes open!* Sweetie, I can't even see ourselves on your phone. It is too dark. *Oh trust me we are there, just look at the camera.*

I smiled at the camera as the intense white flash burned my eyes, but I kept them open. *Hahah, oh my gosh it is better than I thought!* Send it to me! *Sent.* I pulled out my phone and almost dropped it in surprise. I had completely forgotten that I buzzed my hair! Goodness, my hair! *Yeah, you little baldie.* Haha, oh my gosh I look like a little boy. I love this picture. We look like two goofballs! *Hahah.*

I couldn't help but have a laughing attack. My sides started to hurt and I dropped right back down to the grass. Francisco was right there next to me laughing his head off. It was ecstatic, and I enjoyed every minute of it. *This picture is my new favorite.* Mine too, it is now my background photo.

Ditto, but let's go inside now. We have to get some rest. It is already 9 p.m. Are you serious? *Yeah, we spent the entire day outside.* Oh wow, I guess when you are having fun, time goes by fast.

Yeah, so we better soak up every minute of our time in the Bahamas because it will go by in the blink of an eye. Sweetie, this is only the beginning of our amazing life, and how about we start our retreat a little early?

What do you say with me ordering some *Jack in the Box? I say you get me the number, 5. The Bacon Double Smashed Jack? Large, please.* With *Pepsi? Yes, please.* Okay, I'll go ahead and order myself the same thing, but a small version of it! *Thank you, babe. Now, let's go inside my place, and get out of this wet clothes.* Just one second.

I placed the order, and followed Franscio down the block to his apartment. *When will the food be here?* The app says thirty minutes. *Do you mind if I shower?* Go right ahead. I"ll use your guest shower and go ahead and clean myself off too. *I'll be fast just in case the food comes early, but you can take your time.*

I nodded to Francisco and went to his guest bathroom. Unsurprisingly, it was empty, with a thin layer of dust settled in the sink. Boys—they never clean, nor do they ever have supplies. Shit... did he even have shampoo?

I checked the cabinets under the sink and the shower, but there was nothing. Ugh, I didn't want to bother Francisco while he was in the shower, but then it hit me—I didn't have to. I had no hair. Shampoo didn't matter anymore.

The realization made me giggle, and I slipped into the shower. I turned the faucet to a mildly cold setting and closed my eyes, letting the water run down my face. For a moment, it felt calming... but soon, images of my sister and Henry and even Jake crept back into my mind. I pushed them aside and focused on scrubbing my body with the small hotel soap I had found under the sink.

It was enough to keep my mind at bay, and I turned the water off. I then dried my body off, and I put on the comfortable clothes that I would be taking on the plane. An oversized black shirt with tight black leggings. To top it off a large sports bra and compression socks.

Not the most glamorous, but definitely the most comfy. That said, when I arrived in the Bahamas I would have to go shopping. I only packed two pairs of underwear and socks, and pjs. Enough to get me through two more days, but not enough for 3 months.

Not the most ideal situation, but the best under my situation. Plus, I would get to shop from scratch. Hmm, maybe I should change my style up a bit when I get there? *Ding, dong, ding dong.* The sound of the door bell broke my train of thought.

I rushed out of the restroom, but Francisco was already there grabbing our food from the delivery man. *Time to eat.* You don't have to tell me twice. He handed me my meal, and I began to eat. The taste of the crisp bacon was heavenly. The creamy sauce on the burger made my mouth water, and the patties were perfectly well done. Even the bread was soft, but firm at the same time.

You see, this is why I like *Jack in the Box*. It may be pricey, but you get a quality meal. *I'll be the first to admit that I don't normally like burgers, but they make a damn good one.* Oh you don't like burgers?

Is that why you eat one every week? *You little jerk.* Francisco playfully threw a fry at my face. I wanted to eat it, but I didn't want to over eat, so I flicked it back to him, and he gobbled it up.

You know what the good thing about take out is? What is that? *There is no need to wash any dishes after. We just throw everything away.* I know you'll think I'm weird, but I enjoy washing my dishes. It kind of soothes me. *Okay, so you are the permanent dish washer in the Bahamas, and I'll be the cook. How does that sound?* Hmmm, I like cooking from time to time, so I'll have to get back to you on that.

I gave him a little wink, and threw my wrappers away. *Bed time?* Yes, please. *Goodnight, babe. Tomorrow our lives will forever change. Get some rest.* You too, sweetie. I headed to his spare room where I had slept plenty of times before.

I walked into the carpeted room, and opened the closet. I had stashed a blanket and a pillow there about a year ago. That way I could be comfortable any time that I slept over. I grabbed them, and shut the door behind me.

Before I dove into my bed I plugged in my phone and then I hopped into bed. I was out before my head even touched my pillow. I guess I didn't even realize how tired I was, but I slept the entire night without waking up once.

Unfortunately, I was awakened bright and early by the sun. I had forgotten to shut the blinds before going to sleep, but oh well. Now what time was it? I picked up my phone. It was 6:00 a.m. Ugh. I wasn't planning to wake up till 8 a.m. Oh well. At least I could do my yoga comfortably before the flight.

I lazily crawled myself out of the bed. I folded the sheets, and my blanket, and then I laid on the carpeted floor. Not the best place to do my yoga, but it would do. I started today's routine stretching my hamstrings and calves.

I then went and stretched my glutes. I wanted my lower body to feel nimble since I would be sitting on a plane for almost six hours. Next I did a five minute downward dog session to ensure that my back and core are firm. That definitely woke me up, and I ended up doing a forty minute yoga session.

I felt refreshed afterward, but very sweaty. I guess it was time to rinse off. I walked over to the restroom and turned on the cold water. I got into the shower and rinsed myself off. I felt so fresh, and at peace.

Now it was time to brush my teeth. I pulled out my tooth brush from my bag and brushed away. I then applied some moisturizer to my face, and some spf. I was now done, and it was exactly 8 a.m. now, and I wasn't the only one awake now.

I could hear Francisco in the living room, but before I went out to greet him I grabbed all my things and repacked my bag. I made sure that I was not forgetting anything, and then I quickly made sure the water and all the lights were off. Everything was in order, soI left the room.

Good morning, babe. Slept well? I slept great, but I forgot to shut the blinds, so I woke up a little too early. What about you? *I slept like a baby. I woke up about an hour ago, but I was making sure my room was empty, other than what I needed to take with me. Is everything good? Yeah, it's all good. What time do you think we should go to the airport?*

I think we should go now. I know we are only fifty miles from the airport, but those fifty miles can easily turn into three hours of traffic, instead of one. *You're right. Let's go, but should we eat breakfast first?*

Um, what if we stop at *Ralph's* right by *LAX* and pick up snacks to take on the plane? *Oh gosh, I love that Ralph's. They have the best baked goods.* I know. They do. Let's go ahead and do that to save us some time. *I'm definitely getting a croissant.* Ah! Let's go, Francisco. I am so happy.

As am I babe, but let me just do one more quick look around to make sure I didn't leave anything behind. Sounds good sweetie. I watched Francisco scan his apartment, and then we were in the *Uber* on our way to the airport.

Sweetie, we are lucky that your landlord let you keep your two parking spaces till we are back in town. *Yeah, she's a cool gal.* She really is. *Mhmm. Hey, there isn't much traffic right now.* Yeah, most people are at work by eight.

We should get to the *Ralph's* by LAX right at 8:40. *Perfect, that gives us 20 minutes to look for snacks.* "Where are you two going off to?" The Bahamas, and I can't wait! The driver looked back at me and smiled. "Now you two don't be having too much fun out there." *No promises sir.* Francisco winked at the driver, and we all started laughing. My new life was already starting off great.

Our *Uber* driver was kind and a talker. He looked to be around sixty based on his forehead lines, and crows feet, but he looked like a strong sixty. A man that you wouldn't want to disrespect. Someone that can still stand their ground with the younger crowd. I liked seeing older people like that. It gave me hope that I could hopefully look and feel good at an older age.

"Okay guys, we are here." The driver interrupted my daydreaming as he pulled into the parking space of *Ralph's*. *Are you able to wait twenty minutes for us while we get snacks? We will tip you thirty dollars.* "You got it."

Thank you so much, Francisco and I both said as we stepped out of the car. We closed the door behind us and started toward the store's entrance.

We were no more than fifteen feet away when it happened—something that would haunt me for the rest of my life.

Time seemed to freeze. I saw it coming, but it was too fast. My body wouldn't move. It rushed toward us in an instant, yet somehow it felt like an eternity before impact. I know the truth, though—it all happened in milliseconds.

Milliseconds that would stay with me forever. I can still see it clearly: a plateless 2027 Chevy Silverado with dark, tinted windows speeding straight toward us. It didn't slow down. It didn't stop. It all happened in a flash.

CHAPTER 14

The Death of Francisco

In all honesty, all that I truly remember was Francisco shielding me with his body as the truck rammed both of us head on. The next thing I recall was the pain that I felt after being slammed into. A pain so severe that no one word can describe it, but if I had to try I would say excruciating.

It was like I was being murdered over and over again. The ironic thing was that it probably lasted a second before my adrenaline soared through my body. However, the mental trauma that followed will always leave scars in mind.

Imagine hearing your own ribs break into pieces. Followed by hearing your pelvis shatter, and then seeing your own shins pierce through your skin. Truly a living nightmare, and if things couldn't get any worse, I went airborne.

The truck must have hit us so hard that Francisco and I were flung into the sky. I must admit that I do not remember seeing Francisco flying, but he must have since he had been shielding me. I did my best to look for him as I flew through the air, but the last thing I remembered seeing was the shopping carts as I landed on them.

Surprisingly the impact didn't hurt, so as soon as my head stopped spinning I began to call out for my best friend. Francisco, where are you? I tried yelling, but then everything went black.

Wee oh, wee oh. She is waking up. Stabilize her head now. Give her the anesthesia now! Red and white lights flashed like a swirl right before my eyes. *Is she going to be okay? Please save her! Don't let her die like that poor man.*

That voice. It was the *Uber* driver, but what did he mean by "Don't let her die like the poor man?" WHAT POOR MAN? I yelled in a fear that I had felt once before, when my parents died.

Was Francisco dead? NO! NO! FRANCISCO! FRANCISCO! WHERE IS FRANCISCO? *Sedate her now! She is injuring herself!* Get off of me! I tried to move whoever was trying to sedate me, but I couldn't move. Was I that badly injured? *She is going under now. Let's get her to the hospital and save her life!*

Huh? Save my life? What? My eyes grew heavy, and it all went black again. *Beep, beep, beep, beep.* That noise. That annoying noise. How long had it been beeping? Where was my phone to turn it off? I opened my eyes to locate my phone, but all I saw was a bright white ceiling. A ceiling with little pocket holes. Where was I?

Oh yeah, I was in Francisco's guest bedroom, but wait. His ceiling did not have pocket holes in them. Where the hell was I, and why did I feel so confused? I needed to find out what was going on. I tried to control my panic as I attempted to get off the bed. Woefully, it was to no avail. My body would not move! What was going on? Was this some sort of sleep paralysis? Was I dreaming?

Wake up Lucianna! I tried as much as I could do to wake myself from this nightmare, but my body wouldn't budge. It was as if I were wearing a rope of heavy metal chains around my body, but no, it was worse than that because I couldn't feel my body!

I never had a dream where I couldn't feel my body! All I could sense was my head. It was as if I were a floating head in space. HELP ME! I yelled in frustration as I began to realize that this wasn't a dream after all.

The car! I had been run over at the *Ralph's* parking lot. FRANCISCO! FRANCISCO! I yelled in pure mania. HELP ME! SOMEONE PLEASE HELP ME! Why is no one coming to help me?

I felt tears rush down my face. My eyes started to itch, and as much as I tried to scratch the itch away it was in vain. I was motionless. I was powerless. Why is this happening to me? Try to calm down, Lucianna. You will be useless if you are panicking. I told myself.

My small pep talk helped me calm down a bit, and that was when I realized the true extension of my situation. When I tried calling for help again, I noticed that my voice was incomprehensible.

Instead of forming words, I was only letting soft groans out. I was not able to speak. This was hell. I had to wake up from this nightmare. I closed my eyes, but I quickly opened them back up when I heard footsteps near me.

She's up! She's up! Doctor! Doctor! Please come! I felt a rush of air come in as people began to enter the room. Suddenly, lights were being flashed into my eyes. Just like in the movies.

I couldn't believe what was going on, but when I heard someone say, "I have been pricking her on the legs, arms and torso to no avail." That got me out of my loop. I was now in tune to what was going on.

I was in a hospital. Obviously I had been asleep, or maybe even in a comma for some time, and I had just awoken. It was a miracle. That is what they were saying, but in reality it wasn't a miracle.

I wanted to be dead. How could I live like this? Why had I survived? Why? *Doctor, she is crying. Look at her tears and eyes. Can I have a minute with her to try to explain what is going on? Of course. Come get me when you are finished. I will.*

Suddenly, the rush of wind hitting my face, and the voice of many people crowding the room vanished. My room was silent again. That is, all except the soft patted footsteps heading to where I was. A smile.

A friendly smile staring down at me. His almond shaped eyes looked at me with empathy. It was nurse Benson. *Hello, Lucianna. I am glad that you are awake. You put me through such a huge scare.*

What is going on with me? I tried to speak again, but this time nurse Benson brushed the side of my face, and spoke. *Don't strain yourself. Your vocal diaphragm was injured during the accident.*

You won't get any words out right now. Please, just know that I will do my best to take care of you. I know you are scared and confused. Just know that once the doctor runs all the exams I will personally explain everything to you in a way that you can understand.

There was no way for me to acknowledge his comments, and quite frankly they didn't make me feel any better. I was not in control of any of my functions, but at least nurse Benson was there.

Once more he caressed my hair, and I was glad that I was at least able to feel his hand across my face. It gave me a tiny glimmer of hope that maybe my body was just in shock and that I would feel everything again? I mean it only took one day for me to recover from my stroke, right? Wrong. I soon learned that wouldn't be the case.

For the next two days I was pricked with needles. Not that I felt them. I was scanned and x-rayed. Light was flashed into my eyes. My limbs were massaged and picked up. My bandages were changed and I was given a sponge bath. Thankfully by an older woman nurse. Needless to say on the third day I was still completely paralyzed, and I was a nervous wreck waiting to see what my diagnosis was.

Knock, knock, several footsteps entered the door. I turned my head to the left. A man in a white coat. He must be my doctor, and nurse Benson. I was relieved to see him there. *Hello, Lucianna. I hope you're doing fine this morning.* I was glad he was acknowledging me like a person. *Before I start, I want to say what a brave person you are.* He paused as if he were waiting for a response from me, but then he continued.

My name is Doctor Ukermann, and I will be your primary care provider during your time here. Firstly, I wanted to inform you that you were in a nine day coma. It was induced by us at the medical team. We needed your body to heal from all the trauma that it undertook.

A nine day coma? My ears heard a ringing. How in the world was that possible? I thought I had only been here 3 days. My head was spinning, but almost on command knowing that I needed him, nurse Benson came over and caressed my hair.

Being able to feel his hand brought me back down to earth, and the doctor continued. Secondly, as you know we ran every test that we could on you. We wanted to ensure that we gave you the most accurate information that we could of your current state. Once more he paused. He was giving me time to understand what he was saying.

Your results are in. I want to start with the positive. I am glad to say that your cognition exams and brain are absolutely intact. Your brain function is normal. Your head is healthy. Which means that intellectually speaking you are good as new.

I felt joyful hearing that. *Furthermore, your vocal chords are quite damaged now, but you should be able to regain your voice, or at least most of your speech when they heal and with therapy.* Happiness, if I could communicate then that makes life easier. *Now comes the hard news.*

Nurse Benson recommenced the caressing of my hair. Something bad was about to come. *Your spinal cord was partially severed. You have no motor function from your neck down. Your injury is just right below the C5 vertebrae.*

That is why you are thankfully able to breathe unassisted. This makes the possibility of recovery, or I should say some recovery more of a reality. That said, I am an honest person, and an honest doctor.

You are in for a ride. Your entire life will change, and you will need 24/7 assisting until you learn how to adapt to your new life. Lucianna, I want you to know that I will do all in my part to get you the best quality of life, and to help you recover to the best of your abilities.

I know that this is all so hard to hear, but we must be real. The journey that lays ahead is hard. You will be in this hospital for at least another month. I want the bruising in your spine to fully heal. That way part of your severed spine has the best ability to heal.

Lucianna, I want to give you some time to absorb all of this. Nurse Benson will be with you. I know he is a friend. He will explain everything to you again. I will come back and see you in about two hours.

Doctor Ukermann walked out of the room. His pity over me was obvious. It made me upset, but not at him. He was just being a decent human being. I felt upset because I would never be seen like I was before. My eyes blurred once more.

The tears stung my eyes, and I couldn't even remove them myself. There was nothing that I could do. What kind of life was this? Why couldn't I just die? DIE, Francisco? Like a light switch being turned back on, Francisco came into my mind. I had been in such a state of suspense and trauma for the last three days that I hadn't forgotten everything and everyone, but now I remembered. Was my sweetie really dead?

I became frantic once more. I began to moan. Trying to scream, trying to let out my own words, but it was to no avail. Now that three days had passed, I could clearly hear that I was speaking gibberish. Thankfully, this did get nurse Benson's attention.

Lucianna, dear, I am here for you. I know you want to communicate, and I know you want to know what exactly happened to you, so I will go ahead and call the police chief and let him know that you are awake and aware. That way he can explain everything to you because dear, I really don't know anything either.

What I do know however, is that we need to have a system of communication. You can't talk, but you are able to move your head. How about when you want to say yes you move your head to the right, and if you want to say no you move your head to the left? That was a fantastic idea on his behalf. I moved my head to the right without hesitation. *Just to be clear you understand?* Once more I moved my head to the right. *Okay, trick question, my name is nurse Rod?* I turned my head to the left.

Perfect. We have a basic way of communicating. We will add more gestures throughout your stay, okay? I am here for you Lucianna. You are not alone. I felt so much gratitude that nurse Benson had at least figured out a small way for me to communicate.

However, I wanted answers. I wanted to know where Francisco was. The wait was killing me. Why, oh why did this have to happen to me? "Knock, knock, knock, this is chief Hocker, May I come in?"

Of course chief. Lucianna, this is the chief of police running your investigation. He will break down everything that happened to you. If you want me to stay you know what to do. I turned my head to the right. *I'll stay right by your side.*

Before the chief started talking, nurse Benson gave him an update on my health, and my current form of communication. He nodded his big head, and looked me straight in the eyes. I glared back at him.

He had a very authoritative look to him. His eyebrows were big and bushy. His face was clean shaven, but his five o'clock shadow was quite visible, and when he introduced himself his voice was so commanding that it made you want to listen to him.

"I'm chief Hocker, I am sorry we are meeting in these circumstances ma'am." "I know this is not ideal, but I have to let you know what is going on." I scrunched my lips together to show him that I was ready for him to start speaking.

"I am sorry that this has happened to you." "It is awful, and no one should have to go through this, but I want you to know one thing, ma'am." "I will catch whoever did this to you, and your friend." My mouth dropped open when he said friend. Chief Hocker must have noticed because instead of looking straight at me he turned his head slightly to the side.

"There is no easy way to say this, but Francisco is dead." "He was pronounced dead on the scene after the first hit." "It was too much of a shock to his system."

My entire world stopped. The room turned upside down. My breathing became difficult. My eyes were rain clouds letting out a storm. I tasted salt in my mouth. My head felt like a thousand pounds, and my mouth opened wide.

I wanted to scream, but I knew nothing but groans and moans would come out. Instead I stood there like a caged bird. Motionless. I didn't know what else to do. I couldn't and wouldn't believe this.

I couldn't phantom the reality of Francisco being dead. *Maybe you can come back when she absorbs this news?* "I wish I could, sir, but I have a schedule I must follow." *I understand.* Nurse Benon's voice was a distant spec at this point, and so was Chief Hockers'. My mind was in a different place now, but when I heard him say Jazmine's name, I was brought back into reality.

"We have informed your sister Jazmine of your circumstances and she is currently trying to get emergency authority over looking after you." My jaw dropped to the floor, and I started to scream-moan as loud as I could. I shook my head in all directions. There was no way in hell that I wanted Jazmine taking care of me.

I would rather die right here and now. She was the last person that I wanted to ever see. NO, NO, NO I groaned, but of course no one understood me which made me even more agitated. So once more, I began to bobble my head left to right, and up to down. I wanted nurse Benson, and Chief Hocker to know that I did not want Jazmine in my life!

This of course, caused the bed side monitor to start to beep uncontrollably. Nurse Benson ran in with wicked quickness. "Is she okay?" Chief Hocker's voice was low and collective. Nurse Benson ignored him and injected something into my IV. The bed monitor started to beep less, and I felt more at ease.

My eyes felt heavy, but before I drifted to sleep I heard nurse Benson say, *"She has a hostile relationship with Jazmine."* Then everything went dark once more. I don't know how long I was out for, but I awoke to another nurse giving me a massage.

She was happy to see that I was awake, so she began to talk my ear off. I let her talk away, but I did not pay attention to anything she said. The only thing that I could think of was Francisco. Which caused my eyes to fill with tears.

The talkative nurse was nice enough to wipe them away when she would come check in on me throughout the late afternoon. I appreciated that, but gosh it was a horrible few hours of me being alone in my thoughts. Thankfully nighttime came soon enough, and I cried myself to sleep.

I ended up waking up once thinking that I was at Francisco's house, but the reality soon came in when I smelled the strong antibacterial hospital stench. I had lost the last person who cared about me in this world, and to add more wood to the flame Jazmine wanted to take "care of me."

There was no way in hell that I could let that happen. I was sure all that she wanted was to have access to my finances. I was not rich by any means, but I did have a little over 110 thousand saved in the bank. One hundred and ten thousand dollars that she would waste in months.

Ugh! Why couldn't I have just died with my brother? I thought to myself in pity as I closed my eyes once more and drifted off to sleep.

CHAPTER 15

Learning To Live With My New Reality

I awoke right at 6:00 a.m. to a terrible smell. It was an undeniable stench. The strong order of urine and feces. Sadly, I knew exactly where it was coming from, and it was me. I had soiled myself.

That had happened three times since being at the hospital, but every time it had occurred there had been a nurse besides me to help out. This was the first time that I was alone with my accident, and that helped me realize one thing.

I truly did not have control of my own body even at that level. I really was just a head staring off into space. Once again, like so many times since I awoke from my coma I started to cry.

I was sitting soiled on a bed, and there was nothing I could do. The smell was making me nauseous, and it took almost an hour for a nurse to come in, and who out of all people arrived? Nurse Benson.

Good morning Lucianna, how are you? He was so cheerful, and was smiling from ear to ear. I was shocked that he did not mention the smell.

Instead he was professional, and told me., *"It's the start of the day, let's get you changed."*

I couldn't feel what he was doing, but I could vividly see how he changed me like an infant. It was the most humiliating thing I had ever experienced, but still Nurse Benson treated me like a person, an equal. *Your catheter fell last night, but I will make sure to report it, so the night nurse pays more attention.*

I smiled at him, and he came over. *About yesterday, I know you don't want Jazmine to take care of you, and I was looking up legal information on how to prevent this.* I turned my head to the right 3 times, and he smiled again. *I knew it, so here comes the tricky part. We have to prove to the courts that you are well in your mind, and that you can make that decision of not wanting Jazmine as your power of attorney.*

Since she is your only living family member, and has evidence of you guys living together, and even of you attending her wedding, the courts will favor her. I turned my head to the left. *I understand, and this is off the books, but she has been granted permission to visit you at the hospital.*

I suggest that you do not allow her to know that you are able to communicate until we develop a way to truly prove to the courts that you are able to, so for now this stays with us okay? I turned my head to the right to signify YES.

I'll do everything I can to help you, Lucianna. He told me as he walked over and put his hand on the side of my face. I felt pleasure in that. It made me feel alive, and his smile was soothing for my soul. I guess it was because his upper lip curved in the middle when he smiled, and it gave him a childlike appearance.

I want you to know that I know you are grieving over Francisco, but I can't keep secrets from you. Someone came to the hospital this morning regarding his estate. He has named you as the sole inheritor. Thankfully, no one saw the lawyer come in, but me, so I told him to come back in a month. That way we have a way to communicate with him.

I was appreciative of Benson. I wanted him to know that I was grateful, and I think he understood that I was. *Once more, off the record, I know things are just awful Lucianna. I know Jazmine will make things worse for you. However, I am doing everything I possibly can to stop her.*

Also, I can't imagine the immense pain you are going through with losing your ability to move, and losing your friend, Francisco, but just know that I am here for you. I have taken 2 extra days of work for the next month, so you can count on me being here at least 5 days a week for my 12 hour shifts, okay? My vision blurred. I felt grateful for him.

Don't cry, we will get through this together. He wiped the tears from my face. I will be back to check up on you later. I did my best to nod "okay" at him but my head was too heavy to bring back up.

Your neck muscles are still a little too weak for that nodding up and down motion, but don't worry they will get stronger. He said as he slowly stabilized my head. I smiled at him again, and he left to see his other patients.

Which left me alone for almost two hours. I didn't do anything during that time other than wait for nurse Benson to come back. When he did he checked my vitals. *Everything seems to be going well. Doctor Uckermann will see you this evening, and I wanted to tell you personally that Jazmine is in the waiting room. She will come see you after I give her the all clear, but before that I wanted to tell you something.*

I was thinking there are 26 letters in the alphabet, we can use that to our advantage. If you want to spell something, maybe you can move your head up however many times to signify a letter.

For example, if you want to say "A" move your head once up. For "B," twice up, and for "Z" 26 times up. I know it is inconvenient, but that will at least give you the independence to say what you need to say. Plus you should be able to control those upper neck muscles since you are not nodding up and down, and it will fortify them.

How does that sound? Instantly, I nodded up once for A, and then I waited 3 seconds to nod again for M so nurse Benson could understand. 13 for M, waited three seconds, one more nod for A, three more seconds 26 for Z until I spelled AMAZING.

Ha! I will document all of this. We will get you your independence back, Lucianna! You can't count on me. I grinned slightly at him. *Okay, Lucianna, I must go, and your sister is coming in.*

If you want to fake sleep go right ahead. Nurse Benson gave me a little wink and left my room. Not even a minute later I heard the sounds of heels clicking and clacking on the tile floor. I recognized my sister's sound.

She was definitely wearing the *Gucci* heels that she always wore when she wanted to look important. The ones that I had gifted her that cost me 700 dollars. A birthday present wrongly spent.

"Lucianna!" "Big sister!" "What has happened to you?" My eyes were closed as she walked in, and as strange as this sounds, simply hearing the sound of her voice made the tiny hair on my face stand up. She really triggered me. I wondered if the rest of my body had goosebumps?

I wouldn't know. "I can't believe this has happened to you." "How awful, sister." "Never in a million years did I expect this." If I could move at that moment I would have slapped her. I was the one in the bed, and she was already making it about herself. "Lucianna." Jazmine stopped talking mid sentence and began to sob.

"I wish you were okay, sister." "You don't deserve this." "You are too much of a good person for this to happen to you." Wait. Was she actually being sympathetic like when we used to live together?

Should I open my eyes so she can see that I am awake? I pondered briefly, but soon got my answer. "Unfortunately, I guess karma does exist." "You weren't being a good person, so you had to pay a price." My head started to pulse. She was implying that karma was the one who did this to me!

"We will get through this together, Lucianna." "I'll be extra strong for both of us, and I won't let you see me cry because I need to be strong for you." Confusion and hate was what I felt at that moment. I hated my sister for who she was, but I felt comfort in knowing that she did care about me, or so I thought.

"I just need to gain access to your finances." "If I am going to be taking care of you, then I better be getting paid for it in some way." "I mean I will have to change you apparently." "Yuck." "I don't even want to change a baby."

There it was. The true reason she had come. Thank goodness that I had not opened my eyes for her. Fuck, I am such an idiot for thinking that she cared about me. It has always and will only be just about her, and there was no way in hell that she would get access to any of my funds. Let alone any of Francisco's. Thankfully, Benson had shooed the lawyer away. He had thought in advance.

"Sister, I hope you don't mind, but I am going to wake you." "I want you to see that I came in to see you because I sure as hell won't come back for at least another week." "They told me that you are going to be here for another month, and I don't like coming to creepy ass hospitals that are full of sick people." "It just grosses me out." "Thankfully, they have you in the recovery section of the hospital so I guess I don't have to see too many sick people, but anyway, wake up."

My head started moving back and forth. I heard Jazmine's laugh, and then she said, "Oh shit, you really can't feel me touching your shoulder can you?" I hated her. She then tapped me on the forehead.

"Sis, it's me Jazmine." "Please wake up." "Her voice was softer now." I had no choice and opened my eyes. Jazmine was staring at me with a look of confusion in her eyes. She looked sad to me, almost empathic, but she also looked triumphant." She really was a terrible human being.

"Sister, I came here as soon as they let me in." "I am so glad that you are alive. She embraced me. "Please, I am sorry for all the hell that I have put you through, and I have put everything negative that you have put me through into the past." "We are sisters, and I will be here for you." "I will take care of you, and with my help you will walk again!" She hugged me again, and I simply stared at her blankly.

She looked like a smudge to me. I didn't want to focus on her, so I looked through her. She kept talking. "I won't stop hounding the police until they find that maniac who ran you over, and killed Francisco!" "It is unbelievable that they still haven't caught him!" "Oh and I say him because it has to be a guy of course!"

Her voice was starting to hurt my ears. I wasn't able to move, but my ears still worked. "Can you believe they told me that they have no leads?" "Is this why we pay taxes?" "I am thinking about hiring a private investigator, Lucianna, but of course I will need money for that." "I was informed that I can have access to your finances while I take care of you." "If you agree then I will look for the best investigator now!"

There was no way in hell that I would ever agree to that, and there was no way in hell that I would ever let her take care of me. I mean the entire reason why I was leaving the damn country was to get away from her. Sigh.

Why did life have to play such a cruel joke on me? From the cheating, to now, leaving me paralyzed, and taking Francisco from me. Was I cursed? Maybe, I should just let myself die? It would be better than having Jazmine take care of me.

"Lucianna, I want to talk about the elephant in the room." "I am sorry for attacking you the other day." "I know it wasn't your fault." "Henry told me that he was the one who forced himself on you." "Look, I really thought

I was pregnant." "It turns out I had a phantom pregnancy, so my body did go through all the symptoms." "Anyway, things are better with Henry and me now." "We are on a break, but we are back on speaking terms." "I'm sorry, again." As Jazmine blabbed on, I couldn't help but think about my Francisco.

If it wasn't for me he would still be alive. I mean it was my issues that caused all of this. If it wasn't for my bitch of a sister I would never have wanted to leave the country. Francisco would still be with me. He was my ride or die, and sadly he died being my ride, and it was all because I never cut ties with this abomination that was yacking on and on right in front of me.

Beep, beep, beep, the monitor tracking my vitals starting to go off. *Beep, beep, beep,* fast paced footsteps raced into the room. *Ma'am move away now!* I heard nurse Benson yap at Jazmine.

"I am allowed to stay here!" "She is my sister, and I am her caretaker!" *If your sister dies because you stressed her then you will be charged with man slaughter!* "I have done no such thing to my sister!" "I love her." "I will go and file a complaint against you to the hospital manager!" *Go right ahead, so I can show them how Lucianna's stress levels have gone through the roof since you came in to speak to her.*

Jazmine didn't say anything after that. I heard the clicking and clacking of her heels leave the room. Nurse Benson didn't say anything after she left. He was huffing and puffing loudly as he silenced the vital monitor.

I, of course, didn't say anything. I just watched him as he injected something into my IV. *You'll be okay now. I'll let the staff know to not let any more visitors in for the remainder of the day.* I gingerly smiled at him and closed my eyes.

Lucianna, wake up. This is Doctor Ukermann. My eyes fluttered open. They were heavy. Whatever nurse Benson put in my IV must have knocked me off for a good while. *Sorry to wake you darling, but I want to let you know that your swelling has gone down a lot since last week, and if all goes well you should be able to start physical therapy within a week.*

Nurse Benson has also told me that you are able to communicate. Is that correct? I nodded my head to the right. *That is amazing! You should be able to make decisions on who cares for you based on this.*

Nurse Benson has also confided in me that your sister may not be the best person out there for the job of caring for you, considering the stress she put you through today. However, I am not the judge for that. I will make notes of your communication methods in my report, but ultimately it is the state who will decide whether they allow your sister to be your primary provider. I turned my head to the left.

I see that you don't want that. Alright, then I will refer you to an in house care facility that is affiliated with this hospital. I turned my head to the right. *Perfect. I'll make a note out of all of this, and next week we will see the outcome. I'll be back tomorrow to check on your progress.*

For now, I just want to let you know that you cannot eat any solids yet. All your nutrients will be through IV for at least the next few weeks, maybe months. This means you will lose some weight, but you are strong. You can do this!

With that he left, and I was alone momentarily. Another nurse came in shortly after and set up my nutrient IV filled with all the vitamins and proteins that my body needed. It took 3 hours for my body to absorb it all, but when I was finished I really felt better. I felt more energized. I even tried moving my body, but of course it was useless, so instead I just sat in bed wasting away until I eventually fell asleep again.

That same cycle repeated itself for the next week. Waking up, getting my vitals taken by various nurses who changed almost daily. The only thing that made my days better was seeing Nurse Benson. There were three days that he wasn't my nurse, yet he still came to see me. Which brought me joy.

Whenever I saw him it just made me forget my hell. Plus he even found more ways for me to communicate easier. For example, biting on my lip meant that I wanted to be alone. Little things like that were making my life more equitable.

I just wish he could just be my nurse at all times. Not just because he treated me kindly, but because I had developed a small crush on him. However, I digress. I shouldn't even be thinking that way. I should be focused on getting physically better. Which by the looks will hopefully be happening soon.

Doctor Ukermann, believes that I can start my physical therapy tomorrow. He was pleased with my slow improvements. Like being able to nod up and down now. That made me happy. Nonetheless, being stuck in my new reality was overwhelmingly depressing. I just felt sad.

I cried most of the time when I was awake and alone. My mind kept thinking of Francisco, and his boyish charm. His innocence and selflessness. His dreams and aspirations that were all wasted and cut too short.

The unbearable dread of knowing that it was all my fault. The wishing that it was me and not him was too much to handle. In fact, one night my blood pressure shot through the roof. I thought I would die, but nurse Benson was on his shift that day and immediately saved the day.

Soon after that, it didn't take him long to realize what was going on with me, so he set up an appointment with the psychologist in the hospital which I was having today. It would be interesting to see how it would pan out. I couldn't communicate much, but hopefully hearing from a trained professional would help me out somehow? We would see because it was time for the rendez-vous.

Knock, knock. Ms. Lucianna, my name is Louise. I am the psychologist here at the hospital, and I am delighted to make your acquaintance. I couldn't see her just yet, but her voice was soft and soothing. She slowly walked her way next to me.

Her bright smile filled the room. She was a little old lady. Her curly permed hair nestled into a bob. Her bright dark eyes were glowing even though they were small. The wrinkles on her face lit up as she gazed upon me. She brought some sort of peace to me.

CHAPTER 16

Back To The Gates of Hell

I've heard a lot about your recovery from nurse Benson. I am glad that you are getting better day by day. I wrinkled my eyebrows together at that remark. *Oh, I don't mean to lower the gravity of your situation dear.*

I felt my face get red. Louise had read my facial expression to the tea. *Now, no need to get embarrassed.* I felt my face get hotter. She was good, and it made me happy. She could see and read my emotions by just looking at my face!

I want you to know that I respect you fully. Don't think for a second that I have pity over you. I am, however, empathic to what has happened, okay? I slowly nodded my head. I believed her, and it made me feel at ease that she was straight forward, yet compassionate.

Since you can't verbally communicate right now, I will ask you a series of questions and you can respond with your yes or no method, or even spell the word out with nods, okay? I nodded once, and waited for her questions.

Are you feeling grief for what has been done to you? Right head turn. Are you mad? Do you feel jealous? Do you want revenge? Do you miss Francisco? I turned my head right to all of those answers. She jotted down notes.

I heard you have a sister. Would you like for her to be at your physical therapy appointments, starting tomorrow? I nodded my head to the left. She jotted notes down. Do you have a strained relationship with her? I nodded my head to the right. I felt myself get agitated.

I didn't want to talk about Jazmine. I began to bite my bottom lip. *I can tell that you do not want me to mention her. I respect that, but as your psychologist I must be up front with you. I have worked with patients in the past who are in a similar situation as you, and sometimes insurance takes a while to kick in. Which means the patient ends up living with that specific family member for a month or two before they can go into an inhouse living facility.*

I know it's not what you want to hear, but helping you deal with the trauma that your sister has caused you will help you deal with that situation if it arises. I felt my eyes begin to twitch, and Louise quickly changed the topic.

Was Francisco like a brother to you? Yes, I nodded. *What was one of the things you liked most about him?* 8 nods for H, 21 nods for U. I smiled at the end of spelling, humor.

I can only imagine how funny he was if he had you smiling just thinking about that. Louise's wrinkled face shriveled together to form an empathetic smile. It made me feel seen. *Now you don't have to answer this, but what was the silliest thing he did to you when you two first met?*

So many memories flooded my mind. Like the time where we both did a 10k race and Francisco had diarrhea and had to poop in the park. I had to cover him. It was hilarious, and just thinking about it made me feel like Francisco was still here.

Psychologist Louise asked me a few more questions regarding my parents, and when she found out that they were also gone she used the same formula. Which was asking me about silly things that they did. It really did make me feel better, and by the time she left I actually felt motivated to regain my life back.

My parents and Francisco were no longer here. They didn't have the chance to live, but I did. Even in this state, I was still alive. I couldn't just throw my life away. I had to do the best of what life has thrown at me. I owed it to myself, to my parents and most importantly to my brother, my best friend, Francisco.

With that positive mentality I drifted off to bed with no issues. I supposed it was because I felt happy to reclaim my life, but the next day I quickly learned how in the shit I was. I had my first physical therapy appointment, and it was awful.

I hated saying this, but I felt like dead weight as the nurses picked me up and wheeled me over. I had no control over myself. I guess I thought I would be able to at least wiggle a toe or something, but no. I couldn't even keep my own head up. Which caused me to have breathing problems while at the therapy.

I didn't realize that my breathing would be affected since I had been laying on a bed in the best position to support my oxygen intake. The physical therapist told me to keep my morale up, and that I would be okay once my lower jaw muscles got stronger. She sounded hopeful.

Which gave me enough motivation to not give up. I would keep trying because once I was able to strengthen those muscles I would be a tad closer to independence. Moreover, while in therapy I learned about wheelchairs that you blow air into, and they move. I didn't know about that, but many quadriplegic people used them to move themselves around.

Also, I was informed that I could even use a computer by using a mouth operated joystick! I had no clue that these technologies were available, and it made me happy that there were at least some decent people out there creating things for those with disabilities.

People like me, I should say. Even though it's hard to think of myself as being disabled. Nonetheless, as the days go by I am growing to accept it more and more. In fact, the more I went to physical therapy the more I learned that disabled people have the biggest hearts. We are trying to do things that our bodies don't want us to do.

That made me proud, and motivated me to try harder. Which I did. Eventually my days at the hospital went from days to weeks, and at last the last couple of days of my stay arrived. By this point, I was over the moon because I was finally able to keep my head up on my own!

I could even hold a computer joystick! Woefully, I wasn't able to talk yet because sadly my vocal chords were still heavily damaged, but I could communicate with a computer now! I could even write with my mouth, but very sloppily.

Nurse Benson was super excited for me, and even though he wasn't coming in to see me every day like before we started to text, as friends of course. It was nice to tell him how I really felt. Especially after learning that my insurance would indeed not kick in for another 6 weeks.

Nurse Benson, or I guess I should call him Benson now since we are friends, offered to house me, but unfortunately Jazmine won a legal battle to have me in her care until my insurance kicked in.

It was hard hearing that news. It sent me down a terrible spiral, but I was strong. I could handle six weeks of her. For crying out loud a truck hit me, and killed my brother. I could now handle the world.

Still, it didn't take away the fact that I was beyond livid about having to live with Jazmine, but I have had a few days to process it. Louise, my psychologist, was a ton of help with aiding me in dealing with that new hell.

Yet, I must admit that even with all the support that I received upon learning my new fate, it didn't take away my true feelings. It frustrated me how the disabled community was not seen as equal to ablebody people. When I had my virtual court hearing with the judge, not only was I treated like a lower citizen by the judge, but Jazmine was praised.

Even though Benson, Doctor Ukermann and Louise clearly stated how I did not want to be in Jazmine's care the judge ignored it. He brought up how some time together could help save our sibling relationship.

Especially after Jazmine presented a lot of proof of how we lived together, and how until recently she was my next in kin. She convinced the court that Francisco had negatively influenced me, and that is why we had gotten hit. She told them that it was a targeted attack.

Unfortunately, she brought in Francisco's ex who was almost as diabolical as her to testify. He lied through his teeth about Francisco. He said everything in the book from him being a con artist to him taking advantage of me. The judge bought it all.

Ultimately, he ruled in Jazmine's favor, and gave her access to me, and my care for one full month, or until my insurance kicks in. Needless to say I was really in the shit now. I had prayed for death at that moment. If it wasn't for the fact that I couldn't do anything on my own I probably would have ended it all.

However, I was doing better now. Even so, I felt a sharp irritation, knowing exactly what awaited me at Jazmine's. She wasn't going to take care of me, and she was never going to change. The truth was simple: she only wanted custody of me for my finances.

Well that and so she could be seen as the heroic hero who saved her "sister." I could bet all my money that she was making it seem like she was my savior. Ugh, just the thought of it was making me feel unwell. I had to relax.

I took in some deep breaths, and... *Knock, knock,* "Hello, Lucianna." "How are you?" Doctor Uckermann walked into my room. He was smiling from ear to ear. It momentarily helped me forget Jazmine.

"I am happy about the progress you have made." I typed in "Thank you" on my tablet. "I am giving you the all clear to be discharged tomorrow." I don't want to go with Jazmine. I hurriedly typed for the doctor to see. "Honey, I am sorry that you do not want that, but legally there is nothing that I can do."

Am I allowed to just die? Can I do that? I surprised myself by typing that. I didn't know I felt that strongly about not going with that witch. "Don't talk nonsense." "You are one of the strongest patients that I have ever had the privilege to work with."

"You can survive this month with your sister, and then once your insurance kicks in, you do not ever have to see her again, ok?" Okay, I typed on my tablet. Doctor Uckermann looked at me woefully, and then said, "Off the clock, if anything happens to you at your sister's, I will make sure she pays for it!" "You will be okay."

He then came over, and held my limp hand. "Please do not give up." "You are making great progress." "Don't let it all go to waste." I didn't bother to type anything, and just closed my eyes. Trying my best to not let my tears escape, but it was in vain.

My pillow was drenched by the time the doctor left. I wouldn't be seeing him for two entire weeks. I felt sad. He was a good man, and he deserved to be thanked for helping me, but I just couldn't look at anyone right now.

Instead I kept my eyes closed until I eventually drifted off to sleep. I was awakened in the middle of the night the next day by Benson. *Lucianna, I am about to clock off for the day, but I wanted to say bye to you.*

You have grown to be a big part of my life. Please stay strong my friend. If anyone can survive a month of hell it is you. Please believe it. He looked at me with so much tenderness. It made me feel protected. I had to show my gratitude to him.

Wasting no time I began to type, "Promise me you'll be the one to take me to the in-living care facility as soon as my insurance kicks in." *I'll drop everything I am doing, and will run right over.*

That gave me hope and steadied my mind. I could survive this hell. And when it was over, I would heal from losing my only friend—my brother. I would also get justice for him. A month had passed with no leads. That was unacceptable.

I'll see you soon. Benson gave me a hug. It was awkward because I couldn't feel it, but I liked it anyway. He soon left, and I ended up dozing off back to sleep. "Lucianna, I am here to get you ready to leave." "Your sister is waiting for you in the parking lot."

One of the female nurses who had helped me a few times was smiling at me. She looked happy to see that I was leaving. She was excited with all the progress I made, but little did she know that I was going to hell.

"Aren't you so excited to be going home?" I forced a hint of a smile for her. I did not want to make her feel bad. She was a kind person, and treated me well. "I'm so happy for you." Thank you, I managed to type. "Now do you want to wear this white shirt or blue shirt that your sister brought for you?"

I nodded towards the blue shirt. The nurse put it over me. It was extremely oversized. It hung over my thighs. "Gray sweats or black ones?" I nodded towards the black ones. "Great, you are all set." "Now are you ready to be wheeled out?" I turned my head to the right, and the journey started.

I was wheeled out of my little home. It felt bittersweet. I hated being there because of my circumstances, but it was also a safe haven for me. I met many amazing health care workers, and I have a huge respect for them now. They dedicate their lives for their patients. Granted some are total stuckups, but the majority truly care.

I'll mess all of you I thought as we entered the hallway. *Hip hip, hooray! Hip hip hooray!* Confetti was thrown all around me. Doctor Ukermann, Benson, Louise, and several of the nurses and my physical therapist were out there greeting me. I couldn't believe it. *We wish you the best Lucianna. We are so happy that you are getting stronger and stronger.* They all came and hugged me tightly.

Once again like so many times before tears flooded my eyes. Thankfully, this time they were tears of joy. I moved my head toward my tablet that was hung on the side of my wheelchair on a metal pole. I grabbed my stylish and began typing. "You all mean the world to me." "You have saved my life, and I will forever be grateful for that." "I hope that the next time that we all meet again, I will be able to have some mobility."

They all clapped and cheered for me, and with a big smile I was wheeled off to the outside of the hospital. Instantly, a fresh breeze hit my face, and it felt heavenly. I had not been outside in over a month now, and now it was the perfect time to be outside.

It was almost fall so the morning air was nice and fresh. "Does it feel good to be outside again?" I turned my head to the right. Answering my nurse. "I'm so glad." "Enjoy every minute of it because as you know life is short."

That was exactly what I wanted to do, but then I saw her again. My sister, Jazmine. She was coming out of her truck. She was smiling so big that I could see her gums flaring in the sunlight. "I see your sister." "Let's get you wheeled over." My nurse wheeled me over. "Lucianna!" "My big sister." "I am so happy to see you healthier!" "I missed you so much!"

I gave Jazmine a small smile. I didn't want to fight with her during this time. I had to be on her good side. That was the only way that I could stand living with her. I had to forget how much of a horrible human being she was. "Do you have something to lift her chair, or do you need me to help you lift Lucianna to the seat?"

"I am going to need you to help me." "I don't have any money to get a crank to help lift my sister, but I am sure we can both talk about purchasing one later." Yep, there it was. She was already thirsty over my savings, but she was stupid if she thought I would ever give her another dime. My money was my money. The days of letting her "borrow money" were gone.

"Stabilize your head while we pick you up, Lucianna." My nurse said as she and Jazmine lifted me up. "Sister, you have gotten fat!" "I need to put you on a diet!" "You almost threw out my back." "Hahaha!" There was an awkward silence as my nurse did not laugh instead she handed Jazmine my tablet.

Another mistake. Now I would not be able to communicate. "Can you also put her chair in the back please?" "Ugh, okay." My nurse looked hesitant. That wasn't her job, but she did it anyway.

"Is that everything?" "Yes, but please do not forget her two week follow up." "It is scheduled for 2 p.m." "Yeah, I won't forget." "Bye!" Jazmine drove off leaving my nurse talking in mid sentence.

"Sister, finally you get to go home." "Did you miss me there?" "I missed you." "I missed you so much that I used every resource that I had to get you into my care." "Don't worry I do not hold any grudges against you trying to get into *the in care living facility.*" "I know Francisco had your fragile mind manipulated, but he's dead now, so we can start repairing our relationship."

CHAPTER 17

Complete Access To The Savings

I would have loved to say that I couldn't believe what I was hearing, but I'd be lying. Jazmine was wicked and only cared about herself. "Sister, guess what?" I looked at the rearview mirror so she could see that I was paying attention to her. "Henry finally started talking to me again after I told him that I was taking care of you!" "He is actually at home now waiting for us to arrive."

I nodded my head at her. I had to be smart. Make her think that I was on her side. "I knew you'd be happy for me, sister." Yeah, keep on thinking that I thought as we made our way to her place.

"We are here, and look, Henry is already outside waiting to help get you off." I faked a smile for her. She parked the car and got off. My insides turned as she opened my door. "Please be careful with her head, okay?" "It is the only part of herself that she can move." "I will."

Jazmine unbuckled me and came inside the truck. All the while Henry stared at me like a deer stuck in headlights. "Her hair is taking its sweet time to grow back, no?" "It is, and she has also gained weight!" I felt my cheeks burning.

They were talking about me as if I wasn't there. That surprised me. Henry was a coward, but he had never been this crude. "My poor sister." "Her mind is no longer there, but I know that her soul is still there, and that is why I will do my best to keep her healthy and safe." Ah there it was. Jazmine once again had weaseled her way into the minds of others.

She had Henry thinking that I was no longer myself. However, that didn't give him any right to think of me as less than him. "Let me get her chair down." Jazmine huffed and puffed as she got my wheelchair down from the truck.

"Jazmine, I was thinking, what if I move back in?" "What do you mean, Henry?" "I mean what if I come back and live with you?" "It seems like Lucianna will be a lot of work to care for, and I don't want you to have that burden all your life." "Maybe we can try to patch things up between us?" "I think I was wrong about you." "It is clear that you have a big heart."

"To be honest, it makes sense why you had a phantom pregnancy." "You are just that sensitive." I slightly turned my head to face Jazmine. The amount of happiness on her face was impossible to contain. Her eyes were glowing.

Her smile had become enormous, and her cheeks had become rosy. "I don't want to pressure you, Henry, but I would love some help with my sister." Oh she was smart. She had made it seem like she only cared about helping me, and that everything else came second. Yeah fucken right, I thought as I slowly turned my gaze toward Henry.

He had eaten it all up. He was also smiling. "Well okay then." "Let's get Lucianna all set up." They wheeled me up their messed up driveway. My head shook violently with all the bumps on the pavement, but they did not notice. They were too busy talking about how cruel life could be. "I lost my parents already, and I was so close to losing my sister." "I have a second chance to make things right with her, and I will."

"Don't take all the blame, Jazmine." "I'm also to blame." "I flirted with you too, but what is done is done, okay?" "We have a second chance to help Lucianna., so let's do it!" "Alright!"

Jazmine opened her old rustic smelly wooden door. It creaked as it opened, and as she slid me in, we got stuck. The bottom of the door's frame was about 2 inches too tall. My wheel chair would have to be lifted for me to get through. "This is what I was afraid of." "My entire house is not suitable for a disabled person."

"I know." "That is why my lawyer will fight tooth and nail for you to get a hold of Lucianna's finances." "How much does she have?" "She has over 111k in her savings from what I am told." "That would be enough to at least buy a crank for her to be put to bed, and to shower."

"It is insane how they are making it this hard to gain access to her funds." "I mean it's for her own good!" "Because of Francisco." "He manipulated her, and brainwashed her into putting everything under his name." "The jokes on him though, he's dead now."

"Then why can't they just put everything back to your name?" Tell him, Jazmine. Go on and tell him that I am aware. "She switched banks before getting in the accident." "The bank didn't even know she had family until the hospital reached out to them concerning a bill that had to go through." "That's when the bank found out about me." "I understand." "Should I call my lawyer?"

"Not yet." "Why not?" "Apparently there is an easier way." "The judge says that if after a month of living with us we can prove that she is in good hands he will award me full custody over all aspects of my sister's life!"

Oh, so that was her plan. Treat me nicely for a month, get my money and then let me rot. Couldn't expect less from her. Nonetheless I just couldn't sit around and do nothing. I had to find a way out of this situation before then, but how?

I closed my eyes and started to think of ways out of this shit hole, but there was nothing that I could do! I would lose my money, but not all was lost. Jazmine did not know about the inheritance that my brother left me. Apparently it was a little over $450,000 that Francisco left for me. At the bare minimum I could relax that neither Jazmine or the judge knew about this.

Benson had explained to me that Francisco's will would only become public knowledge when I personally went into his estate's handler's office, and proved my identification by answering personal questions. That meant I did not have to worry about my brother's money getting stolen by Jazmine. That idea eased my mind.

"It kind of looks like she is happy." Henry's voice caught me off guard. I guess the thought of Jazmine not knowing about 450,000 dollars had lit up my face. "She probably senses the positive energy in the house."

Yeah fucken right! "I'm sure that is it." He said with an upbeat voice. "Now, where do you want me to put her?" Henry was talking about me like I was some sort of pet. "You can put her in her old room."

"I removed all the furniture but the bed." "That way I can easily move her in and out of there." "That is sweet of you Jazmine." "You really did everything you could to prepare for your sister's comfort." "Your gratitude means a lot, Henry."

Crunch, crunch, crunch the noise that my wheels made on the broken tiles of my childhood home made my ears squeal. "Here we are, sister." Jazmine stared at me with a huge smile. She then placed me dead center in our old childhood room that now contained nothing but a futon bed.

"Sister, you must be so tired." "Let me put you in bed." At least that is one thing she got right. I did feel tired. This was my first time out of a hospital room in a month. *Click, click,* Jazmine unstrapped me from the seat, and then she began to pull me out of the chair. She huffed and puffed causing Henry to come to her help.

"That's it, there is no way that I will leave you alone with all of this baggage." The word stung my heart. I was called baggage. I felt tears swell in my eyes, but I would not let them escape my eyes.

Instead I let my head fall forward as my coward of an ex scooped me out of the chair like a baby. He then placed me on the bed where Jazmine arranged my body. I felt like an absolute useless disaster. "Okay, now that she is all tucked in, shall we have something to eat?" "Of course, I haven't had lunch." "How does Mac & Cheese sound?" "Amazing."

They both left my room, and closed the door behind them. I was left alone with nothing to do. With no way of communicating, and with my body slightly twisted to one side of the bed, and the other side towards the wall.

I know I couldn't feel anything below my neck but being in a slanted position was not good for my body, or the IV that was attached to my right arm. Hopefully it would fall off so Jazmine could take me back to the hospital. Wishful thinking I know, but what else was there to do?

Nothing! I couldn't even entertain myself since Jazmine took my tablet away, so I simply laid on my bed until my room was pitch black. Which meant that at least 8 hours had passed since I got home from the hospital.

For a second I thought Jazmine and Henry had forgotten about me, but soon enough Henry came in to check up on me. "It is time for someone's food." "Jazmine went to go pick up some things at the store, so she asked me to set up your IV."

"Apparently, I just need to press this button and you should get your nutrients." I looked at him as he pressed the button, and he caught my eye. "It looks like you still have some life in you." "That is crazy to think that you are not who you once were." "You are just a shadow of that beautiful woman."

"Maybe one day you will get healed?" "Who knows, but speaking from soul to soul, I will do my best to keep you healthy." He came over and rubbed my head. "Your hair needs to get growing!"

"I hate seeing you look like a little boy." "Oh well, but I don't want to be negative." "Your sister and I have decided to recommence our relationship." "I think it is best for the three of us." "It is kind of a full circle moment." "Maybe this is why I cheated on you?"

"Maybe it was in our destiny for me to be together with your sister?" "Somehow I think a higher power knew what Francisco was influencing you negatively." "You know, I blame him for taking away the time you used to give me."

"That is why I even began to cheat on you." "He put ideas in your head about how you have all this potential and to make your dreams come true." "That took so much time away from us." "Yeah you eventually became a principal, but at what cost?"

"Look at you now, and look at Francisco." "You can't even survive on your own, and he's dead!" Tears began to swell in my eyes. I felt like there was a ball inside my throat. My breathing got heavier.

How dare he say that about me? How could he be so idiotic, and who the hell was he to even mention Francisco? "Anyway, I'll let you get some rest." "I am going to call someone to help make this home accessible for you." He gave me a wink like if he were some sort of savior.

He really did think that. How arrogant of him. If he had any sense he would see how miserable I truly was. I mean for crying out loud my face was wet from tears, yet he did not even bat an eye. How was it possible that I had been engaged to him? Had I been that much of an idiot?

I didn't want to know the answer to that, so instead I closed my eyes, and cried myself to sleep. When I woke I was not greeted by sunshine and rainbows, instead I was welcomed by a strong fecal scent. I don't know how I knew, but I knew that my catheter had fallen out. There was absolutely nothing that I could do.

I believe a few hours passed until Jazmine came in to see me. "It smells like shit in here!" "Ugh gross, there is poo and piss everywhere!" I felt my face get bright red. "You are so disgusting, Lucianna!" "Henry, please call the hospital and let them know that her catheter fell off!"

"On it." Jazmine left the room and came back a few minutes later with latex gloves, a face mask and wipes. She didn't talk to me while she cleaned me. Which somehow made it worse. It made it seem like I wasn't human.

Even as my tears clouded my vision she did not say a single word to me. Instead once she was done she left me alone, and only came back into the room when a nurse came and set up the catheter again. *I think you guys should invest in adult diapers. At least until you figure out the best position for her catheter to not fall out again.*

You should be fine as long as you don't let her body slant, but just in case this is my number to call me directly. "Thank you nurse." *No problem. We have you all cleaned up and ready to continue healing, Lucianna.* The nurse gave me a pitiful smile and left.

Again I was left alone, and that is how the first couple of days went. Jazmine never bothered to have a real conversation with me. I was wasting away physically and mentally. I was never stretched or moved from my bed.

My only source of entertainment was the distant sound of her and Henry laughing and arguing. It echoed through the silence, reminding me just how alone I was. I was miserable, and for the first time, I understood how people could go mad when left to fend for themselves.

By the third week in that cage, time had begun to blur—until one morning, Jazmine came rushing in, far too cheerful for that hour, my tablet clutched in her hand. "Sister!" she said brightly. "I have some great news."

"My attorney says all you have to do is agree to give me access to your care and money, and then I'll officially be your provider." "Here is your tablet." "It is all set up for you." "I am going to ask you the questions, and you just respond with yes."

She brought over my wheel chair, and easily lifted me up into it. I was at least 15 pounds underweight now, so I wasn't surprised about the ease of her lifting me. Once I was strapped into the chair she put my tablet on the bar, and wheeled me to the living room where the sun was beautifully shining.

The beautiful sun hitting my face filled me with joy, and emotion that I started to cry. Jazmine noticed this time and wiped my tears away. "Let's go ahead and do this, I have a lot of things to do, sis."

She turned my tablet on. I could hear notifications going off. It was probably all from Benson, but of course I wouldn't be able to see them. "Okay, your voice is set up." "I'll ask the questions now."

"Lucianna, do you give your sister Jazmine permission to be your sole care provider?" I slowly typed "fuck no." The look on Jazmine's face was priceless. It was almost worth the slap across the face that she gave me.

A smack so hard that it sent my head spinning. I was left in utter shock. She had hit me before the accident, but I saw it more as her being in a passionate state. This time it was plain abuse. My left cheek ached, and my jaw hurt.

"Lucianna, do you think I want to hurt you?" "Of course I don't, but I know you have this insane idea of me that Francisco implanted in you." "If I have to slap some reason into you I will." "I love you sister, but don't play with me." "We need your money not just for you, but for us as a family."

"We can renovate this entire house, and even get fertility treatment, so I can become a mom." "Don't you want to be an aunty?" NO! I typed with my joy stick. Please let me go live on my own. *Slap!* Everything went dark for a second. She had struck me so hard that I briefly lost consciousness.

"We can do this the easy way, or the hard way." "Do you think anyone but us will care if you die?" "I don't want you to die sister, but I will let you rot away if it means I get your money and I can become a mom." Jazmine's eyes started to twitch, and I could see how serious she was.

It was apparent that one of the reasons why she had changed so much in a year was her desire to become a mom. She didn't have to tell me, but from the phantom pregnancy to needing the money for treatment. It was obvious.

I now understood her more, and I also understood one thing more clearly. She would definitely leave me to die without regret. Any doubt that I once had was gone. Nonetheless, something else was also crystal clear for me now.

There was no way in hell I was going to let someone else decide whether I lived or died. I would play along with Jazmine's game—for now—but if I ever chose to quit living, it would be on my own terms. With that, I nodded in agreement. You can ask the questions again, sister, I typed, as the tablet spoke the words aloud. "Thank you so much, Lucianna." "You will not regret this sister!" "You'll see, we will become a great family." I smiled in agreement to appease her. Her gums flared and she asked the questions again.

I agreed to everything. I said yes to losing my savings. I agreed to give up my insurance "live-in. I even helped her verbally submit an application to be paid for her services of taking care of me by the government. She was all smiles when it was finished.

All in all she would be getting my one hundred and eleven thousand dollars. Plus she would get monthly checks of 3700 dollars for being my full time caregiver. On top of that she will have access to my 401k. All my hard work was gone in less than an hour.

"Okay, sister I am going to put you back to bed." "I am sure you are tired." She wheeled me back into my room, and carried me effortlessly into the bed. "Oh, I can't forget this tablet." She grabbed the tablet and left my room.

Leaving me alone once more, but this time with severe pain to my head, neck and face. A pain that felt like the back of my neck was being burned. This wasn't good. Had she hurt me enough to die? I really hoped not.

Like I said before, I wanted to be the one who decided whether I lived or not. I didn't want her to think she had that over me. Gosh, how awful to even be saying this. God, why me? I know I never was religious, but please God help me get out of here. Help me, or take me with you.

CHAPTER 18

Stuck in Limbo & Hope

Please, take me with you, God. I quietly said out loud. Wait, what? Were my ears playing tricks? Had I really said my name out loud? Lucianna, I whispered again. Yes! My voice, my beautiful voice!

It sounded groggy like if I had smoked a pack of cigarettes and then tried running a mile after, but it was my voice! I could talk again! How could this be? Did the beating that Jazmine give me fix something? I didn't know, or was it God giving me a signal to not give up in my life? Maybe? Or maybe it was a mixture of both?

I had no clue, but tears of joy washed down my face and onto my shoulders. What? My shoulders? Did I really feel tears falling onto my shoulders? Only one way to find out! I slowly moved my head side to side, which caused my ears to spread on my shoulders! I was able to feel some sensation there. Oh my goodness this was a miracle. Like I said, I wasn't religious, but I think this was a sign of God to keep me going forward.

I promise you, God—I won't give up. I will keep fighting. I will survive... no, more than that—I will thrive. My first step was to regain full access to my voice. Jazmine and Henry could never know that I could speak. And by the time my voice returned, I hoped I would be able to feel more than just my shoulders.

Despite the sharp pain radiating across my face and head, I felt something I hadn't felt in a long time—hope. No one, and nothing could take away this feeling. Not even when Jazmine invited her friends later that day to celebrate that she was now fully in charge of me. They came a few hours after she had slapped the life back into me.

They watched with amazement as Jazmine set up the "nutritional IV." They took videos and pictures. She was praised as a hero, and she loved every minute of it. She was even gloating that I did not have to go to the hospital because she had somehow secured five box refills of my IV meaning that I didn't have to see a doctor for at least six months.

I was flabbergasted upon hearing that, but I shouldn't have been. She was cunning. *Jazmine do you have to wipe her ass?* "I do everything." *You are such a saint! You must really love her.*

"I do, she is my sister." "It is my responsibility." *Girl, but don't let her stop you from doing what you like in life too. I mean it must be a burden to have Lucianna. Like the bitch can't even move. How will you travel?*

"I'll find a way to take her with me!" "Besides I am not all alone, Henry and I have gotten back together." "We are stronger than ever." *Bitch! You didn't tell us!* "Ha." "I was waiting for you ladies to come over so I could spill." *Well, spill!* They walked away from the room and left me alone.

Alone—something I knew all too well. As the days passed, I saw less and less of Jazmine. Some days, she forgot to feed me entirely. Those were the ones that scared me most, because I no longer wanted to die. Still, in the back of my mind, I knew she wouldn't let that happen—not with all the money she was getting. Especially once she gained full control of my estate.

Three weeks after she recorded me giving her access to it, she finally got what she wanted. Not even a day later, I heard a furniture company arrive. They hauled out her old couches and tables and replaced them with new ones.

Surprisingly, they even brought a new bed for me. I didn't know if Jazmine did it to give me a better life, or if she just wanted new things in her house? It was probably the latter, but I was so happy that she did because when they brought in the new bed she asked the moving men if they could lift me to my chair. Of course they agreed, and that changed my life forever!

As the man picked me up he accidentally slipped sending me tumbling down with him. My left arm hit the floor with a thud. It hurt so bad, but it hurt! I felt it! I had felt the pain in my entire left arm.

I was so ecstatic that I almost yelled for joy. Thankfully, Jazmine interrupted me by hammering the man. She called him every name in the book, and even got the move in fee and removal of old furniture waived.

While she was happily gloating about that. It gave me enough time to regain control of my own emotions. I became a soulless shell once more, and patiently waited for her and the men to leave. Once I was alone, without even thinking about it, my left hand started to move.

My hand slowly wiggled. It took every ounce of my mental strength but my fingers moved too! I had movement in my hand and arm! Tears of joy ran down my face as I slowly lifted my arm!

This was beyond amazing. I wondered if any other part of my body had feelings? I slowly moved my hand across my legs and feet. No sensation there. I then moved it to my right arm. None there, but on the shoulders yes.

Hopefully that meant that I would gain access to both my arms soon. I could only wish, but even with just access to one arm I could do something that I had not done in months. Touch my own face. With a heavy and shaky hand I reached for my face.

My fingers trembled as they touched nothing but bone. My once plumped face was nothing more than a skeleton. I was shocked. I had not seen my reflection in months, but I could imagine how I looked. Hmm, but what about my hair?

I reached for my head and I definitely was not bald anymore, but my hair was still short. I felt like I may look like a Chia Pet. The idea made me laugh, but that was cut short as my left arm started to spasm.

It fell from my head right back to my thigh. It shook violently for almost a minute and then I was able to move it again. I must have pushed it too hard. I needed to be slow and steady when it came to dealing with it.

That is right Lucianna, slow and steady. Gain your strength and you can leave this hell soon enough. With that thought in my mind and a big smile on my face I went to sleep, and for the first time since his passing I dreamed about Francisco.

In my dream we were both in the Bahamas. We were swimming in the ocean as we got our tan on. We laughed and smiled. It was a beautiful dream, and it gave me the strength to get through the next two weeks which were tough.

The honeymoon stage of Jazmine and Henry were over. They were arguing like dogs. Henry even came to my room one night. I was shocked since I had not seen him in at least a month.

"I don't know what to do anymore." "I know you can't understand me, but your sister is becoming unbearable again." "The only thing that is making me stay is her big heart." "I mean she is taking care of you, and you are nothing but a nuisance to her."

"Ugh, sorry I did not mean to say that, but Jazmine has been under a lot of stress." "We are trying to have a baby, but I know she has a lot on her plate." "I mean, you are basically a baby again." "For crying out loud she has to wipe your big ass every day!" "But you know what?" No, I don't you dumb ass bitch. I quietly thought.

"I shouldn't be blaming you." "At the end of the day you are the one showing me how much of a good person Jazmine is." "I appreciate that." "Besides, I know I hurt you, so the least I can do is give you a good life." "You'll be okay with us, and once we have a kid I am sure they will love you too."

Henry left after about 30 minutes, and went back to the living room. I soon heard laughter from both of them. They had made up, and sadly it was apparent since my ears bled as I heard them having sex.

It was awful, and dehumanizing. They were moaning and groaning like if the house was alone. At one point Henry even walked into my room butt-naked. I guess he had forgotten his charger in here. "Oh don't mind me." "I mean you've seen all the goods before right?"

I stared through him and waited for him to leave. He smiled and walked away leaving me feeling pathetic and useless. I will always hate him for that. Before I thought he was just a coward, but now I knew better.

He was a terrible person. I just never saw it before because I had never seen him with a disabled person. People show their true colors when they are with a disabled person. I always knew this, but now more than ever. However, I digress. Enough of those two pieces of shits for the day. I needed to relax.

My head was spinning again, and the only way to elevate the pain was sleep. I closed my eyes once more, and this time I was able to drift to sleep with no issues. *Thump, thump, thump,* the sound of heels and what

I thought were boots hastily walking to my room. "Wake up, "Lucianna!" "Look who is here to see you!"

"Hi." Jake slowly entered the room. I was surprised to see him. The last time I saw him he was helping me off the floor. He was the only one to defend me at Jazmine's wedding. I thought Jazmine had cut him out of her life for that. I guess I was wrong. "Sis, Jake wanted to speak to you." "I told him that you can't understand anything, but he still wanted to speak to you."

"I appreciate that, Jazmine." "You think we can speak in the front yard?" "It is beautiful with all the leaves covering the floor." "Yeah, sure, but you have to put her in her chair." "I don't feel like straining my back today."

"I will have to buy you something for your back." "I don't want you getting hurt, Jazmine." "Oh really?" "Yeah." Jake smiled at her. Jazmine looked ecstatic. She loved others feeling bad for her, and also getting her gifts.

"Okay, if you need me I'll be in my room." "I need to catch up on my shows." "I haven't had a free minute in months." "You are a life saver, Jake." She winked at him, and then left us alone.

"Hey, Lucianna." "I don't know how much of you is still there, but this is Jake." I felt a tingle go down my spine. Jake the one who had played with emotions. "I'm sorry, Lucianna." "I am really sorry for what I did." "Ever since the day of the wedding I have been thinking about you." "I can't believe I did that." I listened carefully as Jake walked to my wheelchair. He kept his head down as he prepared it for me, and he continued to speak.

"It all started as this sick joke." He came closer to me. His arm shook a little as he reached for me. "I'm going to carry you know okay?" That surprised me. He was actually treating me like a person. He wrapped one of his arms under my legs and the other under my shoulders. He easily placed me in my seat.

"There is no excuse for what we did, but I will tell you that your sister was hurt. "She told me how you ruined her life for exposing her in public." "I didn't know that you were still dating Henry when Jazmine slept with him."

I kept my head to the side as Jake strapped me into the chair. "Honestly, it was all a mess." "I was wrong for doing that, and so was Jazmine." "You were also wrong for ruining her wedding, but you know what?" "What is done is done." "The important thing now is to do the right things, and move forward by learning from our mistakes."

He started to wheel me out of my room, and I could smell that cinnamon. "I'm making cinnamon rolls, Jake." "They'll be done in two hours, so feel free to walk Lucianna to the local park if you want." It's funny because this entire time I had not been physically hungry at all, but something about smelling the cinnamon triggered hunger in me. This was a good sign. I was healing.

"I can't wait!" "We will be back by then." "Alright, now don't have too much fun." "Lucianna is in no way in shape to do anything naughty, okay?" She gave me a sly wink, and then opened the door for us.

Henry was easily able to lift the chair over the small platform that separated the door to the outside. The platform that Jazmine and Henry were supposed to make into some sort of ramp for me almost 3 months ago. "See you."

Jake shut the door behind us and we commenced our way to the park. Immediately, a nice fresh breeze hit my face, and my hair started to move! A warmth of happiness engulfed me. It is crazy how the simple things are the ones we appreciate the most when they are taken away from us.

The little things like seeing the squirrels running up the trees. It was beautiful to all my senses. Especially my nose. I had forgotten the smell of the outside world. I had learned to live in the smell of my own waste.

Pee has a strong smell, but so does nature! The fresh smell of dust flying in the air, to the smell of dying leaves. It was beautiful, and it gave me more motivation to keep on living.

"Lucianna," Henry interrupted my train of thought. "Look there is something that I wanted to say since I saw you." "I just didn't feel comfortable saying it in front of your sister." I stared blankly at his torso area as he spoke.

I didn't want him to know how aware I truly was because that might ruin my chances of him slipping up, and saying something that I could use against Jazmine or even him. "Look, it is true that I also dated a guy in the past." "I am not going to deny that, but I have also dated a woman."

He rubbed his long hair to the back of his head. "Look, I don't like labels, but what I can tell you is that I fell for you." He quietly kneeled down and picked up my head. He was looking directly into my eyes. There was no way that I could avoid his stare as he was holding onto my chin. "I still love you." "You are beautiful." "I know you are in there." "I don't care what the doctors told Jazmine." "I see the sparkle inside your eyes."

"I was doing some research and I have found rehabilitation clinics on the East Coast that specialize in injuries just like yours." "They have done wonders for their patients." "Some people even learn to speak and use their arms again."

His eyes were starting to water as he spoke to me. "The only issue is that they are private, and don't take the insurance that you have." "Jazmine doesn't have money either, but don't worry!" "I am only 15 thousand dollars away from securing you a spot in their one month camp." "It is thirty thousand dollars, which I have half of" "If I save for the next year, and hopefully this time next year you will have a spot in their next camp!"

Don't let the tear escape, Luclanna. Don't let it escape! Too late. Tears started to fall down my eyes, and before I knew it Jake was wiping them away. "I knew you were in there." "I just knew it."

CHAPTER 19

The Orchestrator is Revealed

Fuck, there went my chance of having him confess any useful information to me. Well too bad. "I have to let Jazmine know that you are aware!" Hmm, trust me she knows. She just doesn't want anyone else to know because if people are aware then she will be forced to treat me better. I quietly thought as Jake pulled out his phone to call my sister.

"Jazmine!" "Lucianna is au courant!" "She cried when I told her about a rehab clinic that can help her!" "Are you serious?" I could hear Jazmine's voice get high pitched. It tended to do that when she was upset. She did not appreciate the fact that Jake knew of my awareness.

"That is great!" "She can tell us how to properly take care of her." "Oh, of course." Her voice pitched again. "Come on over and tell me about it!" "The bread is ready too!" "You got it." "I'm rushing over now."

Jake was all smiles. I felt bad for him. He really thought my sister would take me into consideration now that she "knew" that I was alive! I knew better than to get excited, but I must admit that Jake's enthusiasm made me feel happy.

"I will visit you at least once a week, Lucianna." "I have to work hard to save the money, but I promise I will take you out of the house every chance I get." "I can't have you locked up in the room all day." "It isn't healthy for your mental state, right?"

I shook my head back and forth. "Ah!" "You responded with no!" He joyfully said as we pulled into the house. Jazmine was already standing outside. "Can you take her to her room?" She asked Jake. "She needs to rest." "Of course!"

We entered the house, and the aroma of freshly baked bread filled my nostrils. Butter was in the air. Oh how I wish I could have eaten a piece. Hopefully soon enough. "Do you want me to put you back into bed, or leave you on your chair?" Jake looked at me thoughtfully as I took one last whiff of the air.

He probably thought I was crazy, but I quickly nodded my head at him to show that I wanted to go to bed. Ironically, going outside for the first time in almost three months did make me tired. I felt winded. "Understood." He wheeled me into my chamber and carefully placed me into bed.

"I am going to have some rolls with your sister." "It meant a lot to see you, Lucianna." "You are still so beautiful." "See you next week, okay? I smiled and nodded yes to him. Which surprised me. I never thought I would feel happy to see Jake again, but I was. He tricked me, but he also showed his true colors today.

He was a good person that made a stupid mistake, and he is forgiven on my part. That said, I don't think I would ever want to be more than just friends with him. At some point I would let him know that, but for now his visits will serve a good purpose for me. As long as he comes around then I will be able to go outside.

I felt happy at that realization as he closed the door behind him. Leaving me once again, alone. Alone, but not wasting away this time because now I had some movement. It was time to get to work. I needed to get stronger.

I began to do some exercises. I lifted my hand about three to four inches in all directions. I did this for about five sets of six reps. It was tiring, but I needed to get more powerful. The sooner I did this without struggling, the faster it would be for me to be able to hold a telephone.

As for the strength on my arm, I was able to lift my legs about two inches in the air. Not exactly where I needed to be in order to leave, but I would get there! Regarding my right hand, it too had some movement now. I could now make a fist with a bit of a struggle. My body was slowly healing.

Unfortunately, I couldn't lift my right arm just yet. Nonetheless, my head was as strong as ever. I could move it, and my neck just like before. Also, my voice was getting clearer. It was still groggy and sounded like I had merged with a toad, but I was understandable! That was a true win for me because I knew deep down that I was still too weak to even be able to drag myself onto my chair, let alone escape.

But! A big but, if Jake really did come to see me maybe I could yell for help from someone at the park? Yes, I see it clear now. I could let a stranger know that I was not being treated well at Jazmine's!

Yeah, that was what I would do. I felt another giant smile form on my face, and with that happiness I closed my eyes and drifted to sleep again! That night I slept like a baby, and I would have continued to sleep if it wasn't for Jazmine's yells.

"LUCIANNA!" She shouted. "Sister, I have some awful news!" She rushed into my room, slamming the door open. She looked distraught. Her wig only half ways on. "I just got a call from the doctor." "I thought I may be pregnant because of some cramps that I have, but no." "Apparently, my uterus is filled with tumors!" "The doctor said I will never be able to carry a baby!."

She looked at me like she wanted me to save her. She resembled that little girl she once was. Honestly, I felt bad for her. She was crying. She was shouting. Her face was red and swollen from all the tears. At that moment she was my little sister again. My sister who was tired of being teased for her lack of hair.

I had to control myself from reaching out and caressing her as she fell to the floor and just wept. She wept for what felt like ten minutes. I wanted to talk to her, but I didn't. I guess she realized that I wasn't much help because she soon got up and left the room without saying another word.

I was left feeling confused. How could I still feel empathy for her? She treated me like shit, yet I wanted to hug her, and tell her that everything would be okay. Sadly, I knew that was impossible.

Ugh. I did not like feeling like a terrible person. It made me feel uneasy. Which caused my shoulders to cramp up. Ah! I quietly yelled as a cramp set in, sending my right arm up and down. I slowly steady myself.

Wait, what? I moved my right arm? Slowly but surely I watched in amazement as not only did I move my right arm, but I brought both my arms together. This was a miracle. I couldn't believe it. I would have clapped for joy if I had not been startled.

Thump, thump, thump, the sound of heels clacking the floor in the living room filled my ears. They were headed in my direction. I immediately stopped moving. "Sister!"

"Oh my gosh!" "I have some excellent news!" "You will be so happy!" Jazmine was beaming with joy. Her tears were gone, and they were replaced with a smile. I was confused. It had not even been five minutes since her breakdown, and now she was happy? What was going on? As if she had heard me talk in my mind, she answered.

"I know how I can get pregnant! "Even with a tumor filled uterus!" "A surrogate!" "The doctor said some of my eggs are healthy, so with the money you have given me I can have at least ten trials!" She was jumping up and down in the room. It was making my small bed shake. *Hmmm.* I pondered as she leaped for joy.

How the hell would she afford a surrogate? They are easily over 100k! That was pushing the limits of what I had in my account. I guess Jazmine read my expression because she quickly spoke up, and said something that shook me to a core that I thought I no longer had.

"Lucianna, I want you to be my surrogate." She flashed her gummy smile at me. I swallowed my spit, and out of pure shock I tried to speak. Thankfully, I did not say a word because I began to choke. "Sister, we know that you cannot talk!" "Don't force yourself because you will get more injured."

"I know this is a lot to drop on you at once, but I'll go ahead and let you soak everything up." "Once I have all the logistics of everything I'll talk to you about it, but for now I am going straight to the doctor's!"

She joyfully skipped out of the room, and this time quietly shut the door behind her. I, on the other hand, was left dumbfounded. Firstly, because of the news that she had just given me, but most importantly because I almost spoke to her!

If it wasn't for choking on my own spit I would have blown my cover. I needed to be smarter than that! I had to stop letting her get the best of my emotions. I mean look where it has gotten me!

Secondly, who the fuck did she think she was? There was no way in hell that I would ever be her surrogate. Maybe in another lifetime, but now?

Hell no! Sweat dripped from my forehead onto my lips. My chest was rising and falling rapidly. The back of my neck started to feel hot.

This wasn't good. I had to calm myself down, but how? I knew Jazmine. She would get her way one way or another. Either I listened to her calmly, or it would get ugly. What should I do? Should I use my voice and let her know that I didn't want this? That would never work!

Ah! Think Lucianna, think! I told myself as I closed my eyes and thought about what to do. About a minute into my pondering a clear answer had formed, and that was "Hell fucking no would I ever be a surrogate for her!" I would rather die! I mean, I had movement of both my arms now. I didn't need any assistance if I wanted to end it all. Ugh, why was I thinking this way?

Why was life so unfair to me? Why? I yelled to the empty room. Screaming was risky, but I knew no one was home, so I yelled and I yelled, and I yelled till my throat hurt. I cried till my eyes were dry, and I must have fallen asleep at one point because the next thing I recall is hearing the door being banged.

Thud, thud, thud. Jazmine you bitch! Open this door now! Where the fuck is my money? I've been patient with your bitch ass, but I need my fifty grand now! That voice got me up. Well my head anyway. I lifted it straight up, and I perked my ears.

If you don't open the door I will break your windows and enter myself! Thud, thud, thud. The man sounded furious. He meant business. Jazmine must have done something to really tick him off. I wasn't surprised. She had a phase where she thought she was a gangster.

She got a good beating back in the day, before leaving all that behind. I guess she didn't officially cut ties with that side of her because this man was serious. He was breaking into this house one way or another.

Creek, crack, the living room door was pushed open. He was inside. I should have been scared, but I wasn't. I secretly wanted him to beat me to death as horrible as that sounded, so I shouted back to him. "In here!"

I'm here! I hallowered again. *Thump, thump, thump,* heavy footsteps walked toward my room. See you soon, Francisco. Boom! My door shot open. The gush of wind that came in reached my face. I had my eyes closed as I waited for the beating, but silence.

What was going on? I opened my eyes. *Oh, wow. It's you!* He looked at me with wide open eyes. His mouth slightly widened, and the crows' feet around his eyes tightened. *I thought you were dead.*

He walked closer to me, and inspected me from head to toe. I did not flinch. I wanted him to end it for me, but instead he looked confused. *This isn't right. Who are you? How do you know, Jazmine?*

He watched me carefully waiting for an answer, and I gave him exactly that. She is my sister. If you have any issue with her, go right ahead and give me the punishment instead.

My answer must have caught him off guard because he took three steps back. *This isn't right. Why would she do this to her own sister? Why do you want to take your sister's beating when she has already caused you so much pain?*

What do you mean? He looked at me, and was about to answer, but instead walked away. Where are you going? Answer me please! *Don't trust Jazmine. You are in a wheelchair because of her!*

With that he started to walk away again, but with all my will and strength I picked up my left arm and I grabbed his hand. He looked at me with pity. Please tell me what you mean, I cried.

I can't! Just don't trust the bitch! He shook me off and tried to walk away, but not before I used my right arm to gently touch his back. Please don't tell her that I can talk. He shook his head up and down, and left. Leaving me feeling completely enraged as his words became clear in my mind.

I felt like the inside of my body was being stabbed with tiny needles. My head was spinning, and I felt the weight of the world on my shoulders. What this man, this creep had said was obvious. He had insinuated that Jazmine was the reason why I was in a wheelchair. She was the reason that Francisco was dead. How despicable!

This wasn't right. Could it really be? I needed to know if it was true. I required actual evidence because if it was then all hell was about to break loose. I mean all hell was already breaking loose inside of me. My stomach was in knots. My body felt hot. I felt like I needed to throw up.

My arms were shaking from anger. I slowly stabilized them and to my amazement, I noticed that I was able to keep them up longer without much effort. Quite possibly it was because of all the adrenaline running through my veins. Who knows?

Regardless, that was a good thing because it meant that I was possibly powerful enough to pick up my own body. There was only one way to find out. Using my left arm as the lever tool, and my right arm as the stabilizer I picked up my heavy legs. One by one I placed them over the bed.

Ah, I had some independence again! I cried from the joy of it all, but in doing that I did not pay attention to how close I was to the edge of the bed and I stumbled to the ground. In that exact moment I heard Jazmine yell. "Someone broke into the house!" I laid frozen. I could not let her know that I moved myself, so I waited till she found me.

"Oh my goodness!" "Lucianna!" "Sister!" "What did he do to you?" My mind went numb. The only way for her to know that it was one person, and a man was because she knew this individual.

Whether this creep of a man was lying about Jazmine or not, there was more to the story. I mean for crying out loud when he had first seen me it was as if he had seen a ghost! He had been surprised to see me alive!

Fuck, there was no denying it. Jazmine had to do something with my accident. How awful! I wanted to beat the shit out of her right then and there, but I had to be smart. This had turned into more than just a sibling rivalry. This was murder!

The killing of my best friend-my brother, and there was no way in hell that I would leave his death in vain. The times of wanting to kill myself were over! I had a reason to live again, and that reason was to put my "sister," and all the scums who were her accomplices in jail.

"Sister, are you okay?" The demon came toward me, but I closed my eyes. I wanted her to think that I was knocked out. Maybe she would slip up and say something?

CHAPTER 20

Forced Impregnation

I felt disgusted by Jazmine's touch as she lifted me back onto the bed. I wanted to beat her head in as she tucked me back in. It took all my will power to not scream at her, but at the end of the day I couldn't, and I needed to be 100% sure that she indeed did this to me. There was no room to be wrong because what I had planned for her was not to be taken lightly.

"Yes, someone came in and broke into my house." "They even threw my quadriplegic sister to the floor!" "Please send someone this way!" The police arrived within ten minutes. They performed a wellness check on me and made sure I was okay.

While they were doing that I was so close to letting them know that I was not safe here. I wanted to tell them that I needed to be removed from Jazmine's custody, but I kept my mouth shut.

I was not going to leave this house until I found out if Jazmine actually killed my best friend. That was my top priority now! Get justice for Francisco, and vengeance for myself. "Are you okay ma'am?" The officer looked at me emphatically." I had not realized that my breathing had gotten faster, but I did my best to slow it down as the officer put me back into bed.

We have written down everything in the report. We will do our best to find this person. For the meantime we will leave a police officer to patrol your home for the next two days, okay?

"Thank you officers." "I appreciate everything." Jazmine was using her fake kind voice for the police officers. They soon left, and she called the insurance right away. With the reference of the police the insurance company agreed to put a new door and new windows in every room. Jazmine of course was through the roof about that.

She loved that she was getting new things. On top of that Henry was treating her with so much care. I guess she had lied to him that the man had roughed her up. I don't know how he believed her, but he did.

He was as kind as could be to her for the next two days. In fact he didn't leave her side for two entire days. It was a long 48 hours where they left me to rot, or so they thought.

Being alone gave me the courage to learn how to independently move myself out of bed and onto my chair. I even changed my own catheter and diaper without them knowing. On top of that, I started my own IV.

They probably thought I was weak as hell, when Henry finally came in on the third day to "feed me." Hey Lucianna." "Sorry for not putting your IV in for a few days." "I'm sure you are fine." Yeah, no thanks to you, coward.

"Besides, your sister needed all the attention she could get." "She was almost killed." "Can you believe that?" "Anyway, I have to get to work." "Jazmine will come change you once she is done at the doctor's." "See you soon."

With that sorry speech he left me, and this was my chance. I waited to hear the front door close and then I dragged myself onto my wheelchair.

This was going to be a mission. It was one thing to drag myself onto my chair, and a whole nother thing to use my arms to wheel myself around, but I had to try.

I undid the breaks on the wheelchair, and using all my force I began to wheel myself forward. It was exhausting. I felt like my muscles were slowly being ripped off my bone. No one tells you how strong wheelchairs users are, until you try wheeling yourself!

I'll forever see the disabled people differently. They are super human. I just hated that it took me being disabled to empathize with their struggles.

For example, an able-bodied person would never know the struggle that I felt. I was currently grappling with exhaustion as I tried leaving my room. From opening the door with one hand, while holding the wheel with my other took a lot of strength. I even started to sweat!

Funny enough that wasn't even the toughest part. The most challenging thing was getting myself over the small platform that separated the door and the floor. Just lifting my chair was torture. I truly thought my arms would fall off, but I managed.

With sweat dripping from my forehead onto my face I wheeled my way into Jazmine's spare room aka my parents' old room. That no longer looked like their old room. The once violet walls were now a dull gray. Sigh.

Why did I ever let Jazmine keep this place? She quite literally sucked the life out of the room. The only thing that remained that was similar to how my parents once had it was the frame.

The family picture right in the middle of the room. Our last family picture together. We were so happy then. I was even holding Jazmine. What a pity, but enough of that. It was time to find evidence against the baby girl I once held. With determination and sadness I began to wheel myself into the room, but I was caught off guard instantly.

Jazmine had put in carpet. The once tiled floors now contained a boring black carpet. There was no way that I could wheel myself though. Fuck! To make matters worse, I was not nearly strong enough to crawl all the way in the carpet while dragging my chair.

I needed help. Also, at that moment I realized that any sort of proof that I was to find of Jazmine's involvement in Francisco's death would not be wheelchair height. I needed to ask someone for their aid in that too, and the only person that I remotely trusted now was Benson, but would he help me?

I hadn't had contact with him since I left the hospital because my stupid sister took my tablet. Would he hate me now? No, of course not. He was so sweet to me while I was there, and he even wanted me to stay with him at one point, but would he even care now? Three and a half months had passed since then.

I didn't know the answer, but I had to try! My palms started to sweat a tad as I wheeled my way over to the kitchen. Jazmine had a house phone still there. She didn't use it, but *At&T* required a landline in order to use the internet for some reason still.

Well here goes nothing. I reached over the counter and grabbed the beige beat up phone. I dialed the ten digit number that I had memorized the day he gave me. I memorized it as a game. His phone number along with the nurses who took care of me while there. *Ring, ring, ring,* my heart was beating out of my chest as I waited for an answer. *Hello?* Benson? *Who is this?*

By the simple sound of hearing his calm voice my racing heart stopped. It brought calmness to me. Benson, this is Lucianna. *Lucianna! I am so glad you're speaking! When did this happen?*

Benson, I have to be quick because I don't know when Jazmine will be back, but I need your help. *What's wrong?* So many things are wrong, but is there any way that you can come to Jazmine's house tomorrow between 1 p.m. to 4 p.m? That is the time she does her grocery-errands run.

Why can't I just come now to speak to you? I am off work. No! Jazmine can't know that I am speaking to you. I think I found out something awful. Are you able to come tomorrow? *For you, of course! Do you want me to ring the door bell when I arrive?*

NO! Please, I will find a way to signal you when the cost is clear. *Alright, if you are in any danger, call 911! I am worried about you Lucianna. I tried to go to your home four times already, but Jazmine said you didn't want visitors.*

His statement brought me into tears. Benson, I had no clue that you tried coming to see me. I thought you had forgotten me. *I would never!* I can't wait to see you tomorrow. *The same, Lucianna. Bye for now, and please if anything call 911.* I will. I silently told him as I hung up the call, and deleted the history.

Feeling more at ease I began to wheel my way back to my room. It was pointless to be out in the open when I couldn't do much. Besides I was tired, and needed a break, so back to the room it was.

Which was definitely more challenging wheeling my way back this time with sore arms and hands. I stopped quite a few times, and the last stop before reaching my chamber was right at the edge of the hallway.

Exactly where a large mirror was hanging. My stomach knotted up. I had not seen myself since the accident. While at the hospital it had been by choice, but here at Jazmine's it was because I was not allowed. I needed to see myself now! I slowly lifted my head toward the mirror.

I couldn't believe my eyes. I knew I was skinny, but my round face was gone. It was replaced by a bony face. I could visibly see my cheekbones. My goodness I looked just awful. On top of that my unibrow had grown quite a bit.

I have always been a hairier girl. Wow. To add to all of that, my body was severely malnourished. I needed to eat real food. My collar bones were so visible that it took me aback. The only good thing in my entire appearance that I liked, was that my hair looked cute. It was in the shape of a pixie bob.

That made me smile, but it was short-lived because the sound of a car pulling up into the driveway filled my ears. Dammit. That had to be Jazmine. I needed to get back to my room! Using all my might I wheeled myself back into my dungeon, and I shut the door behind me. Wasting no time I lifted myself off the chair and onto the bed.

My arms were trembling from fatigue by the time I got back into bed. Which was not a second too late because my door swooshed open. "Lucianna!" "Sister!" "I am going to be a mom!"

"Today my baby will start to develop!" My arms were still trembling furiously. I had overexerted myself. "Aw sister, are you having one of your muscles spams?" Jazmine came over and massaged my arms. Surprisingly, it brought comfort to me, and the spams stopped.

"There you go all better." "I talked to a doctor today about trying to feed you solid foods too." "He thinks it's a good idea if I start with liquids and take it from there." "I showed him pictures of you, and your history." She gently rubbed my hair. "Your hair is growing out beautifully." Why was she being so nice to me?

I looked at her with one eyebrow up. I wanted her to know that I didn't trust her, but she completely ignored me, and continued to talk. "I talked to my boo today after my visit to the doctor's and he is so excited!" "He really wants to be a dad too, and the fact that you are making this happen for us has him through the roof."

"It is a full circle moment." Fuck she was being an idiot again. There was no way in hell that I was going to consent to being a surrogate. Even if it meant that I had to leave before getting my evidence against her.

It is one thing to do something to me, but another thing to bring an innocent life into the mess that was my current life, and of course the life of Jazmine and Henry. Francisco would not want that. He would have rather died again than to see an innocent life being brought to this world to just suffer!

"Doctor, you can come in!" Doctor? I thought in my head. What was she talking about? "You are going to be okay, sis." "Relax." In the flash of an eye Jazmine struck me with a needle.

I immediately began to feel dazed and confused, but not before I saw a large man dressed in all black step into the room. He had to be at least 6'5 and a good 400 pounds. *Can you push her chair and IV out of the room so I can have space to move around?* His voice was deep and hollow. "Of course."

I vaguely remember Jazmine taking my chair and IV drip away, and then it all went black. *Wake up, ma'am, wake up. I need to make sure you are okay, so I can leave.* That booming voice penetrated my ear drums. I slowly opened my eyes, and saw the "doctor" staring down at me.

Alright, she is up, and I am out of here. I did my part! Just remember to feed her healthy foods so the babies can grow. "When will I know if she is pregnant?" What? *Between 10 to 14 days give or take a day or two.* "Thanks Doctor, and your money is in your account." "Forget this address."

Forget my face. Their laughter filled the air, and they left the room. Jazmine shut the door behind, leaving me alone. I immediately began to examine myself, and I was mortified to see that I was naked on the bed.

To make matters worse my legs were elevated on a stack of what seemed to be like six pillows. I wanted to kick them out of the way, but that would have been in vain as I couldn't move my legs.

This had to be a nightmare. Had they really implanted me with embryos? This couldn't be true, but it was. Fuck, there was no way that I would ever see this forced pregnancy through! I had to do something, but what could I do? Think, Lucianna, think! Maybe if I removed my legs from the pillows?

It could possibly give the embryos less of a chance to attach? There was only one way to find out. Using all my will power I fought through the groggy feeling that the anesthesia had given me, and I tossed the pillow stack to the floor. It sent my legs down with them.

That was not what I wanted to do, but good! I didn't know much about IVF, but I did know that elevation was good for it, and nonelevation was possibly bad. "Lucianna!" "Sister, you shouldn't be on the floor like this!"

"You just had my embryo implantation!" "Fucken muscles spams!" Jazmine ran toward me, and like a body builder she lifted me back up the bed. Her face was purple and flustered as she struggled to put the pillows back into place.

Not so easy manipulating someone while they're awake, is it? I thought as she finally put me back into place. "Sister, the doctor does not want you to move at all during the next three days, but I know your spams are involuntary."

"I am sorry that I will have to do this, but he did give me these restraints for you." Before I even had a chance to understand what she was saying, thanks to the anesthesia. She kneeled down by the bed and pulled out these straps.

There was no fucken way that I would let her do this! Screw staying here any longer. L e a v e m e a l o n e. I tried to say, but my voice was muffled from being put under. "Sister, you know you can't talk!" I had to fight my way out! I lifted my left arm, and as I swung she strapped my arm down.

"Man the anesthesia must've really brought out your spams." *Click, clack*, and I was strapped to the sides of the bed. H E L P. I D O N T W A N T, I tried to scream, but my words were slurred with spit.

"You're safe now sister." "Go back to sleep." I felt a prickle on my arm, and I was out once more. "I just put her clothes back on." "Go ahead and come in." Huh? "So our babies are in there?" "How much was the doctor able to attach to her?"

"We did two of them, and still have four in storage just in case these don't survive." "Do we have enough funds for those two tries?" "Yes, I got control of her account, and we have enough for all tries." "That is perfect babe."

My eyes fluttered open to a disgusting scene of Jazmine and Henry kissing. "She's awake, Jazmine." "Feed her, please." "I'm on it." "Sister, I'm glad you are up." "It is dinner time."

"The doctor wants you to try eating real food mixed with your IV now, okay?" "He suggests liquids, so I will start with your favorite juice, orange." Okay, look, I know that I was in an awful situation, but the fact that I was about to drink orange juice after almost five months of literally nothing had me ecstatic!

"I can tell by the look on your face that you are excited." "How in the world can you tell that?" "A sister knows." Jazmine walked over and sat next to me. She lifted my chin, and pressed the glass around my lips. The juice started to flow slowly, and it was amazing.

My taste buds were going to over drive. The acidity of the drink was bitter, but sweet at the same time. My mind instantly cleared, and even though I had been put under twice my body felt better. "There you go."

"We will start with four ounces and see how your body reacts." "Goodnight sister." "See you tomorrow after I do my errands." I waited for both of them to exit my room, and then I began to squeeze my arms from beneath the straps. There was no way in hell that I would stay here any longer. I had to get out! I had to prevent the embryos from attaching to me!

I tugged and pulled with all my might. I twisted and turned my arms as much as I could until finally I was able to squeeze one arm from under the strap. Once my right arm was untied I quickly untied my left arm.

Much better, but where was my chair? I scanned my room and it was nowhere to be found. Dammit! How was I supposed to leave when my chair is not in my room? A faint memory of the doctor asking Jazmine to remove my chair because he needed space entered my mind. It must be right outside the door, but how would I get there?

I panically searched the room for anything that could help me, but it was useless. There was nothing in this gray room! Nothing that could help me escape, but maybe that was a good thing?

I mean, I didn't want to bring innocent life into this world, but after drinking the orange juice my mind had cleared a lot. Was it worth escaping and leaving Francisco's murder go without punishment?

I had no clue what the answer was to that now. Everything was so confusing. I needed to think, so I closed my eyes and thought about him. What would he do in this situation?

Would he run away to save himself, or would he stay against all odds in order to protect me? The answer was obvious, he would stay. He was family after all. I couldn't just leave this house without finding what I needed. Which was the proof to see if Jazmine was involved in our demise. Besides, Benson was coming tomorrow. I could wait till then.

CHAPTER 21

The Keys

After an awful night of waking up from nightmares of being pregnant by Jazmine and Henry's child it was finally morning. It was a cold morning. Winter was near and I could feel it. The tips of my fingers felt numb, and even though I couldn't feel my legs I knew that my feet were numb.

My toes were bright red. This wasn't good. I only had one lousy blanket, and if I stayed in this room any longer I would surely get sick.

"See you later babe!" Henry called out to Jazmine as he left for work. I brought my toes near me and rubbed them till they were no longer red. "Do you need anything from *Walmart?*" "Get me some of those *Uncrustable* peanut butter sandwiches."

"You got it." The door slammed shut. If my calculations were right it was 7:30 a.m, and I had two and a half hours before Jazmine left. It was time to do my stretches while I waited. Left arm across right for one minute. Right arm across left for one minute. Left arm behind neck for two minutes.

Right arm behind neck two minutes. Opening my hands one hundred times. Rotating my wrists for two minutes. I repeated these stretches for a total of five reps or about forty minutes. Now my neck stretches. Head forward, head backward, head side to side for two minutes. Much better I was feeling more agile. Now my mouth stretches.

I opened my mouth, and closed it repeatedly. I was sure that I looked silly doing it, but I noticed that if I didn't do this stretch I found it hard to speak. Alright, now to stretch my legs. Legs that I cannot feel, but needed to be moved.

I unstrapped my right leg then my left. I then carefully lifted each leg about five inches off the ground and held my leg in the air for one minute. This was not only stretching my leg, but also helping me develop the muscles in my arm.

I lifted my legs up and down for a few more sets, and then I heard the front door open. Jazmine was on her way out of here. That meant that it was time to see Benson! I steady myself up onto my bed, but I did not get off yet. I had to make sure she was really gone, so I waited to hear her car leave the driveway. Once I heard it pull away I got myself ready.

Very carefully I pulled my legs over the bed. Once I did that I used my arms to push my body forward, while at the same time scooting my legs further and further away from the bed until I was on my knees. After that I let my upper body fall forward. Once I was on the ground I straightened my legs, and I was on my stomach. It was time to crawl out of my room.

One arm out, one arm in. One arm out, one arm in. I felt like I was a spy that couldn't stand up or they'd trigger the lasers up above. No standing till you reach the gem. I told myself sarcastically. One more push, and bam! I was right by the door.

Thankfully my room was wood and not carpet flooring, or that would have been one nasty rug burn, but I digress it was time to open the door.

I pulled myself up against the wall—it was extremely hard, and I couldn't help but let out a faint squeal. It was a good thing I hadn't tried this last night, or Jazmine and Henry would have caught me. And honestly, if I hadn't done my stretches earlier, I wouldn't have even had the strength to try.

On top of that, I had to keep reminding myself—I couldn't feel my core at all. I was doing this using nothing but my arms and shoulders. But somehow... I did it! I was propped up where I needed to be.

Now it was time to try to open the door. I touched the knob, and turned it, but it did not budge! What the hell? I shook it furiously from side to side, but no luck. I was locked in! No! This couldn't be. My room never had a lock before? What was going on?

Upon further inspection of my door knob I realized that it was different. Jazmine must have replaced it while I was under anesthesia. Why did she do this? To keep her "embryos" safe. It was obvious she still feared that man who came into the house. The man that she probably hired herself to kill me, and who ultimately killed my Francisco.

This was too much for me to handle again, and I let hate blur my mind. I began to hit the door with my bare fists, and after the fourth hit I stopped. The pain that I caused myself made me cry.

My knuckles were bleeding. That was stupid of me. I couldn't let my emotions get the best of me like that. I couldn't be stupid enough to risk getting hurt when I needed to seek justice for Francisco, and you know what? For me too.

Even if Jazmine didn't kill anyone, or whatever, she still stole for me. She has left me in neglect for weeks. For Pet's sake she lets me sit in my own feces! She deserves to be thrown in jail, and so does Henry!

So cut the shit out Lucianna, think before you act. You need to be smart about this. Now, how can you leave this room without destroying the door, and your hands? I furiously thought. Hmmm. Was there anything here that I could use to my advantage?

I turned and looked at every angle and every detail that I could of the room, but it was useless. The only thing in the entire dungeon was my bed. I had no windows, no objects to even try to unlock the door, nothing.

It was hopeless, and I felt worthless. I was a mere shadow of the person who I once was, but even at that I couldn't give up. There was too much on the line now. From Francisco, to me, to potentially having innocent beings brought to this world, no. I couldn't give up, but what now?

Did I have enough strength to punch Jazmine in the face when she came back? I did, but was it enough to knock her out? That I didn't know, but should I take the chance? If I did end up knocking her out I could escape, but then I risked losing access to discovering any information with her involvement in my accident, and Francisco's death.

Ugh, what to do? I muttered again as my breathing got heavier, so I closed my eyes to try to clear my mind. Calm yourself, and think. I thought. Let's see? Escape and prevent an innocent soul being brought to a life of hell, or get justice for the most kind hearted individual to ever exist?

Breathe in, breathe out, Lucianna. Let the answer come to you, and answer that was yours before being locked up again. Fuck! Maybe taking a nap would clear things up? Yeah, that is my only option now. Unfortunately, that meant standing up Benson. That was not what I wanted to do, but I had no choice.

I began to crawl back to my bed feeling like an utter failure when I heard a faint whisper. If I hadn't been near the door I wouldn't have heard it, but it was clear. Someone was whispering my name.

Lucianna, where are you? It's Benson. Don't be afraid. It's not a trick. Benson? I yelped. My voice cracking with emotion. Is that you? *Yes!* I heard footsteps near my door, and through the small space between the floor and door I saw a shadow. My heart was racing with glee.

Are you behind this door? He knocked on the door. Yes! Jazmine locked me in! Please let me out. *Give me a second!* I heard him run away from the door, and I am assuming he dashed to the kitchen because I heard the sound of utensils being moved around.

Alright, let me try something. The door knob jingled back and forth, back and forth, and surprisingly after what only felt like ten seconds I heard the door unlock. *I got it. I am coming in.*

The door slowly opened. *Lucianna, where are you?* Down here, Benson. Oh my goodness! What are you doing on the floor? Why are your knuckles bleeding? Please, get my wheelchair.

It should be by the hall somewhere. Benson stepped out, and in a flash, he was back—wheeling my chair into the room. Without hesitation, he carefully lifted me and strapped me in with an ease that made it all feel routine.

Tell me... what is going on? Benson—sweet Benson—looked at me, worried filling his big, almond-shaped eyes. A sideways smile softened his chiseled face as his hand came up to gently cup mine. And just like that, I lost it... before I could even register what was going on.

Let it all out. I am here now. You are safe. I cried so much that not only my shirt was wet, but also his. I am so sorry. I said after about ten minutes of crying when all my tears were dried up.

I have just been through hell these past four months. *Tell me everything you feel comfortable with.* I will, but how did you get in? I looked at him. I was perplexed. *Well, let's just say when I was a kid I wanted to be a spy, so I learned how to pick a lock or two, ha. Don't worry there's no broken locks or windows. I locked the door when I came in too. No one will know that I was here.*

I couldn't help it, and I lunged over and hugged Benson. *Woah! You regained movement of your arms? That is amazing. I am so happy about that, Lucianna. What else can you move?* I can speak, total head and neck movement, shoulder, arm, and hand movement. The rest I still can't feel. *Wow, that is just phenomenal. I am sure if we get you to the right rehab centers you may be able to get control of some of your core too. Which leads me to my next question.*

Why did you never come back to your appointments? What happened? Please sit down, Benson. He sat on my bed, and I told him everything. Absolutely everything. From having to live with sleeping and eating in my own feces to being looked down upon by Henry and Jazmine. I even told him about Jake coming and being the only decent human being.

Words can't express the anger and sadness that I feel right now. How could they have done that to you? There is more. *What do you mean?* Jazmine hired a person to impregnate me with her and Henry's embryos.

Benson looked at me with utter shock. His rosy lips opened wide. His muscular shoulders throbbed up and down from anger. *We need to go to the police now, and get you to a hospital!*

I can't go yet, Benson. *Why not?* Two days ago a man showed up and broke a window, and part of the door. He came demanding money from Jazmine. She was not here, but he came into my room. When he saw me it looked like he was seeing death itself, and needless to say he said, "Don't trust your sister, basically."

Benson, I think Jazmine put out a hit on me. I don't have the evidence to prove it yet, but I know in my heart that is what she did. Why else would that man have reacted that way when he saw me? He was probably the one driving the car that hit me. *That is why we need to go to the police now.*

Oh how I wish, but I learned something in these past four months, Benson. *What is that?* People with disabilities are treated unfairly and not listened to. We are treated like second class citizens.

I know they will take Jazmine's word over mind, unless I have actual proof to my accusations. I can't let Francisco's death go in vain. *I understand, and I will do everything that I can to help you, but the first thing now is to get you a day "after pill."* You are a savior. You really are. In all my confusion I had not remembered about the day "after pill."

Do you know when your sister comes home? Yeah at 1. *Alright, it is almost noon. There is a CVS down the road that I saw. I will go grab one and be right back!* Thank you so much, Benson. I really did miss you. I felt my cheeks reddened as I said that.

He smiled at me, and left my room. Without having to tell him he closed the door behind him and locked it. Just as a precaution if Jazmine walked in. He didn't take the wheelchair however, but that was fine.

If Jazmine did come back early I was sure she would forget that it wasn't in my room. No need to worry about that. Now what I needed to do was focus on getting justice for Francisco, and myself.

Graciously, that justice was near. Benson was back from the pharmacy before I even had the chance to notice that he was gone. *Here is the pill. You simply swallow it. Here is some water.* Water, I thought in my mind. I wouldn't tell Benson this, but I had not had drunk water in four months. My mouth was craving it, but first things first I had to swallow the pill.

Would I even be able to? Only one way to find out. I gingerly grabbed the pill and placed it on my tongue. I then positioned the bottle of water in my mouth and swallowed the medicine whole. Phew, no issues, and as a matter of fact I felt great. I now had one less thing to worry about.

I like seeing you smile. My face warmed up from Benson's compliment. I didn't want him to notice, so I quickly asked him if he could wheel me to the hallway. *Of course!* There is a room there that used to belong to my parents that I want to explore. I believe if Jazmine is hiding anything it will be there. *Let's go find out.*

Benson carefully wheeled me to the hallway until we reached the room. *You want to open it?* Yes, please, and can you help me get inside the room? The platform is too high for me to wheel into, and the carpet will make it impossible for me to move, so I will also need you to wheel me around.

No worries. He gently rubbed my left shoulder as he lifted the back part of the wheelchair. I got light goosebumps on my arms from that. I prayed he wouldn't notice. Which I don't think he did because he was looking around my parents' old room. He was specifically staring at the family portrait. I saw him smirking over it.

You are so cute here. Thank you Benson. I said a little too excitedly. *Now where do you want me to wheel you to?* The couch please. *May I ask why the couch?* My mom used to hide any important documents under the cushions. I have a feeling that if something is hidden it will be there. *Understood.*

My heart began to race as I got closer and closer to the couch. Did I really want to find evidence against her? A part of me wanted her to be innocent of all my accusations, but a part of me wanted her to rot in hell.

Do you need help removing the cushions? I shook my head back and forth, and I began to remove the cushions. Almost instantly as I lifted the cracked leather cushion a set of keys with a phone number attached to them fell to the floor. Keys that looked like they belonged to a truck. Was it the truck that hit Francisco and me? My heart froze, but I didn't show it.

CHAPTER 22

The Violation

Instead, I stretched my arm down and picked up the keys. Benson, these keys belonged to my father. I am so happy to hold them. Benson smiled at me, and gave me a hug. Instantly, I felt guilt for lying to him, but I couldn't let him know who I thought these keys really belonged to, so instead I asked him to take me back to my room.

Are you sure you don't want to look some more around the room to see if you can find any proof against Jazmine? After seeing and holding these keys I think I need some time to think. Is that okay? *Anything you want.*

Once again he helped me over the platform, and then he closed the door behind him. *We have around forty minutes before your sister comes back, or a good thirty just to be on the safe side. Tell me what you plan on doing?* He said as we entered my room.

I stared at him blankly. Even though I felt horrid about lying to him about the keys, I couldn't reveal anything to him right then and there. I had to figure out who they belonged to first, and that meant calling the number on them.

Well Lucianna? What would you like to do? Am I able to live with you? I surprised myself at my directness, but my gut told me that I had what I needed. There was no need for me to stay here a minute longer.

Of course you can stay with me, but we have to be smart about it. The last time I checked Jazmine had a conservatorship for you until you were able to communicate by yourself. Which you are.

I will talk to the lawyer of the hospital and ask what we can do. I should have an answer by tomorrow evening, so call me after then and we can figure out what to do to get you out of here, okay? I nodded my head yes. *In the meantime, just know you will be okay, alright? I am here for you, and I won't leave you alone.*

You don't know how much I appreciate that Benson. You are an angel. *I am not an angel, but you are. Now do you want some help to get back into bed?* Yes, please. Benson slowly came over, and swept me off my chair. His strong body felt rock hard as my head touched his stomach.

I felt safe with him, and weirdly enough, his strong masculine aroma did something to me. For the very first time since the accident, I was turned on. The strong scent of a man... oh gosh, what was happening to me?

I could feel my body getting warm, but I wasn't embarrassed. Not when I could see that Benson's cheeks were bright red. He must have enjoyed picking me up, and that made me happy, but it also left me feeling some-what awkward. I felt relieved when he started talking.

Lucianna, yes? I am leaving you this butter knife so if you have to get out of here, you will be able to simply break the lock like this okay? Sounds good. I watched as he demonstrated how to break the lock from the inside.

Thanks, Benson. I hope I get to call you within the next two days. *It will be okay.* I hope so. *I'll get going now, but next time we see each other it will be because you are coming to live with me.*

Fingers crossed. Oh, before you go, can you put my chair where you found it? *Certainly. See you soon, Lucianna.* He slowly walked out of the room and left me alone with the keys. Keys that had the *Chevrolet* logo on them. The same type of truck that rammed into Francisco and me.

There was no doubt in my mind anymore that Jazmine had caused all of this. Nonetheless, I just had to know for sure, and that's why I would call the number on them, *661.849.3194.* I repeated the number till it was engrained in my head, and then I placed the key safely under my bed and strapped my arms in.

Which was perfect timing because Jazmine was home. "Sister, I'm home." "I have a surprise for you." She unlocked my door and entered. "Look, I have some prenatal vitamins for you." "Do you want to drink them with juice or water?" "Nod twice for orange and one for water?" I nodded twice and she gave me a glass of oj with one giant vitamin. "Open wide."

I opened my mouth wide and she placed the vitamin in. I then swallowed it with the juice. "You are looking much better." "I think the anesthesia is out of your system." "I am going to go ahead and unstrap you." She unstrapped my legs and arms. "Alright, I'll come change you and feed you a jello with your IV before I go to bed." "See you later."

She was glowing. As she walked out of the room I noticed the spunk in her walk. She really thought she was going to be a mother. It was hard to not feel bad for her, but then I remembered what she was.

An egocentric maniac. I highly doubt she even wanted kids. I was positive that it was the fact that she couldn't have kids that was killing her.

Since, of course she deserved to have them. If most people could, why not her, right?

How pathetic. If she really wanted a child there were plenty of programs where you can adopt for free. Nevertheless, it was obvious that wasn't in her plans. She wanted to have a child who she could mold to be her little robot.

A child that she could use to get Henry to do what she wanted. I was glad that I wouldn't be the one doing that for her. In fact, I would be the one bringing justice to her. I couldn't wait to see her behind bars.

"Lucianna, dinner time." I nearly screamed in surprise. I had been so in my head since Jazmine left that I did not realize that I had spent hours thinking of all the ways I hated her. This wasn't healthy.

This wasn't me. I really wished I could change that, but something in me knew that I had changed as a person. Life made me bitter, and that truly broke my heart.

"Here is the jello." "I hope you like it." "Open wide." Jazmine gently placed a spoon in my mouth, and I momentarily forgot my troubles. My taste buds went into overblast. The squishness of the jello felt so silky in my mouth.

My tongue was smeared in sugar. My eyes started to water with the taste. It was overwhelming, and I guess my face looked funny too because Jazmine started to laugh. "Haha, you look like a baby trying food for the first time."

"Ah, I just can't wait to see my future child trying food for the first time." "I am sure they will look as silly as you do, Lucianna." She laughed and laughed as she fed me more. At one point she rubbed my head and said, "That's a good girl."

It was apparent that she didn't see me as a human being anymore. She just saw me as an oven. An oven who gave money, and who produced children. "Bye, bye future baby." "See you tomorrow evening after I'm back home from San Diego."

She rubbed my stomach and left. A wave of relief flowed through me. She wouldn't be here tomorrow. Her alopecia doctor was in San Diego, and she usually left early in the morning, and spent the majority of the day in the city visiting around. This was perfect.

That meant that I could call Benson. Hopefully he had good news because my time here was running short. I was soon to get a pregnancy test, and if I wasn't pregnant then things would surely take a turn for the worst.

I didn't want to be here when that happened. Well, let's not think about that for now, Lucianna. Just close your eyes, and get some rest. I shut my eyes, and as I went to sleep I began to dream about Francisco, and about me.

It was an out of body type of dream where I was seeing myself with Francisco, but they couldn't see me observing them. Francisco was telling me how to not hold grudges as he braided my long dark hair. His gentle slender fingers easily slipped through my hair. "It is not worth your time." I smiled and agreed, but then the dream took a turn.

We were right in front of the truck. The truck that took him from me. In that truck I could see the driver. The driver and the passenger. The big man who warned me against my sister was driving, and she was his passenger.

As they hit me I saw the laughter that she had. She thought I was dead, and that made her feel powerful seeing me as I flew to a lake. The childhood lake my parents used to take us during the hot summer days. It was refreshing. I felt the water hit my legs as my dad slightly dipped me in the water.

The water felt warm, too warm. Oh no. My eyes shot straight open. I could smell it before I felt it with my hands. I had peed the entire bed up to the point that it reached my arms. The smell was intense.

I felt embarrassed. I didn't even have control of my own bladder, but you know what? I didn't have to sit here and lie in my own urine anymore. I gently removed the covering from beneath me, and then I carefully placed it under the bed. Hopefully it would dry down there without Henry or Jazmine seeing it.

Thankfully by removing the sheets most of the piss smell went away, but unfortunately my underwear were still damp with pee still, and so were part of my sweats. There was nothing that I could do about that.

Jazmine only changed me once every two weeks, and I had no way of accessing clothes. Oh well. The only way to dry myself was by fanning my wet clothes. At least it would be a good workout for my hands.

I began to fan air onto my pants for about thirty minutes until I heard Henry leaving for the day. "Babe, just to confirm you aren't going to San Diego today after all, right?" "No, I am not." "I have a meeting with our lawyer in an hour." "About what?"

"I just found out that Francisco named Lucianna his sole heir." "Our lawyer said it is about 450k dollars." "Whooh, are you serious?" "Yes." "We can use that money to buy a new home, babe."

"That is incredible." "Will you know by today if you have access to that money?" "I should." "How about if we meet for lunch at that one Chinese restaurant by your work, and I'll tell you all about it?" "Sounds perfect." The door slammed shut." I knew they were both gone after a minute because I heard both cars take off.

This was not good. Not good at all. I had no clue how Jazmine had found out about this money! However, it didn't matter at this point because there was no way in hell that I would ever let her access it. I had to do something now!

Wasting no time, I crawled out of bed with my butter knife and I dragged myself to the door. Using all the muscles that I could call upon I unlocked the door, and I crawled my way to my wheel chair.

To my luck my chair was up against a wall, and it was locked in place, so climbing onto it was not that hard. Once I was in, I went straight to the phone and I dialed the number on the keys.

661-849-3194, the phone rang, and rang, and rang, but no one answered. The call hung up, so I dialed again, and again, and again, until the fifth time someone answered. *Who is this? How did you get this number?*

That voice, it was him. It was the man who came to my room. A lump formed in my throat, but I swallowed it back down. I am the paralyzed woman, Jazmine's sister. I heard a gasp come from the background.

Please, don't hang up. I want to speak to you. I have money that Jazmine doesn't know about. Can you please come to her house? Please. Dead silence for almost a minute, but then, *I am on my way.*

My heart started to thump like a humming bird's wings. I was about to discover the truth. My palms started to sweat. What was I going to tell him? I did have money, but I didn't have access to it. Would I be able to convince him?

I sure hoped so because if I didn't then I would never get any answers. I had to play smartly. I could outwit this criminal. At the end of the day he was just a thug. I had to make him feel like he was all powerful.

I would have to play the victim part, and give him his flowers. It was important that I made him believe that he was not to blame in any of this. *Knock, knock, knock,* the pounding on the door took me by shock.

It had not even been ten minutes since my call and he was already here. That meant he lived nearby. Cautiously I wheeled my way to the front door and opened it. The man didn't even wait to be greeted. He pushed his way through and slammed the door shut.

How much money? I have fifty thousand that I can give you once I have all the info I need. He looked down at me and smiled as his crows' feet covered his eyes. *You expect me to believe you? Your whore of a sister hasn't even paid me the full thirty thousand that she owes me.* Why does she owe you thirty thousand?

Don't take me as a fool! His loud voice boomed. *I need a guarantee that I will get the money, or an advance.* Sir, I promise you that I will get your money by tomorrow. I just need to get to the hospital now. When I am there I can talk to my lawyer to keep Jazmine from taking control of my estate any longer.

I didn't know if this was the case. I hadn't even talked to Benson yet, but I was desperate. I probably wouldn't get a chance like this again. *Your whore sister called the cops on me.*

She thinks she can pin all of this on me. If you want information beforehand you will have to do something for me. He gave me a wink, and rubbed his genitals. Which was hard to do because his big belly covered them.

I felt anger and disgust at the same time, but I knew that I had to do what he wanted. Francisco was way too important for me to not get justice. I didn't matter at that point. What do you want?

Take your shirt and bra off. I didn't think twice about it because if I did I would have had to tell him off, and swing at him. I couldn't. I needed him.

With my shaking hands I removed my giant shirt, and then I tried to remove my bra, but my hands could not reach up to my back. It didn't matter, he ripped my bra off. The back strap cut my back, but he didn't care.

He immediately started touching my breasts. His pupils got wide and he went into a trance. His double chin bobbled up and down as he came closer to me. He was like a dog eating a piece of steak.

I on the other hand had an out of body experience. I felt like I was floating on the ceiling watching everything go on. From him putting his disgusting frog lips on my breasts to him finishing off on them. It was gross, but I didn't cry. There would be time to cry later.

Alright, girly you kept your part of the deal, so I'll tell you everything you want to know. I put my shirt back on as I began to ask him questions. Did Jazmine hire you to kill me? How much did she pay you? Do you have any evidence that I can use against her?

She did hire me to kill you and your friend. I would like to add that I had no clue that you two were related. That is some fucked up shit. I watched him carefully as he talked, and I surprised myself.

I was quite composed on the outside. All I did was nod my head, but inside I was dead. My own sister called a hit on me. She killed my best friend. My heart completely shattered. If I had not been sitting I would have fainted.

Anything else? Yes. I quickly regained my composure and asked one last thing. Lastly, I have a favor that I would like. *What's the job?* I quietly told him the job that I had for him. Something that I dare not repeat. *Cool. Anyway, I have all the evidence against Jazmine. I have a recording from her when she called the hit. I have video evidence as well when she came to my house.*

Why didn't you tell the police? Especially if she hasn't paid you? *She eventually did pay me, but I don't like to be played with.* Oh, I see. Well, if you give me the evidence that I need then I will pay you fifty thousand. *If you give me the money you will get everything you need, plus that favor you asked me for.*

Thank you. I would be lying to you if I said, I wasn't thankful for having you tell me everything that that bitch did. He smiled at my compliment. I felt sick inside pandering to this monster, but I had to make him feel powerful.

No problem, sweet tits. My stomach turned as he mockingly said that, but all I could do was force a neutral face because I needed him. *Well you know my number.* He winked at me, and started to walk back to the door. I quickly grabbed his arm.

Can you please drop me off at the hospital? *Only because it means that I will get my money.* He laughed as he wheeled me out the door and onto his truck. Immediately I felt nauseous.

He was not gentle at all. He practically threw my fragile frame into the car. He didn't even tie the seat belt on me. By the time we reached the hospital my body was slanted into a C shape. He didn't even notice because he was on the phone the entire time with who knows who.

We are here, but I am not dropping you off at the hospital. I don't want their cameras to pick me up, so you'll have to wheel yourself there. Thank you again. *Yeah, whatever.*

He parked his truck and tossed my chair onto the sidewalk. He then roughly placed me on the chair. *I'm expecting your call. Good luck!* A smog of smoke hit my face as he drove off in his old dusty truck. Obviously not the one used for the hit, but I digress.

The hospital was probably a seven minute walk away for an able-bodied person. For me, it took about twelve minutes. I had cuts on my hands by the time I reached the entrance, but I felt victorious.

This was the first time that I was on my own since my accident. The freedom that I felt was exhilarating, but I couldn't truly enjoy it because of what had happened to me. I had been violated. I wanted to scream and cry, but I couldn't just yet. I needed to be strong.

Get up there Lucianna. Ask for Benson, and speak to the lawyer before Jazmine takes a hold of Francisco's money. Everything else could wait. I took a deep breath. Here goes nothing.

I pushed the disabled button on the door, and it slid wide open. I was pleased to see that there was no barrier preventing me from entering the doorway, and I simply wheeled myself in.

CHAPTER 23

A Small Glimmer Of Hope

Hello ma'am do you have an appointment today? I need to speak to nurse Benson. It's an emergency! I practically shouted out of breath. The receptionist looked at me like I was crazy, but then another receptionist walked in. He was a young man who I had spoken to a few times during my time at the hospital.

Lucianna, is that you? His eyes gleamed with happiness, but I didn't have time for any small talk. Yes, please, can you call nurse Benson? I really need to talk to him. He nodded his head and called nurse Benson by speaker to the receptionist floor.

He'll be here shortly. I am so happy to see that your voice is back. I smiled at the receptionist, and I thanked him for his kind words. I really appreciated them, but I was in a time crunch. Unfortunately, I could not chit chat. Hopefully he wouldn't be offended.

Ding, ding, ding, the elevator went and out came Benson. He was dressed in his black scrubs. He looked incredibly handsome. His brown hair was combed back like James Dean's. *Lucianna!* He said, shocked to see me there.

Before he even had the chance to come greet me I shouted everything to him, and in front of the two receptionists. Benson wasted no time and asked the male receptionist if he could call the lawyer down. He did, and then he came to me.

My lunch will start in two hours. I will come see you on the admin side of the hospital then, ok? I nervously nodded yes, and he kneeled down toward me. *Everything will be okay. I spoke to him this morning. He knows, and thinks he can get you out of this situation. I'm here, so don't stress, okay?*

Alright, Benson. He left me alone, and I waited for the lawyer to come down. It took him around ten minutes to come down, and my nerves were killing me. Luckily I was accompanied by the two receptionists who at this point knew my story.

They were very sympathetic to me, and promised that if Jazmine showed up they would say I wasn't here. I thanked them for that, and then the lawyer came out. He was the typical bureaucrat stereotype.

He had a suit and tie. His hair line was receding. He had a little gut, and giant glasses. *Lucianna, nice to meet you. I am lawyer Hernandez. Care to come with me?* Yes please. I waved goodbye to the receptionists, and I followed the lawyer to the elevator.

I spoke to Benson, and he explained everything to me this morning. I find it awful what is happening to you, but it is not uncommon. Many people take advantage of disabled patients, and it is just horrible.

I looked through your file and yes, your sister is your caretaker, but you are not in a conservatorship like Benson thought. Those are hard to get, and hard to remove. All you have to do to gain access to your independence is get a doctor's note, and appear before a judge. Here is some good news, your doctor, Dr. Ukermann has already issued the note.

My heart was beating with happiness. Benson, and Dr. Ukermann had already done so much for me. *I have some more good news. The judge seeing this case is my friend. He told me to call him right away when you were here, so without further ado, let's call him.*

My palms were sweating as I watched Mr. Hernandez open his laptop, and sign into *Zoom*. My eyes were watery as the judge appeared and asked me question after question until he said he was ready to make a ruling.

Lucianna, I am deeply saddened to hear what has happened to you. Though, I can't get any money lost while you were under Jazmine, I can momentarily stop her from gaining anymore access for an emergency thirty days.

During this time I suggest you meet with two more doctors because she will have the chance to appeal my decision if she wants to. That said, as of now you and only you have access to your life again. You can also expect the fax to come in about forty minutes. I began to cry uncontrollably, so much so that I couldn't even breathe at one point.

I had control of my life again! Thank you, thank you so much Judge Hopkin, and thank you lawyer Hernandez. You two will forever be in my heart. Judge Hopkin was appreciative towards me and then wished me luck for my future.

Lawyer Hernandez hugged me, but then had to leave to meet with other patients-clients. He did however let me stay in his office until Benson got out for lunch. That left me with over an hour to just soak up my new reality.

I was free again. I had gotten a second chance, and there was no way in hell that I would not do everything in my power to avenge my Francisco. Oh, Jazmine if you only knew what was coming for you. I smiled at that thought as I began my stretches.

They were kind of hard to do while seated, but there was no way I was going to skip them. Stretching had truly helped me, and I always felt more flexible afterward. More than that, it gave my mind something steady to hold on to—something that pulled me away from the chaos of my life and gave me a sense of purpose.

If I am being honest, seeing how much my body had healed through therapy had even started to plant a new idea in my mind. Maybe... I could change my profession. What better way to motivate those with newfound disabilities than by showing them someone who had endured so much and was still striving for a better future? I smiled at the thought.

This was the first time since the accident that I started to dream of bigger things. I was alive again. *It is nice to see that smile. I hadn't seen it since I was in high school.* I nearly jumped out of my chair.

Well, if I could use my legs I would have jumped out of my chair. *I'm so sorry. I didn't mean to scare you. I did knock, but you didn't answer.* A grinning Benson stared at me. I felt my cheeks get hot. I'm sorry, I was day dreaming, but Benson, I have control of my life again!

Thank you for the bottom of my heart. If it wasn't for you then I don't know what would have happened. *No need to thank me. I did it because it is the right thing to do, and I like helping you. You are special, Lucianna, and look I have something special fresh off the press for you.*

Benson stepped toward me and handed me a document. I couldn't believe my eyes. It was my court decree. Signed, dated and stamped by the judge that I was in control of myself again.

Benson, I don't know how to thank you? This is all because of you, and I hate to ask, but how can I get into my in care living facility when I have no documentation whatsoever. *You are moving in with me until you get everything situated. I don't want to hear no ifs and or buts, got it?*

I nodded my head. *Perfect! I have about 35 minutes of my lunch left, so I am going to take you home right now because I still have an eight hour shift left. Shall we go?* Yes, please. He opened the door for me, and we headed down to the first level of the hospital.

I was expecting to see the two kind-hearted receptionists, but they were gone. Two others had replaced them. I must have looked confused because Benson said, *they are the morning workers, done for the day.*

Ah I see. Which one is your car Benson? *You see that Honda SRV over there? The blue one?* Yeah. *That is my baby. The first thing I have ever paid off.* That is amazing. *It is. It is also super comfortable. You'll see.*

He opened the door for me, and helped me into the front seat. Next he helped put my seat belt on. Thank God. This time I wouldn't be flying around in the back. Once settled in, I glanced over at him. Benson, *yeah?* I must admit your seats are very comfortable. Also, the car smells like fresh cherries. *That's what I was going for.*

Ready? I am. I gave him a thumbs up and we were on our way. It wasn't a long drive. Maybe eight minutes until we pulled up to the newer side of town. He actually lived quite near the movie theater by the giant shopping center.

I am on the ground floor, so we don't have to worry about an elevator. He gave me a wink as he went to get my chair. I quickly undid my seatbelt, and I opened my door. I didn't want to seem like a burden.

Plus, I was able to do these things, so why have someone do them for me? I think Benson sensed this because instead of helping me out he waited patiently for me to move my own legs out of the car. I struggled a bit hopping out of the car while trying to get into the chair, so that was when I asked him for help.

He gently picked me up from the car seat onto my chair. I strapped myself in, and then we were on our way. I followed him on the smooth pavement. It felt like silk. My arms were not even doing much work honestly.

Good, because I was sore from wheeling myself to the hospital. *It is just right around the corner.* Do I turn left or right? *Turn right, and voila.* There was his apartment right on the ground floor.

He unlocked his door and said, "After you." I wheeled inside and I was pleasantly greeted by the smell of ginger. Benson then came in. *Let me give you the tour. I have one giant tv, and that's right in the middle of the living room as you can see. I also have one giant couch right in front of the TV. I have a dining table that sits two.*

I am kind of embarrassed to admit but I don't have any kitchen utensils. I tend to eat out a lot, but I do have two restrooms, and a guest room. That will be yours. Follow me please. I followed him to the guest restroom. It was empty. Not even a towel, but it was large. There was a large shower that I could easily wheel myself to. That made me happy.

The sink however was too big for me, but I would find a way to use it. *Your room is over here.* I continued after him to the guest room, and boy was I in for a surprise. There was a California King decorated with *Sonic the Hedgehog* sheets. I didn't mean to laugh, but I couldn't hold it in.

I'm sorry. I know. This is my bed from my childhood, and yes I still love Sonic, so I didn't get rid of the sheets. Benson shyly stared at me. *We can get new sheets if you want.* No, I like that you like Sonic. It is cute. *Well then good.*

Lucianna, I have to get back to work, but make yourself at home. If I don't see you tonight I wish you a good night. I have tomorrow off, and we can talk, okay? Thank you Benson. *Oh before I forget, are you hungry?* Honestly, no. Not at all. Benson nodded.

I didn't tell him that I hadn't eaten since yesterday morning, but the truth was I really wasn't hungry. Benson wasn't biting though. *I will get a few groceries sent over in about two hours so be on the look out for that, ok?* Alright.

See you tonight or tomorrow. He hugged me and left. I wheeled my chair to the front window and watched him go. I was alone again, and in my solitude I completely broke down and cried. Here I was as a 34 year old woman who had lost it all.

What was the point of my life? I mean I did everything well. I helped others. I stood up for others, and I tried to be kind to everyone, especially Jazmine. Look what that got me?

It got me a wheelchair and a dead best friend. What a wasted life that I have lived. I should have been authentic to myself like Francisco was. He was not afraid to say no. He knew how to set boundaries, and you know what? It was my time.

I vowed that from that day forward, I would do what truly made me feel good. I already had a few ideas on how I would accomplish this. I would help people with disabilities like mine find their voice again—and most importantly, I would get justice for you, Francisco.

However, before I did any of that I had to get in contact with the lawyer who is in charge of Francisco's will. It was research time! I wheeled myself over to the desktop at the entrance of the hallway, and I grabbed the mouse. I needed to contact the lawyer in charge of Francisco's estate.

Without further ado, I opened up an internet page and typed the lawyer's name that Benson had given me months ago. Allison Kipyegon. I clicked on her site. To my happiness she did virtual consultations, and her next one was in 30 minutes.

I quickly signed up for it, and then I headed to the restroom to wash up. I needed to look decent. If that was even possible? Stop that Lucianna, practice what you preach. Just because you are disabled does not mean you can't feel pretty or sexy!

I was beautiful, and I was sexy. With that positive affirmation, I rolled my way to the restroom, and had no issue entering since Benson's doors were quite wide. I then wheeled myself into the shower. This was going to be my first real shower since the accident.

With a trembling hand I reached for the faucet, and set the water to lukewarm. The water hit my face like velvet. It poured down my neck and onto my arms. It felt ticklish and so soothing. It soaked my entire hair. I had forgotten how heavy wet hair was. I loved it. Even though I couldn't feel anything below my neck of course, seeing my body get wet was therapeutic.

Gosh, it was just the little things like this. The little things that many people didn't get to do. It made me emotional all over again, and my eyes started to burn. From water going inside, and my own tears escaping them. Still it was a beautiful moment until I realized that I had no dry clothes. Fuck.

I would have to borrow some of Benson's clothes. I hope he didn't mind. I grabbed the towel that was hanging on the shower door, and I dried myself off. Making sure to hang my old clothes on the shower door.

I then dried my wheels on my chair, and I rolled over to what I assumed was the laundry closet. It was a thin door, and to my content it was. There was a washer and a dryer, and several of Benson's shirts. I grabbed a black polo shirt, and placed it over me. I then grabbed a pair of his white briefs, and some white shorts that he had there.

It felt so nice to wear a different outfit, even if it was guys' clothes. I was tired of wearing the same gray sweats and giant white shirt. Well now that I was all dressed I went back to the computer.

I had two minutes to spare, and I patiently waited until Allison Kipyegon called me. She was right on time. *Hello Ms. Lucianna, even with your short cute bop I recognize you. Francisco was very fond of you. How are you ma'am?*

I skipped the small talk and told her exactly what was happening. She placed me on hold for almost six minutes. *You are right. I see that there is an appeal to get access to his will. Do you have a court decree saying you are able to look after yourself?*

I do! Perfect, what is the case number? 106698091, *great I see it now.* Don't worry ma'am with this your sister cannot do anything. That money is yours, and you can come claim it whenever you want.

CHAPTER 24

Francisco's Estate

We set an appointment for tomorrow right at 1 p.m. I thanked Allison and we ended the call. I felt relieved. The 450k dollars that Francisco had worked so hard for would be safe. I just hated that he wouldn't get to enjoy this money, but I would put it to good use.

Once I got back on my feet I would figure out how to best utilize it to honor his name. Gosh he was just so smart. He even set up his will so it would be nontaxable. I did not know how he did that, but it made me happy because the greedy government would have taken over sixty thousand just in taxes.

Sadly, I would have to use fifty thousand dollars of his hard earned money to access the evidence against Jazmine. To make matters worse it would go to the man who killed him. I hated giving his money up like that, but it would guarantee that Jazmine would pay for her crimes.

At the end of the day she didn't pull the trigger, but she orchestrated everything. Her time would come, but enough of that for now. It was time to rest. *Netflix,* here I come. I grabbed the remote and turned the TV on. This was going to be the first time I watched TV in four months.

I was ecstatic as I pulled up *Supernatural.* In a rush, I turned my show on, and I just began to binge watch. The only time I took a break was to open the door for the groceries. I hated to admit this, but I only ate a banana.

That said, it was the first solid food I had had since my accident. It was kind of hard to swallow the pieces at first, but thankfully it became easier. With time I hoped to be able to eat some tacos because I surely did miss them.

Ha. I laughed at my stupidity and finished season 6 of *Supernatural.* By the time the last episode ended it was 8:30 p.m, and I was beyond tired. I headed to my new room, and with the last bits of my strength I put myself to bed. I closed my eyes and I was greeted with a beautiful dream.

In the dream I was a little six year old. Jazmine did not exist yet. I was as happy as could be. I was flourishing in kindergarten, but then my dream became a nightmare. I was suddenly nine years old, and Jazmine was being diagnosed with alopecia. Suddenly all the attention went to her. I had to become her protector. I was sidelined by my parents. Indirectly, but still set aside.

A dream that was my reality. I woke up from it feeling strangely rested. It was the first time I had ever had a dream where my mind didn't hide from itself. It showed me what I really felt all through my life. I always felt like I had to be Jazmine's protector.

She had to shine while I hid in the shadows. I didn't blame my parents for that at all, but my dream showed me something important. Which was, able-bodied kids may not get the same attention as their disabled-ill siblings. There had to be a balance.

I would implement that to my future job as well. I smiled at that idea as I got ready to get up. It was time to do my stretches. I glanced at the clock on the wall. It was 7:15 a.m. Perfect. I could finish by 8 a.m, and that was what I did.

After my stretching I felt nice and loose, and wheeled myself to the restroom where I sat in the toilet to see if my body would use the restroom without the help of the catheter. After about five minutes on the toilet it did!

That brought happiness to me. I would have jumped for joy if I could. Hopefully this meant one day I would quit using my catheter. Only time would tell, but for now it was time to get ready.

I washed my hands and face. I tried to fix my hair too, but the mirror was too high for me to fully see myself, but I did my best. With luck I wouldn't look like a troll. With all that said, I needed to brush my teeth.

I hated to admit this, but I had not brushed them since my accident. Even at the hospital I was given mouth wash to rinse, since my mouth was damaged at the time. It did not take much imagination to figure out how my mouth smelled. Luckily, brushing was the remedy, but the issue now was that I didn't have a tooth brush.

I'd have to ask Benson if he has an extra toothbrush, and by the looks of it I could ask him now. I heard footsteps walking outside the door. Good morning Benson, I said through the restroom door. *Good morning Lucianna, did you sleep well?*

I slept heavenly, and you? *I could use some more sleep, but today is my off day so it's all good. Are you feeling hungry?* Just a tad. *I'll make us some breakfast.* Thank you, that is so sweet of you. *You are very welcome.*

Benson, do you have an extra toothbrush and toothpaste? *Yes, of course. I'll bring it to you now.* He scurried away and came back not even ten seconds later. *Here you go.* I opened the door.

I was surprised to see that he did not have a shirt on, and I was even more surprised to see his rippling abs and muscular pecs. I felt my face get hot. I had no clue that his body was that nice. His clothes did a good job of covering it.

Well, I'll let you brush your teeth. Your hair looks very nice today. He said with a smile as he walked away. My heart started to beat a little faster. This was not good. I was developing a crush on him again. I had to stop that right away because he had not shown any direct interest in me other than being a kind individual.

Remember Lucianna, don't mix kindness with flirtationness. Instead mix your toothpaste with your toothbrush. Haha, I laughed once more at another one of my stupid jokes, and then I placed my toothbrush inside my mouth.

Wow! I had missed this! The bubbling sensation of spicy bitterness in my mouth as I cleaned my teeth. I didn't know how it was possible, but brushing my teeth made me feel alive. It was like I had mini fireworks going off in my mouth.

I felt like an entirely new woman. Feeling rejuvenated, I left the restroom and joined a shirtless Benson in the kitchen. *I'm not much of a cook, so what do you want me to order?* Can I just have a banana and some juice?

Are you sure? Yes, please. *Well, here you go. I'll have that as a snack too, but I am having a bigger lunch!* He winked at me, and then gave me my breakfast. We ate it together. It was nice, almost tender.

Now that tummies are filled tell me how your appointment with Mr. Hernandez went. It went great. I'm free for at least the next thirty days. There are some things I must do, but one step at a time. *I'm glad to hear that.* Thank you, and guess what?

What? I spent the next ten minutes telling him about Francisco's will. Benson was so supportive. *I can take you to that lawyer whenever you'd like.*

You mean it? *Yes! You don't have to ask twice. I am so happy that you are getting what is rightfully yours.*

Now, how about Jazmine? Are you going to report her to the authorities? I can take you to the police station to file a report on her. I looked carefully at Benson. Could I trust him with my plans, or should I only tell him my partial goals? He was such a good person, and I did not want to burden him, so I would only tell him what he needed to know.

Benson, once I have access to my money I can pay off the guy who ran me over. He has all the evidence against Jazmine. Audio, video and everything in between. *It doesn't sound like it's a good idea to deal with a criminal, Lucianna, but I'll respect your decision to do so.*

That being said, I want you to be careful okay? I don't want anything bad happening to you. It was super hard to go months without getting any news from you. Do you really mean that?

Yes I do. You are a special one, Lucianna. His little cheeks got dark red, but I was sure mine were redder. There was an awkward silence as I didn't have a response to his compliment. *Anyway, I want you to stay with me until I know that you are fully capable of looking after yourself, okay?*

Don't worry about looking for a place for now. Just stay here until you regain your strength. Once again his face got red as he looked at me. Leading me to believe that he did like me more than just a simple friend, but who would like someone like me? Someone so plain, who never lived an authentic life of her own.

Instantly, I hated myself for thinking that. I was as loveable as anyone, and I needed to remember that. *So what do you say?* I love that idea, but I will be paying half the rent. I don't like to be a user. I believe in equal distribution.

Ha, that sounds like a plan to me. He slowly walked over and gave me a hug. I embraced him back. It felt nice to feel him against my face and arms. I liked the pressure, but then I pushed away.

I had to play it intelligently. I didn't want to be hurt if I was wrong with my interpretations of us, so I broke off the hug and asked him about his life these past few months.

Oh you know just working and working. I did get to visit my mom back home. She has been doing super good. She even moved in with her longtime boyfriend. They are happy, and it makes me happy when she is content.

Aw, I am glad. Can I ask what happened to your father? *Oh of course. My dad died when I was twelve. He had pancreatic cancer. He is the reason why I got into the medical field.* I am so sorry, Benson. *Thank you, Lucianna.*

You know my mother didn't date anyone until I finished my Bachelor's Degree in Nursing. That was five years ago. She dedicated her entire life to me, and that is why I am happy that she is finally allowing herself a chance to love once more.

My father would have hated for her to stay alone. The more Benson spoke the more I understood where his good manners, and personality came from. He had been raised in a loving and caring environment. It was apparent, but there was something that was bugging me about him.

How was he single? What was his flaw? I had to know, and it wasn't because I had a crush on him. It was because I was genuinely curious, so I asked. I know you haven't told me, but are you single? If so, how?

Ha, oh gosh. That is a loaded question. How so? *For starters, I am single. It has been nineteen months now.* That is a long time for someone with a good heart like you. *That's sweet. Thank you. The reason why I am still single is because my girlfriend left me. I proposed to her, and she wasn't ready for marriage.*

His voice quivered at the end of the word marriage. *To answer your question, I have been on dates, but when things start to get real I freak out now. I don't have confidence in myself anymore.*

I really loved my ex, and she didn't think that I was good enough for marriage. That really tears your confidence down. He was looking down to the floor now as he spoke to me. It was obvious he lacked confidence in himself, so I wheeled to him and grabbed his hand.

Hey, there is someone out there for you. Don't worry about that. Just believe in yourself, and know that you are a ray of light in so many people's lives. I mean look what you are doing for me. You are a good person, and trust me almost every woman on this planet would want a man like you. Maybe your ex just wasn't ready for that kind of commitment, so keep your head up, okay?

You are too sweet, Lucianna. I'll try to remember that. He caressed the side of my head, and I felt my heart jump. I carefully wheeled back to my spot in the kitchen. Where we ended up talking for almost three hours about our lives. I told him serious things like my parents dying, but also silly things like when my cat pooped on me when I was eleven. It was sweet.

I also learned a lot about him. He actually almost died once. His appendix burst with no symptoms. It was when he was twenty years old. That also motivated him to continue his work in the medical field.

It was such a nice conversation, and before we knew it the time had come to see Allison Kipyegon. Her office was almost an hour drive away, so on the way we stopped at *McDonald's*. Benson had a fit when he found out that I really hadn't eaten anything in four months.

When I told him that I wasn't too hungry he convinced me to try something small with protein. The only thing at that very moment that seemed good to me was a cheeseburger from *Mcdonald's*.

A plain one patty, two pickles, with ketchup, mustard and cheese, burger. Now look I'd be lying if I said the burger wasn't delicious, but I really wasn't too hungry at all, yet to appease Benson I ate half of it. He wasn't too happy, but he was happy that I had some protein in me.

It seems like your body is very fragile. You need good protein in you, and we will work back to having you eating normally. He rubbed my shoulder as we parked in front of the law firm.

Are you ready? I am. *Would you like for me to stay here?* No, please come with me. He nodded and got out of the car. I really liked that he offered to stay behind. That showed me that he was respectful of others' boundaries. It really said a lot about him, and in normal circumstances I would have probably wanted him to stay back, but not now.

I needed someone with me, and no I am not talking about a lover. I just needed someone who cared about me, to be with me during these tough times. I was blessed that Benson was that person, but enough of that I had to get myself out of the car.

While Benson was unloading my chair, I opened my door, and I undid my seatbelt. Then I positioned my legs over the front door. They were feeling lighter than usual. That meant I was getting stronger. That made me feel hopeful.

The breaks are on. You can climb right in. Thanks Benson. I grabbed onto the side of the chair and I carried my body onto it. Once in it, I buckled myself up, and I undid the breaks. I'm ready. *Let's go.*

I followed Benson to the front of the building. It looked like your typical lawyer-legal office. The doors were jet black. You couldn't see inside of it. The lettering of the place was in white letters on the door, including their time of service. Once Benson pulled the door open the familiar *bing, bing* noise rang.

The smell of the place hit my face like a fly on a summer day. The smell of books, papers and office spray. Not the best smell ever, but I didn't care because there was a little ramp to get inside. It was an equitable place..

They were wheelchair accessible. *Welcome in,* a young guy in a suit greeted us. *Do you have an appointment today?* Yes. *With who?* Allison Kipyegon. *Ah, are you Ms. Lucianna?* Yes, I am. *Perfect, right this way ma'am.* We accompanied the young man down the hall and to the fourth door on the right. He knocked twice, and Allison Kipyegon said, "Come in."

I wheeled myself in, and she stood up. She had a sparkling white smile. She gave me her hand and I shook it. *I am so glad to meet you, Lucianna. Let me make some room for you.* She moved one of the chairs from her desk, and signaled for me to take its place. I did, and Benson sat on the other chair. She then thanked the young man, and she shut the door behind him as he walked away.

Allison Kipyegon had an interesting look to her. She was dressed in a beautiful floral dress. Her hair was shaven off, and she had a beautiful pearl necklace on. She looked like a mixture of professional- and "I don't let my profession define me aesthetically." I loved it.

Firstly, I am beyond sorry for what happened to you, and Francisco. He was an amazing man. A pure heart. My condolences go out to you. She handed me a tissue. I didn't even realize that I was crying. It broke my heart hearing someone talk so kindly about Francisco. Especially since he had no one but me in his life.

That poor soul. Wait, what had happened to his body? Throughout these four months my mind had been so clouded that the idea had not even entered my brain. Was he buried? Was he cremated? I asked Allison hastily.

Sweetie, I know you have a lot of questions, so ask everything you want. This is a safe space. She placed her hand on my back, and calmed me down a bit. What happened to his body?

Francisco was a smart and bright man. He was buried per his request. He is buried in Pere La Chaise Cemetery. His tombstone has not been placed because he wanted you to design it. I dried my eyes and smiled.

My best buddy really thought about everything, didn't he? *Yes, he did. He cared so much about you. He left everything to you, and it won't be taxed because all the money is in his account, which you are a co-owner of.*

She handed me a paper. It contained a username, and a password. She then handed me a phone. A scratched up phone, but an intact phone. It was *Francisco's Motorola Razr 60 Ultra. You can use that account and ask for your own debt card, or you can also use his debt card.* She handed me his wallet.

My hands trembled as I took it. I carefully opened his leather wallet. Inside was a license, and two cards. His debt, and his credit card. There were 60 dollars in it as well. I lost it.

The smell that came from his wallet was the perfume that he always wore. I didn't even know the name of it, but it smelled strong enough to make your head hurt a tad. He loved it though. Benson handed me a tissue, and I dried my eyes out again.

Through tears, burgers and lumps in my throat I thanked Allison for being such a great lawyer. I asked her if she had gotten paid for this, and she would soon. Francisco left her a percent of what he had which ended up being around ten thousand dollars. I was glad Allison would finally get that money once I signed the papers. You may sign here. I signed the papers, and swiped Francisco's card.

Allison thanked us, but right before we left her office she told me that my sister had indeed tried to gain access to Francisco's estate. Thankfully everything was blocked, and a cease and desist was sent to her by Allison herself.

I guess this all happened in a zoom call where Jazmine tried saying I wasn't right in my head, and every other thing she could think of. Allison wasn't having it, and hung up the call from Jazmine and her lawyer.

Apparently she was livid. That made me beyond happy, and with that Allison gave us the address to the cemetery, but before we left I took her card with me. Jazmine was a snake after all. I may need Allison sooner than expected.

CHAPTER 25

Paying For The Evidence

With everything taken care of, I left her office feeling secure and content. Not only had I protected everything Francisco worked so hard for, but I was finally going to pay my respects to him. I knew it wouldn't be easy, but I hoped it would bring me some sense of closure.

We're about ten minutes away. Benson's voice gently broke through my thoughts after giving me a few quiet moments to myself. I appreciated that. It had been a difficult meeting at Allison's. It was much heavier than I had expected.

I hadn't realized I would learn where my brother was resting. Somehow, my mind had buried that truth, as if keeping it hidden would make it less real. But now there was no escaping it. He was gone.

Pere La Chaise Cemetery is truly beautiful. I was there once for a friend's grandma's service. There are a lot of wonderful trees, and there is a pond near there as well. Yeah, I bet. Francisco always said, "I'd rather die than look like a slob."

The irony of it all is that he chose the best cemetery for him to rest in peace. Benson nodded, and placed his hand on my shoulder. It gave me strength and comfort as we pulled up into the parking lot.

The cemetery was huge. There were willow trees all around surrounded by hundreds of tombstones. The tombstones weren't crammed together though. They had a good six feet from each other. That made me glad. It would give me some personal space to be with Francisco when I visited him in the future.

I think I will stay while you pay respect to your best friend, Lucianna. I nodded in agreement to Benson. He got out of the car and placed my chair by the door. I dragged myself into it, and then I began to wheel myself to *plot M.*

Plot M was about 400 meters away from where we parked so it took me a while to get there, but I appreciated the exercise. Feeling my muscles put in the work and getting stronger helped me mentally because I felt more independent and comfortable with my body. Regretfully, my under arms were sweating a tad when I finally reached *plot M.*

Plot M, seven spaces from the sidewalk by a maple tree. That was where Francisco was buried. I would have to go on the grass. I carefully tested my wheels out, and I was pleased to see that the grass was quite firm. My wheels would not sink, so ever so carefully I wheeled my way there till I got to *spot seven* by the tree.

The only spot in the entire plot to not have a standing tombstone, or any tombstone for that matter. The sole area that didn't have grass covering it. It was still fresh. I could just imagine how he looked down there. How that sweet innocent boy was decomposing. Why, Francisco? Why did you have to leave me? Why did you have to go?

The world is cruel without you my brother. I told Francisco as I looked down to where he was buried. I wanted him to know that I was having a conversation with him. He deserved that respect.

Brother, it really should have been me, and not you. Your heart was much too big, and I guess it was too enormous for this world. I know you are looking out for me, and just know that I will never let you down.

Brother, I also want to tell you that I am done being the walking pad that I was. I am going to live my life to the fullest, and I'm done caring about Jazmine being in my life. Franisco, I know you would not want me to even seek revenge on her, and I won't do that. What I will do though is seek justice.

Her crimes, and everyone in her little circle that did us wrong will not go unpunished. My brother, your death will not be in vain. And again, I promise you that I will not seek revenge, but justice. Francisco, with the money you left me I will restart my life. I promise you that my brother.

Not only with my mentality, but my career. I loved working in education, but in my heart I know that I will make the most difference working with disabled people. Brother, I want you to be the first to know that I will go back to school for physical therapy.

The money you left me with, will help me achieve my goals and dreams. You are always with me, and I will visit you once a week for the rest of my life. I will travel the world, and you will always be in my heart seeing these new places with me. I will always talk highly about you, and you will live alongside me until my last breath.

Francisco, oh how I miss and need you so much. Why did you have to go? I yelled with so much momentum and frustration that I caused my own body to thrust forward. Immediately, I lost my balance and landed on the floor. I was still attached to my chair as I laid covered in grass and dirt. That should have upset me even more, but I couldn't help but laugh.

This was something stupid that would have happened to me if Francisco had been with me. I could imagine Francisco just laughing at me as I struggled to unlatch my chair, and put it rightside up.

The moment was too funny, and just for a minute or two it felt like he was alive, and that we were having a special moment together. It was beautiful. *Ma'am, we are about to close the cemetery for the day*. Huh?

I turned around and squinted my eyes. There was a security guard flashing a light at me. Woah. I didn't know how long I had spent with Francisco, but it was dark now. Fuck, Benson! Was he still there?

I looked past the security, and saw his car still parked there. Sorry, sir I told the guard, and I began to wheel myself back to Benson. See you soon, my brother, I quietly told Francisco as I wheeled as fast as I could back to Benson.

I was mortified by the time I reached his car. He must be bored out of his mind. That was so rude of me to do, but I didn't do it on purpose. I really lost track of time, and all I could think of was Francisco. He was not with me in life anymore, but I felt his spirit today. He was in my heart.

That thought brought peace to me, and with a smile on my face I made my way over to Benson. *Knock, knock*, I pounded lightly on his car's window. He didn't budge. I peeked through his blacked out windows. I could see that he was watching some sort of cartoon. How adorable I thought, and I knocked a little harder to get his attention.

He swung his head back in surprise. Sorry, I muttered as I opened the passenger door. He instantly got out of the car and came to greet me. He had a smile on his face. He didn't even look mad that I had made him wait for me for so long.

I, on the other hand, felt bad. I am so sorry for keeping you waiting, Benson. I really lost track of time. Benson, being the sweet guy he was, got down to eye level with me and said, *"Don't ever apologize for paying respects to Francisco."*

It was at that moment that I fell head over heels for him, and I didn't know what got the best of me, but his face was so close to mine that I couldn't resist. I kissed him. I kissed his soft lips, and what shocked me even more was that he kissed me back.

He pressed his lips against mine, and it was magical. Sparks beyond sparks. I was on cloud 9. It felt like I was floating in the air. I hadn't felt this way since, well, Jake! This was intense, but I had to be cautious, so after a few seconds I pushed my head back and apologized to him.

Don't apologize, I have been wanting to do that for a while now. My face felt flushed. I didn't know what to do or say, so I just blurted out the first thing that was in my mind. I don't have clothes, can we stop at *Walmart* so I can get a few things?

Anything you want. He giggled, which of course made me even more embarrassed. I didn't say a single word as we drove to the *Walmart*. Nonetheless, I was a mess inside. Had I just ruined an amazing friendship?

Francisco came into my mind and said, *"no."* I didn't believe much in fate but weirdly enough, at that very moment Benson reached for my hand. His hand was surprisingly a tad rough, but I didn't mind that. In fact, I liked it.

It was the first time I held a manly hand. I felt safe with him holding mine, and I think we were both nervous because not a word was said between us until we reached the *Walmart* parking lot.

Shall we go in? Yes, please. We got out of the car, and I began wheeling myself, but unfortunately with just three turns of my wheels I noticed how difficult it was for me to move my chair. The gravel at the parking lot was rough. My chair was meant more for inside than outside.

Also, it was hard to wheel myself through the different departments because some spaces were too narrow for my chair. It was those little things that you didn't notice when you were able-bodied, but when you are disabled they make life much more complicated.

This wasn't right, but maybe one day I could be an advocate for change for the disabled community. One day I would make a difference, but for now it was shopping time.

After about an hour I had five pairs of undies, and socks. I had also secured some plane shirts, and some blue jeans. Lastly, two pairs of pjs. Not much, but enough to get me going until I figured out what would happen next in my life.

The grand total came out to be one hundred and thirty dollars. Not too shabby, but I wasn't quite finished shopping yet. After *Walmart,* I wanted to stop by and buy a cheap phone, but it was already 8 p.m. I would have to wait another day.

I could tell Benson was tired, so instead I kept my mouth shut, and we headed back to his place. *I have to go to sleep now, but I am sure you have a million things to do tomorrow. I have a spare phone that I'll leave on the kitchen table for you tomorrow. You do have to set it up with a service though. Does that sound good?*

It is like you read my mind Benson. I desperately need a phone. Thank you. *My pleasure.* He walked over to me, and gave me a kiss on the cheek. It melted my heart, but I didn't want him to notice, so I wished him a good night and I headed to my room. I was fatigued.

It was 10 p.m, and I had had a very physical day. My body needed the rest, and so did my mind. Tomorrow was going to be a busy day. From sending my court decree to my insurance, and finally getting access to my own care again. To setting up doctor appointments, and everything in between. It was time to go night night. I closed my eyes and went to sleep.

Squeak, squeak, squeak, I awoke to the noise of sneakers gliding against the polished floor. It was Benson. I recognized the sound his shoes made. I heard that noise so many times before when I was in the hospital. It made me smile, and brought some comfort in me knowing I was with him.

Yet, I had to be careful. I had to draw a line between our friendship and a bubbling romance. I couldn't nose dive into anything without taking care of myself first, and that meant knowing more about my condition and the prognosis.

Also, getting Francisco the justice he deserved. Once I did those two things I could focus on the pleasures of life, so without further ado, it was time to get started with my day!

I quietly got off my bed, and I began my entire routine. From stretching for an hour to brushing my teeth and changing. It was all getting easier now. My arm muscles did not ache with every moment, and I felt more confident. I was hopeful that was the proper treatment,

I could even start to lift a bit. Hopefully that would trigger some hunger in me because I had none.

Regardless, I knew that eating was important to recovery, so I ended up eating one banana and a half with some orange juice. It wasn't much, but it would help. After breakfast I grabbed the phone that Benson had left on the table, and I wheeled over to the desk top.

I knew what service I would get. The same one that I had before. It was a reliable prepaid service, *Mint Mobile.* It wouldn't be too complicated to register with them. They offered an esim option, and that would work fine with the old *Samsung 23 Ultra* that Benson had left me.

Done, and done. I had a new number within twenty minutes. Gosh, the independence that I felt after that was incomprehensible. If one did not have a phone in this life, then one couldn't do anything!

Now next on my list was getting my insurance back under my control. I looked up the number online, and after spending two hours speaking to about five different people, *Anthem* was finally able to get me back in charge of myself.

I had to scan my court decree like ten times, but it was easy with a smartphone. *Ugh,* I felt really joyful when I was finished. The insurance was the last thing that Jazmine had over me. I was now fully independent to do what I needed to do, so now it was time to find a doctor.

That wasn't too hard to accomplish. There were a few doctors who worked with quadriplegics, but only two who took my insurance. I chose the one with the best reviews, and I called their office.

I was delighted to find out that they were accepting new patients, and that they had an opening tomorrow because of a cancellation. I booked my appointment, and I took a deep breath. Now that I was done with my things, it was time to seek justice for Francisco.

I had to call the creep of a man. My arm shook as I entered his phone number. Images of him touching me flashed before my eyes. My phone dropped straight to the floor. This was too much, but I couldn't just give up.

I steadied myself and reached down for my phone. I dialed his number and it began to ring. *Hello?* This is Lucianna. I have the money now. When can I get the evidence? *Give me a sec.*

His arrogant deep voice filled me with hate. I hated that I had to deal with him, but I despised myself even more for fearing him. There was no doubt in my mind that I would need therapy when all of this was over.

Meet me at the park behind the hospital in one hour. Don't be late. I confirmed. I hung up the phone, and I immediately made a fake *Google* email. When I was done with that I bought a *Google* gift card and then I downloaded the *Uber* app.

Soon after I downloaded one of those disposable phone number apps, and I had a fake number which I used to create a false *Uber* account, and then I uploaded my gift card onto that. I did this to avoid being traced, and then I was set.

I requested a ride right away. *Your driver is six minutes away.* That gave me enough time to erase my browsing history, and to safely get outside and lock the door. The driver was pulling up to the entrance of the apartments by the time I saw him.

He parked right away when he saw me. He was a sweet older man. Maybe in his mid 80s. He had a hunch on his back. His face was filled with wrinkles, and his hands trembled as he lifted my chair to the trunk. I felt bad for him, but I couldn't put my own chair away.

You have an appointment today? He asked me. I told him yes. I did not want to engage more in conversation, but he had a lot to say. He basically told me his whole life story. He was lonely. Apparently his wife died a year ago, and his life hasn't been the same. His story touched my heart, and made me forget my problems for a while. I thanked him for that.

You are sweet, and you have made my day by sharing your story with me. He smiled at me as he parked his car at the park. *Have a great day young lady.* You too sir. He left, and wasting no time at all, the perverted creep pulled out from behind a large oak tree and drove to me.

He stationed his vehicle, and without asking me tossed me into the driver's seat. Then he tossed my chair to the back of his truck. A loud boom shook my ears. That couldn't be good for my chair. Where are we going? I asked him with a firm, but respectful voice.

I didn't want him to know that I was scared, but I also didn't want him thinking that I didn't respect him. *We are going back to my pad. That is where I have all the evidence. I am not stupid to bring everything out in the open.*

I nodded in understandment, and I stayed quiet the remainder of the fifteen minute drive to his house, and as did he. When we pulled up to his house he hit a button on the remote that was clutched on his visor. The garage door creaked open.

My heart started to pound loudly. My hands started to sweat. I was truly in this man's mercy. He could easily kill me, and I was nervous not because I was afraid of death because I wasn't. I was scared that if he killed me Francisco would never get his justice. That was not something that I wanted to think about.

Let me grab your chair. I watched him as he grabbed my chair from the trunk, and again without asking grabbed me and put me onto my chair. My head got a bit of whiplash as he did that, but I didn't say anything. I just stayed quiet even as he aggressively wheeled me to his back yard shed.

A shed out of all places. The perfect place to get murdered. It even looked like a murdered shed. It was small, maybe only 8 feet tall and 10 feet in length. It was gray in color, and the paint was chipped. Even the door was hanging by a thread, yet somehow it held on as he slammed it behind us.

There was nothing in the shed. Not a single tool. It was just like being in a box. I guess I must have looked confused because the man started to laugh. *You think I'm stupid to have everything I own in a shed? Girl you must be an idiot. All my things are down here.*

I stared at him still confused as he reached to the floor and put out a hidden latch. *We are going in here, so I will have to carry you down stairs.* I didn't say a single word, but I tried to steady my head as he once again grabbed me aggressively, but this time he put me over his shoulder, and down we went.

I counted the steps. There were eleven steps to the bottom of wherever the hell we were. It was pitch black at first so I couldn't see anything, but soon bright lights came on. My pupils dilated to adjust to the light and once they did, boy was I surprised.

This underground room was beautiful. It was basically a computer dungeon. There were computers and screens everywhere. Any computer geek would have been in paradise, but I surely wasn't.

From dark blue walls, to black furniture. It gave me anxiety. Not even the fancy chandelier that hung in the middle of the room calmed my nerves. *Welcome to my world.* The creep said as he put me down on a chair.

I watched him carefully as he walked over to a desk and opened up a laptop. *Here you go, hit play.* My finger shook as I hit play. *Look, don't judge me. She is my sister, and I love her, but she has to die.*

I am tired of being second best to her. Henry still loves her. She has more friends than me. She has a better job! Every time I try to succeed in something she is always there to have the upperhand on me.

My life will never be complete until she is dead. I know it is not her fault! It is life playing a cruel joke on me. The only way for me to truly flourish is to have her gone. Are you sure that is what you want? Look, I told you to not judge me! If I could switch lives with her, and have her be the one to depend on me, I would! I would do it in a heartbeat, but that isn't our life, right?

So take this downpayment, and kill her and her faggot friend! I hate his guts. She loves him more than she loves me. The video turned off before Jazmine gave the money to the man. His face was never visible.

CHAPTER 26

The Re-emergence of Jake

My hands trembled as the psycho took the laptop from my hands. *You get all of this once you pay me.* Where can I send the money to? He handed me a slip. It had his Venmo username. Do you have wifi? *My hotpot is on.*

It should be the only one you can access here. Okay. I joined the network and downloaded *Venmo*. I created an account with a fake name, and then I transferred him 50 thousand dollars. I now had $400,000 left. *Ding.*

Looks like you are the "good sister." It took your ho-ass sister two weeks to even give me the downpayment to kill you. I ignored his comment. *Oh, and to show you how grateful I am, I will tell you that Jazmine came to see me yesterday.* He fidgeted on his laptop and handed it back to me.

I need her back in the house! I don't understand how she escaped! Someone has been in contact with her! I saw on my neighbor's camera that a man walked into the home. Whoever this sicko is, they are trying to get a hold of her finances.

I am the only one that can prevent them from taking advantage of her! Find her, and I will give you $10,000 dollars! You'll have your sister back in your home. I'll guarantee she'll do everything that you want her to do if you pay me right now.

The video ended. I looked at the killer, and he looked right into my eyes. Was he going to take me back to Jazmine? I wheeled my chair back, and I tried to look for any sort of weapon that I could use against him. He began to laugh.

Please, if I was going to take you to your bitch sister you would have already been there. She has no money. No way of paying me! You want to know what she wanted to pay me with? I didn't speak, but he played another video.

In this video Jazmine was completely naked. I felt second-hand embarrassment for her when the killer said. "Maybe if you were your sister, Lucianna, but no thank you. Either give me the money or fuck off. She cursed him out, and he slapped her. The video turned black. *See?*

I would be lying if I didn't admit the satisfaction that I got from Jazmine being slapped across the face. *Don't worry about your safety. You paid, so we are on working terms.* I nodded my head.

Here are the files you need if you want to go to the police. He handed me a thumbdrive. I took it. *Well, if that is it, I'll go ahead and drop you back off at the park.* He started walking towards the stairs, but I stopped him.

There was one more thing that I wanted from him. However, I wasn't sure if I really wanted that just yet, but still, I talked to him about it. He gave me a price. It would cost me $25,000 to do that.

I was willing to pay for that unmentionable service. However, if I wanted to go through with it, I could not report Jazmine to the authorities yet. *How about we meet in one month's time, and then you can decide if that is what you really want to do?* I nodded my head in shameful agreement. The creep was right. I needed time to think.

I had to make my decisions with a clear head. I owed that to myself, and I owed that to Francisco. One thing that I learned right before our accident was that rushing into things gets you shit.

From being embarrassed at a wedding, to being tricked by a guy. All of that happened to me because I rushed into things. I wouldn't make that mistake again. I had to be calculating, and that started now.

With everything said and done the creep took me back to the park, and I ordered an *Uber* back to the apartment complex where Benson lived. Once there I took a stroll around the beautiful park that surrounded the apartment complex.

It looked and felt magical. Fall was in the air. The colors of the leaves were brown, red and orange. The smell of the dying grass was fresh. I could see squirrels running up and down the trees. Doing their best to save for the coming winter.

I also heard the birds chirp here and there. Many of them were going south for the coming cold. It was soothing, and I spent over three hours just outside. I simply parked my chair under a tree, and I just let the fresh fall breeze soothe my soul.

I needed this moment to clear all the clutter in my head. Over the past four months all my brain had done was act on over drive. Thus, the consequences to me as an individual were awful. I was no longer a nice person. I knew this because in my heart, all I wished was the ill will of others.

I wanted to see Jasmine burn in hell. Paying for her crimes was not good enough anymore. I needed to see her suffer to the point that she prayed for death. Francisco would not want that.

That was exactly why I would use this month to heal mentally before I made a decision that quite possibly was already made, but I owed it to my brother and to myself to at least finalize my choice without anger. *Phew.*

I breathed a sigh of relief at that thought, and I slowly wheeled myself back to Benson's apartment. Once there, I turned on the TV, and I watched *Supernatural.* Not worrying about anything in particular but healing my soul.

About 2 hours into the show I ate two more bananas and a cup of water. It was getting easier to eat, and even though my body was still malnourished, I felt overall stronger. My mind was also clearing up, and I didn't know what triggered this, but I decided to google my and Francisco's accident.

I guess I was curious to know why the police never came to a conclusion over who ran us over. Why was it impossible for them to not find that perverted creep? *Hit & Run at Ralphs, 34 Year Old Dead After Hit & Run.*

There were two articles on us, and both had no new information. Just what I knew. Damn. That broke my heart. Did the police not care to investigate further after they found out that I was a quadriplegic, and that Francisco was a gay man with no family?

That had to be it. The police only came once to the hospital, and never again. That was beyond fucked up, but once the truth came to light I would make sure to expose the authorities and their lack of action as well.

As a matter of fact I would start on that now. I wheeled myself over to the computer and I opened up a *Google Doc.* I copied and pasted the articles. I specifically highlighted the part of the news report of the chief speaking on the local news.

He was saying, "We will not stop till that murderer is found." After a quick *Public Records* search I found out that they never even opened up an official investigation. At that point I wasn't even in disbelief. I simply saved the reports, and I logged off the desktop.

Benson would be home soon, and I wanted to look nice when he arrived. I went to the restroom, and I looked at myself in the mirror. My hair was getting long, but still not the correct length for a pony tail, so instead I combed it till it was nice and straight. The natural shine that my hair radiated was slowly coming back.

As for my face I didn't have any makeup, but there was a chapstick in the restroom drawers. I pulled it out and applied it to my lips. It didn't give me any color to my lips, but it did make them appear glossier which brightened up my hollowed face.

I no longer had a washed out look. My natural brown skin was coming back. Soaking up some rays at the park really helped me. I smiled at myself in the mirror. For the first time since the accident, I did not feel totally ugly.

I know we shouldn't get our self worth from our looks, but it felt nice to look good. Especially when one has looked like a foot for months. *Ha*. With a smile on my face I left the restroom, and I headed back to the living room to an exhausted looking Benson.

He was on the couch with his feet on the coffee table. His eyes were closed, and he was breathing heavily. It didn't take a genius to see that he had just had a hard day. I felt bad. I didn't want to inconvenience him with my presence, but I wanted to do something to help him, but what could I do?

Maybe a simple hug would help him? I quietly wheeled myself over to the couch, and I reached over his back. I placed my arms around his broad shoulders and I squeezed tightly. He jerked up in surprise, but once he felt my hands he eased up and brought his shoulders down. We didn't say a single word, but I hugged him until my arms got sore. When I let go I wheeled myself over to face him, but he was asleep.

A warm feeling passed through my body. He felt safe with me so he let his own guard down and went to sleep. He was the cutest. I would let him rest. I quietly went into my room. I got into bed, and I closed my eyes. Slowly but surely I drifted to sleep.

That night I did not remember having any nightmares, but when I woke up I was drenched in sweat. Had I had a terrible dream, or was it the nerves of going to the doctor and getting a proper prognosis?

Probably the latter. Truth of the matter be, I was scared. I was scared to hear that I'd never be able to walk again. The last time a doctor spoke to me, part of my vertebrae were still bruised.

Well we would see. For now I had to try to get myself in a better mood, and that meant stretching. I carefully did all of my stretches, and when I was finished, I made sure to be thankful for all the movement that I did have. Gratitude was key in my life now.

Just five months ago I couldn't even speak. I had to be thankful. That's right Lucianna, be appreciative for what you can do. With my self affirmation out of the way, I wheeled myself to the living room to see if Benson was there, but it was empty.

It was already 8:30 a.m, so he was at work. Hopefully I'd see him tonight, but back to me. I had about four hours until my appointment, and I knew exactly how I wanted to spend that time. Shopping.

I wanted to make myself feel confident again. Even though I was in a wheelchair it didn't mean that I couldn't dress nicely! That's right Lucianna. It was *Uber* time. I quickly ordered one, and then I left Benson's apartment.

I wheeled myself to the front entrance. The *Uber* arrived within five minutes and the driver was almost as sweet as last time. She was a lady possibly around my age. She had similar laugh lines to me.

She was chirpy and had no issue putting my chair in her trunk. She was the type of person who shared her entire life with strangers. By the time I reached the mall I knew that she was doing *Uber* on the side because her ex husband was not giving her child support.

We are here, I am on the clock for another 4 hours. Do you want me to pick you up? Of course. *Here is my number, text me and then I'll request you on the Uber app.* Sounds perfect. I smiled at her as I made my way over to *Macy's*.

It was one of the main stores at the mall. It had its own section. I was joyful that they had a button to press that opened the door. That really helped, and the doors were wide. My chair easily slid through.

Upon entering the store I was overwhelmed with the smell of perfume, but surprisingly this time I enjoyed it. It gave me a sense of normalcy, and at the end of the day that was all that I wanted.

Now let's get shopping. I began to wheel myself around the store, and sadly that was when I saw once again how difficult it was for me to even get through the racks of clothes. Everything was cluttered and tightly jammed. It was impossible to even choose clothes.

For example, I had seen a beautiful blouse, but I couldn't reach it without getting entangled by other attire. I felt frustrated until an older lady approached me. She was also shopping. *Hola, mi nombre es Christina. ¿Quieres que te ayude a buscar ropa?* She was the sweetest thing.

She had volunteered to help me look for clothes. She herself had a walker, yet she found a way to maneuver through the racks of clothes and she helped me pick out a blouse, one nice winter jacket and a cute purple dress. Muchas gracias, Christina. Eres un ángel. *No te rindas mija.*

Jamas! She told me to never give up, and I said never! I thanked her and we parted ways. People like her deserve the world. She put me in a fantastic mood, and I paid for my clothes. However, I still needed one item: shoes. The ones that I had were practically falling apart.

They were the shoes that I got from the hospital donation center. *Gray Nike* walking shoes. Easy to put on and off. I liked them, and I wanted a simple pair like these, but also a pair that I could tie. That way my fingers would get a workout.

Sadly, they didn't have that at *Macy's* so I headed to *Foot Locker, and if my* memory serves me right, it was just next to *Macy's. Eureka!* It was. Things were going my way today, and to make things better the store was empty. I easily got one of the employees to help me.

I told him my size and exactly what I needed, and I kid you not he brought me exactly what I wanted. A nice pair of black slip on *Nike* shoes, and a beautiful pair of purple *Hokas.*

Perfect with all that said and done, I pulled out my phone and I texted my nice driver. She responded immediately, and sent me a ride request on the *Uber* app. I accepted and I began to wheel myself back into *Macy's.*

The store was getting busy now. It was 11:30 a.m, and the makeup personnel were busy applying foundation on several women in chairs. Other employees were busy handing out perfume samples.

I was glad that I was given several samples. It meant that I wasn't being discriminated against. It felt nice that at least when it came to shopping I was still seen as "normal," as horrid as that sounded.

Anyway, by the time I reached the exit I had like four perfume samples. Needless to say, I couldn't be happier as the sliding doors opened and the fresh fall air hit my face. I could breathe again. I laughed to myself as goosebumps ran down my arms.

It was a little chilly, but I wouldn't put on my jacket yet. There was no point since my *Uber* driver was only two minutes away. I could withstand the chill for that time. Plus it made me happy that my arms could feel it. It brought a smile to my face, but that smile soon disappeared.

A duo of women and a man that looked oddly familiar stepped up beside me. My stomach immediately turned as I saw his wavy brown hair bounce up and down. I tried to avoid his stare but it was too late. He had seen me. His mouth shot wide open.

His eyes got wide, and he came to me. *Lucianna!* He practically shouted, getting the attention of the two women. *We have been looking for you for days now! Where have you been?*

Oh my gosh I need to call Jazmine right now and let her know that I found you. I was in shock that I couldn't even speak. *She has been hysterical since that man kidnapped you!* Jazmine I found Lucianna! He was on the phone.

I heard Jazmine say, don't let her leave! She must be in danger! He came over and grabbed my chair. I was stunned. I couldn't believe that I just stood frozen. He was starting to wheel me back to his car, and I couldn't even move!

A small crowd of people started to form after hearing his screams. I don't know how I managed, but at that very moment I was able to yell, "help!" The duo of ladies stopped him dead in his tracks, but he explained to them that I in fact had been kidnapped.

I felt awful for what I did next because I know Jake really believed that he was helping me, but I couldn't let him take me back to Jazmine's. LET ME GO! I SHOUTED WITH ALL MY MIGHT! He stopped dead in his tracks and looked at me. He was stunned. He had no clue what Jazmine had done to me, but I made it clear to him.

Jazmine is evil, and doesn't care about me! I managed to yell at him. She just wants my money! Don't align yourself with her. She even tried impregnating me with her embryos! He backed away, and left me.

The crowd of people who had surrounded us looked at me in disbelief, and then the duo of ladies who I had seen earlier came to me. *Are you okay?* One of them asked. *Should I call the police?* A man inquired. *I think she needs to go to the hospital,* another person said. They were all looking at me with pity in their eyes. I needed to get away but they had formed a circle around me.

I know they didn't mean harm, but they were causing me distress. I was about to cry, but then my *Uber* driver came to the rescue. She broke her away into the crowd of people that were hammering me with questions and she got me in her car. She was like a super woman.

CHAPTER 27

The Prognosis & The Decision

Before I knew it I was safely secured in her car. She had us on the main roads in no time. I didn't know how to thank her, so I simply said, "thanks." She acknowledged my gratitude with a slow nod.

I heard everything you said back there. I am sorry you went through that. You are a brave woman, and you deserve to be heard. Maybe one day. *Why not today?* What do you mean? *I'm part of a group of not just women, but people who have been hurt by their spouses, loved ones and strangers.*

We meet every Sunday morning at the local rec center. Here is the card. If you want I can pick you up next Sunday and the ride is on me. I took the card from her. *Acidulous. Don't get scared about the name of our group. It's a play on words.*

We have had acidic people in our lives, but in turn that has helped us to become individuals that can handle any sour thing that this journey of life throws at us. Acidulous, huh. I like that name, I must admit. *I'm glad you do.* The idea sounds tempting, but I don't want to group myself just yet to any organization.

Oh you won't. If you don't feel comfortable you don't have to come back. I looked at her as she spoke. She seemed so calm and relaxed. Her face was neutral. She didn't seem to be gaining anything from this. She just wanted to help.

You know what? I'll take you up on that offer. What time is the meeting on Sunday? *At 11 a.m.* I'll be there, and I would love it if you took me there. *Sounds like a plan.*

Oh, and before I forget, I am Maribelle. What is your name? My name is Lucianna, and thank you so much for helping me Maribelle. *It is my pleasure. I hope we can become friends.*

Hopefully. I said as she parked the car and got my chair out. *Do you want me to put both breaks on?* Yes, please. She locked my chair into place, and then gave me space as I got back into my chair which I appreciated. It was becoming easier to get into my chair too. That made me glad.

Now that you are safe and secured, see you on Sunday, Lucianna. Bye for now, I told her as I made my way up the small ramp to get to the doctor's office. She drove away as the sliding doors opened. *Hello, are you here for an appointment?* Hi, yes I am.

What's your name? My name is Lucianna. *Welcome, Lucianna. First time patient?* Yes. *Alright, I am going to give you some forms to sign, and when you are done you can go ahead and bring them to me.* Got it.

The receptionist handed me a clipboard with the forms, and a blue pen. I began to read over them, and it was just your basic insurance forms, and health histories. Boring things, until I remembered that I was no longer the same. I was disabled. This was going to be a tricky and personal form to fill out.

My hands began to sweat as I wrote. This was the first time in my life where I had a medical history. It pained me, but I kept on writing until I was finished. I then gave the forms back to the receptionist.

Thank you, a nurse will call you when the doctor is ready for you. Thanks. I wheeled myself over to the waiting area. There were only two other people there. A man who was also in a wheelchair, and the woman who was with them. I smiled at them, and just waited nervously.

After all, this was the moment that I was fearing. Would I ever be able to walk again? My stomach started to twist, but I stopped myself. Focus, Lucianna. Look around you, and don't think negatively.

I began to look around the office. It was nice and clean. The tile floor was shiny. The wooden chairs with pillow covers looked elegant. The large windows in the office illuminated the room. It even smelled nice. Like polished apple sauce cleaner.

The best thing though was that it looked more like a hang out lobby than a doctor's one. I guessed because it was also a big place. *Lucianna? A soft spoken voice pulled me out of my tour of the office daze. *Are you Lucianna?* A petit nurse smiled at me as I said, "yes." *Right this way, please.*

I followed her as she took me to the vitals rooms. She took my pressure, temperature and all of that good stuff. When she was done she brought me to a big empty white room with a desk, a bed and nothing more.

The doctor will be with you shortly. Won't you ask about my medical history? I was confused because she barely said a word to me. *The hospital sent us everything they had on you. Don't worry sweetie you are in good hands.* Oh okay.

Sweetie, I know you are nervous, but you are in good hands. We are here to help. My shoulders eased a bit. I felt better knowing that they had my medical record, and that the nurse was as sweet as could be even though she wasn't as talkative. *The doctor will be here soon.* Alright I whispered as she left.

The doctor must have been right outside the room because not even a minute passed when I heard a gentle knock on the door. *Knock, knock,* the door creaked back open. *Hello Lucianna, this is Dr. Marqueez. How are you doing today?*

A little old man with white hair and big glasses stared emphatically at me. I instantly liked him. Dr. Marqueez looked caring and like a good person. *Are you feeling nervous? In pain?* I am very nervous, doctor. I am sorry. *Oh no need to be. You are in good hands. Lucianna, you know you are a brave and hard working lady.*

I read through your medical record this morning, and your vertebrae damage is right at about C5. Do you know what that means? Kind of, but not really. *It means that had your injury been higher you would have been on a ventilator.* I nodded my head because I already knew that. *I am delighted that you have so much hand dexterity because hand movement is usually reduced drastically with that type of injury.*

Now when it comes to walking, the news may not be so glamorous. I held my breath. *Based on your last scan there was still a lot of bruising on the C5 vertebrae so the doctors could not tell how injured it was, but I will ask the radiologist technician to perform a scan on you right away. After that I will come back and speak to you.* Okay doctor. *Don't worry, I am here for you, and I will do all in my God giving duty to help you.*

I hope so I muttered quietly as he left the room, and the nurse came back. She wheeled me into the imaging side of the doctor's office. My palms were a wet mess. My armpits were equal puddles of water. *The radiologist will come in shortly, okay?* Okay I whispered.

This office moved fast because the radiologist arrived by the time I had parked my chair. She was all smiles. It made me feel safe. She had "Mother Claus" energy, and I really needed that.

I am going to take you over to this machine with your permission of course. May I? Yes. *With your help I will place you on this bed. The scan will last about 15 minutes. Does that sound good?*

Yes, I repeated shyly. She began to wheel me over, and then with her help I got onto the cold machine bed. She punched in some things on the computer and then the CT scan started. *Don't move dear. I'll be back in 15 minutes.*

I felt nothing but fear while I was in the CT scan. So many things were going on in my head. Both good and bad. I felt hope, but also fear. Maybe I could regain the ability to walk? Maybe my vertebrae were just bruised? Or, maybe I would never walk, and maybe my bladder will always have a mind of its own? So many thoughts. Not knowing was killing me inside.

All done. You did fantastic. Can I help you back into your chair, or do you want to do it yourself? You are fairly strong. I smiled at the radiologist. She was probably tired of carrying patients, and knew that I could get myself off. I got this, ma'am. Just hold my chair, please. She held my chair in place, and then she wheeled me back into the lobby. Now there were three other people there.

Wait right here and when your results are in someone will come get you. Okay, ma'am. She left me, and now it was a sit and wait game. My nerves were killing me, so I pulled out my phone to distract myself.

Surprisingly, there was a message from Benson. *I hope you are feeling great. Whatever they tell you we will get through this together (heart emoji). The message was sent two hours ago.* My heart began to flutter, and I responded back to him.

Your message means the world to me. I just finished a CT scan and they will get the results soon. I'll keep you posted. Sent. Benson's message made me feel cared for, and once again the emotions came flooding back to me. Here I was feeling cared for while Francisco was dead.

He had no one with him. No one but me. Now he was no more. My sweet boy was gone. My tears flooded my face, and I began to sniffle. Gosh I just missed him so damn much. My stomach knotted just thinking of him being in a morgue. No one looking for him. No one.

All thanks to the demonic, reptilian, Jazmine. She would get what was coming to her, but for now the best thing to do was focus on my health. I had to calm myself, so I wheeled over to a table that had magazines.

Hmm. I hadn't read an actual magazine since like 2012. Funny. I picked up a celebrity mag and began to read it. I need a distraction from my real life. Ironically, it was nice reading gossip that wasn't about me.

Lucianna, the doctor is ready for you. Coming I said, and placed the magazine down. The soft spoken nurse greeted me as I wheeled my way toward her. *Come to this room please.* I went inside, and immediately noticed that this room was different from the other two.

It was bigger, and there was a large 60-inch monitor in it. There was also a big table with medicines, and medical tools. *The doctor will be right with you.* Before she left she put my file on the cabinet that was hanging on the door. My heart began to thump. I wanted to reach out and read my files, but they were too high up, so I waited.

I waited for an agonizing seven minutes and then the doctor came in. He pulled my file out of the cabinet. *Hello, Lucianna. Your results are in. Let me have a seat next to you.* He pulled his spinny doctor chair and sat next to me.

The sweat in my temples was getting into my eyes. He began to read my file. I could not read his expression thanks to his giant glasses. The wait was killing me as he flipped between pages, and back to the same pages. He did this for what felt like an eternity until he at last stood up.

Lucianna we have some good news, and some bad news. The cliche. *What do you want to hear first?* The bad. He nodded slowly. *As of now, with today's technology you won't be able to walk again. Your spinal cord is severely damaged in the C5 vertebrae.* I knew it. I knew it, but it still hurt.

Hearing it out loud sent my head spinning. I felt nauseous. The old me was truly gone, but to the doctor I said, "Go on." *The good news is that all your organs are working perfectly. With proper care you can live a healthy normal life.*

Even your bladder is great. We can work on getting you into a normal eating schedule that will help predict your bowel movements. There are a lot of things we can do, and with your own personal observation you can learn when your body needs to go.

I nodded my head, and faked a smile. The doctor went on talking for what felt like hours. He referred me to a therapist that would help keep my muscles from deteriorating at the rate that they were. He also put in a word to my insurance to get a new chair.

A chair that would allow me to live a more independent life. Furthermore, now he wanted me to stay with a catheter at night, but he also wanted to see me in a month to see if it could be removed. I could then go on with diapers.

There was so much said. I got pamphlets, and everything one could think of. I thanked the doctor, and his staff, and then I went outside. My world was spinning again. I had a lot of information in my head that I would have to pick apart when I was feeling better, but for now I just wanted to talk to Benson. It was already 5 p.m, so he should be off work.

Bring, bring, bring, the phone rang as I dialed his number. *Lucianna,* before he had a chance to say another word I broke down. Through tears and sniffles I told him everything that the doctor told me. *Where are you now?* At the outside of the office. *Stay there. I am coming to get you.*

He hung up the phone. He sounded worried. I felt bad for making him feel that way, but at least he was coming to get me. It'd take him a good thirty minutes to arrive though, so I moved away from the front office. I didn't want to block the exit of anyone leaving or arriving.

I wheeled myself over to a shady area of the building where I could still see the upcoming road. There I let my mind go blank as I waited for Benson. He ended up coming in twenty minutes instead of the thirty. The poor guy looked flustered and tired when he saw me, yet he still came over and gave me a tight hug. A hug that made me feel warm and protected.

Once I was in his car I cried all over again. I let everything out, but this time I wasn't alone. Benson was holding my hand. He didn't say a single word while I cried. He just held my hand and drove.

We drove until we left the city behind, and until we got near the mountains. There he finally parked and got out of his car. He opened his trunk and came back with a cooler. I was curious at this point, so my tears stopped flowing.

He came back inside the car with the cooler, and then he let his visor down from his car. *Look at the beautiful sky.* I looked up, and I was flabbergasted with the amount of stars that I could see. I didn't grow up in a large city, but still the light pollution in my town was great. This was the first time in my life that I ever saw this many stars.

Lucianna, you see all those stars? Yes, I do. *None are as beautiful as you are. You are more than just physical beauty. Your soul is beautiful. I want to be a part of your life.* He pulled my face towards his and smiled. He had a beautiful smile.

Maybe not the straightest teeth in the world, but there was a charm to his lip curvature. *Can I kiss you?* Of course. I closed my eyes and leaned in. His moist lips pressed against mine. I could taste his cherry chapstick. I had butterflies in my stomach that had their own butterflies.

It was beautiful, and we kissed until our lips were dry. It's funny to say that, but it's true. After that he pulled out a vanilla popsicle and gave it to me.

I was not sure how he remembered, but during my stay at the hospital I had told him that I loved vanilla popsicles. What a full circle moment. Here I was holding his hand now while eating one. He, on the other hand, was eating an ice cream sandwich.

You know this is our first real date, right? Benson looked at me as he spoke. I nodded my head. He was right. This was our first true date. A date where we ended up talking for hours.

We didn't get back home till 1:00 a.m, and it was crazy to think that an entire month has passed since then. A month where I have grown so much as a person. I now have a boyfriend, a dedicated health team, and a support group of friends in *Acidulous.*

Life was getting better in every way but one. Francisco was not here and I needed justice for him and myself. Five weeks had gone and come since I last saw the creep of a "man." It was time to pay him a visit.

CHAPTER 28

The Trial

In my purse I had ten thousand dollars. I would give the creep who killed Francisco ten thousand dollars to teach Jazmine a lesson. That was my dirty secret. The favor that I had asked him for, and needed a month to think about.

Well, now I had a clear answer. I would never be happy with life if Jazmine didn't get more than just jail time. I needed her to also suffer for what she did to my brother, and to me. Even though in my heart I knew Francisco would not have wanted that. Woefully, there was no going back.

I wheeled my newly customized wheel chair to the park near Benson's apartment. Away from any camera. By the time I got to the edge of the park the creep was there waiting for me. He took me back to his place. Where Jazmine would be arriving in the next ten minutes.

She thought that this pervert had found me. He told her that I was pregnant and she couldn't resist getting me back. Cynically, as I sat in the underground shed watching through the cameras a part of me wished that she wouldn't show up.

Maybe she had changed? Maybe she didn't want to kidnap me, and make me become her oven? So many maybes, but in the end I was still a fool to have those hopes. She arrived right at the dot. The creep took her to the shed and closed the door.

She couldn't see me since I was underground, but I heard the beating. Her screams were horrific as she yelled for mercy. He laughed and laughed as he beat her mercilessly. I had advised him to only hit her in the T1-T12 vertebrae.

I wanted her to be paralyzed, but still retain the functions of her upper body. That way she could also serve her time in jail because in one weeks' time I would go to the police and report her with my evidence.

"AHHHHHH!" One last horrified scream and then everything went silent. I was sure that she had been knocked out. A guilty wave of satisfaction flowed through my body. I hated it, but I felt so much relief. Finally she got what she deserved.

As awful as this entire situation was, I did feel happy. In fact I felt so content when I saw the creep carrying Jazmine out of the shed and back into his house. I could see blood dripping from her pink jacket.

Her wig slipped off as the creep carried her away. Phase one was completed, and I would never be the same. The old Lucianna was dead, and a new one was born. A better one. A free one with a dark secret that no one would ever know. Well, I shouldn't say no one. Franscico knew. I hoped he wouldn't hate me. He wouldn't. He knew my heart and soul meant well, right? Yes he did.

Don't feel shame, Lucianna. Move on, I told myself, but before then I had to wait for the pervert to come back. It took him over two hours to return from "the hit." I had instructed him to leave Jazmine in her front door and then call the ambulance. He did just that, and he also scouted out the area for information.

She was being rushed into surgery, but she was not in any critical condition. That did bring me satisfaction. I did not want her to die. I just needed her to hurt. However, who I did want dead was the creep. I had a special surprise just for him.

When he came back and told me everything I took out shots to "celebrate." Like the fool he was, he drank not only his, but my non poisonous one without asking me for permission. As we got into his house he started to compulse. Foam came out of his mouth, and I just watched him.

I watched him and smiled as he dropped to the floor. He tried calling out for help, but I ignored him, and went back to his shed, and I took my money back. Now with a smile on my face, I grabbed a hammer that he had on the wall and I began to smash all the screens and monitors that he had.

I ensured that everything was left in pieces before I left. Now there was no evidence to use against me. Especially since I never got out of his car, and his windows were tinted, so there's nothing proving that I was ever here.

Plus, there was no way that I could be traced back here either because the creep's home was in front of a forested area of the town that bled directly into a local park. I used that to my advantage. I simply left through the back yard and after twenty-five minutes I arrived at the park where I ordered an *Uber*.

I was home before I knew it. I felt happy. I felt excited, and a tad too jittery. I needed to shower to calm myself down. My brain was going a million miles an hour. What was going on? Relax, I told myself.

I took in a few deep breaths and held them in and then let them go. I did this for a few minutes until I was calm enough to look into the mirror. I had a smile from ear to ear. My face was glowing. My skin was bright. I had a sort of light radiating from me like I never had before.

What was this? I thought to myself, but I knew the answer. I had put myself first. I also felt powerful. Moreover, I was almost finished with my justice. The last stop was filing a report against Jazmine. Nonetheless, I had to be careful.

The police would ask how I got this evidence. I couldn't let them know that I paid for it. What could I do? Think, Lucianna, think. Ah! Yes! If I mailed the evidence to myself from the creep's house it would make it seem like he was reaching out to me. Perfect!

I ended up going back to the creep's house the next day, and I mailed the evidence to myself from his home, with a letter. In that letter "he confessed to what he did," and why he beat Jazmine. He also tried to "bribe me in finishing the job."

It was all perfect, and six days later I received the mail. I showed Benson in a hurry. *Oh wow, Lucianna. I am so sorry, dear.* He hugged me tightly. I embraced him, and I cried. I cried, and I cried.

I didn't fake a single tear. I really felt the pain of it all again. Seeing the death of Francisco. Watching myself get hit. It all struck a chord in me, and I was pissed because I had to lie to the only person that I now had. That was fucked up, so through tears and sobs I said, "We have to go to the police."

I am grabbing the keys. Benson ran to the kitchen and grabbed his keys. We were in and out of his apartment in no time. He was the sweetest thing through it all. He kept asking if I was okay. *Lucianna, I am here for you. Please, just know that okay?* I nodded and put my head on his shoulder as he drove to the police station.

As we reached the parking lot I asked Benson to do all the talking. It wasn't that I didn't want to do it, but I truly couldn't. Seeing everything again had put me in a state of shock. It was traumatizing reliving all of that again.

In fact, the sheriff ended up calling the ambulance for me because my pulse would not go down. They gave me a sedative, and took me home. Benson came back about two hours later. *Jazmine, and Henry are reported.*

The investigator that I spoke to said they had enough evidence to get a warrant for their arrest. That said, Jazmine will be in hospital arrest because she is still there recovering for another week.

What do you mean? I asked. Feeling like a horrible person for lying to Benson. *Apparently her hit man did some damage to her.* Oh no. Are you serious? *Yes, but she is expected to make a full recovery.* A full recovery? My voice cracked as I asked the question.

Benson came over to hug me. He probably thought I was worried. I wasn't. I didn't feel bad for Jazmine. I felt upset because she was expected to make a full recovery. That sucked! That wasn't my plan, but hey, at the end of the day she was at least going to serve her time. It would be a fight though.

Benson informed me that we would go on trial for this. Jazmine, *and Henry will fight with all that they have. I know that this will hurt you, and the investigator said he will do his best to keep you out of it, but there will be a time where you must testify against them.*

Okay, Benson, but before we get into all of that, can you cuddle me? *Always.* Benson wrapped his arms around me. I felt secured and drifted off to sleep. The next few days were a blur.

Nonetheless, what wasn't vague in my mind was when I met up with *Acidulous* and told them everything. The group gave me great advice. "Do something positive that will change your way of thinking." That was exactly what I did.

I applied to an online university to become a physical therapist. Shockingly within just eights days of sending in my application I received an acceptance letter. I was ecstatic, and as happy as could be.

Congratulations sweetie. I knew you'd be accepted. Now how about we go and celebrate with some popsicles under the stars? I would love that. We went to the place of our first date and looked up at the stars. *You are still the brightest and most beautiful star, Lucianna. You are the kindest soul. You would never harm a single soul, and that is why I love you.*

My heart stopped. Not only had he said he loved me for the first time, but he said he loved me because I would never hurt a single soul. If he only knew that I had not just paid to have my sister hurt, but that I had killed a man. He would hate me.

That thought made me lose it. Benson was like Francisco. A kind-hearted human. I did not want to lose him like I lost my brother. I had to stop my ways now because here I was thinking of different schemes to hurt Jazmine even while she was in jail, but no, prison would be enough for her.

I had to stop while I still had the chance. I couldn't go deeper into the abyss. *Why are you crying, Lucianna?* Benson asked while looking at me with his beautiful eyes that were filled with curiosity and hope.

Once more, and for the last time I lied to him. I am crying because I love you so much too. I, of course, loved him as well, but that wasn't the reason why I had cried. *That makes me so happy!* He kissed me softly, and we gazed up to the stars until 12 a.m. We then went home.

The next day I was in for a surprise. I video chatted with his mom for the first time ever. She looked like a lovely woman. She was happy to see that her boy was gleaming with joy. I was very shy, but I loved her compliments. *You can call me mom from now on too!* My cheeks reddened when she said that, but I shook my head okay. Life was going great in every way.

I really didn't want this feeling to ever end. I was discovering new things about me. My classes were going amazing. Organic chemistry was brutal, but it kept my head active and I liked that because if it wasn't active then I would over think about my past demons.

Nonetheless, not even learning about the periodic table and balancing equations could ease my mind when I learned that Jazmine and Henry were currently incarcerated with no bail possible, and that their trial was set for six months from now.

I had a panic attack upon finding that out, but as soon as I got to Franciso's resting place my soul and mind eased. I was frequently visiting my brother during this time period. I knew that his soul was with me, but I just needed to be where his physical body was too. Especially when Jazmine started to write letters to me via her lawyer.

She wrote letters upon letters saying that it was not how she wanted our relationship to go. She had been mistaken. She was depressed. She was confused. Everything, and anything she could think of. All, but never taking accountability for her actions.

Are you reading another of Jazmine's letters? Yeah. *Do you need to be alone?* No. I smiled at Benson, and wheeled myself over to meet him at the front door. He had a smile on his face. What's so amusing huh? *Your cute face.* Oh stop. I said like a shy school girl.

How was work today? *Well, work was work, but having you to look forward to after it makes it all worth it.* You're too much. *How was your day? How did classes go?* My day has been really good. I even got an online job correcting essays for college students. It is only part time, but it will help me get some income.

That makes me happy my dear. He gave me a peck on the cheek. *Have you had dinner yet?* Yes, you will be proud. I had one entire fish fillet. *Wow.*

That is amazing Lucianna. You really are getting healthier. I love that. I am happy too.

My body is adjusting perfectly to the new therapy, and with my personal yoga my appetite is slowly returning. *That was what I was praying for. Maybe in a few weeks you'll be eating as much as me.* He gave me a sneaky stare, and I started laughing.

Yet like so many times before I felt instant guilt. Here I was laughing when my brother was dead. That thought always floated in the back of my mind, but like so many times before I did my best to correct my thinking. Francisco would not want that for me. He wanted me to be content, but something was lacking.

I needed to do something to help those who were like Francisco. Ridiculed, and abandoned for being who they were. Not necessarily just gay people, but anyone who had been discriminated against, and that's what I did. I created a foundation under my brother's name to help others out. *Fresco in Cisco Foundation.*

This foundation would give some money to those who shared a similar story to Francisco. It would only be 500 dollars and limited to 6 people once a year, but it would grow.

I would make sure of that, and that's what I did! At the six month mark, I gave away the first six scholarships, and when I met the winners I knew my heart was finally whole.

This was what I needed. Sharing Franisco's story really healed me, and it made me forget the negative. Until it was time. The day of the trail had arrived. I would see Henry and Jazmine once more.

I truly did not want to see her face ever again in my life, but I had to. The investigator told me that if I didn't testify then she could just serve a lower sentence by claiming insanity drove her to hire a hitman on us.

That was something that I could not, and would not allow. *I am here for you, Lucianna. I am with you. You are not alone.* Benson held my hand as they brought in a chained Jazmine. She was wearing a bright orange jump suit, and she had no wig. Her face had become pale.

My stomach turned upside down. I hated myself for feeling sorrow for her. She was not a good human. She was evil, yet the way she looked at me tore my heart into pieces. Her face said it all. "Save me."

Her eyes were filled with tears. My cheeks were swollen from crying. This couldn't be happening. I couldn't feel sorry for her all over again. I was cracking again, but when they brought Henry out everything changed. Jazmine started to scream hysterically.

IT WAS ALL HIS FAULT LUCIANNA! HE IS THE MASTER MIND BEHIND THIS. I WAS AN INNOCENT GIRL CAUGHT UP IN HIS LIES. PLEASE BELIEVE ME SISTER. BELIEVE ME.

"The bitch is lying!" Henry shouted back. It was all her plan. She seduced me, and ruined my life. I am sorry Lucianna for everything that I did to you. Henry looked me directly in the eyes, and I knew he was being sincere.

I ignored Jazmine's gaze for the reminder of the trail. Even as she shouted that I was lying about her impregnating me. It was rough, but by the time I was done I looked directly at the judge and told her, "Ma'ma my sister has done all these crimes, but if she agrees to see a counselor and a psychologist for the remainder of her sentencing then I will drop my charges against her.

I will only keep the charge of the murder of Francisco. The judge noted my decision, and now it was just a wait and see game. The trial had ended, and the fate of Jazmine and Henry would be revealed the following day.

What made you decide to drop the charges against your sister, honey? Seeing her so miserable, and staring at me with so much pity made me feel sorry for her. She lost her way, and deserves to serve her time in jail for what she did to Francisco, but I am not going to make her life anymore complicated.

Plus I have to keep my kind heart. That is what you love about me, don't you? *One of the thousands of things that I love about you.* Thanks, Benny, but all jokes aside I really want her to become better. *Whatever you want, I'll support you.* I know you will.

With that said and done, we went home to home to rest up for the sentencing. By the time we got home I was mentally exhausted. I was glad that we went to bed early because the next morning I was a complete mess. My head was hurting. I felt confused and nauseous. My nerves were killing me. Today was the day.

CHAPTER 29

The Trip Is Booked

Jazmine Abalos-Roberts you are hereby sentenced to 20 years without the possibility of parole for your involvement in the murder of Francisco Ontiveros. Henry Roberts you are sentenced to five years of prison with the possibility of parole after serving two years for the theft, and impregnation of Lucianna Abalos.

There it was. Loud and clear. Jazmine got what she deserved, and my Francisco got his justice. I felt at peace even with Jazmine crying and begging the judge that she was not in her right mind.

The judge told her if she didn't stop her yells her sentence would go up. That shut her right up, and she was removed from the court room. I had to leave too. I couldn't stay here any longer. Benson, can we go?

He stood up and I followed him out of the court before the crowd disbursed. Unfortunately, the local news, and to my shock the national news channels were right outside the court building. Microphones were jabbed right at my face.

Intense bright light blinded me, and my ears were filled with hammering questions. Word had gotten out of the SISTER-SISTER NOVELA as it had been titled. I wanted to just leave, but I didn't. I stopped and took the time to speak about Francisco.

Francisco was a man with nothing but kindness in his heart. He always had a smile on his face, and he put everyone before himself. My foundation *Fresco-Cisco* is here to support people like him. Those who have been abandoned and marginalized, but somehow never give up on making their dreams come true. Please support it. That is all I have to say, and that is all that I will say ever.

With that, Benson and I left directly to visit Francisco. There, I spent the entire day with my brother. I told him all about the trial, everything that had happened, everything that had led me here.

As the words left me, something inside finally settled. I felt at peace, like I could finally start living again. It was in that quiet realization that I pulled out my phone and booked two tickets to the Bahamas. Benson would need a passport.

As for you my brother like I said you will see the world through my eyes. We are going to the Bahamas, sweetie.

www.ingramcontent.com/pod-product-compliance
Lightning Source LLC
Chambersburg PA
CBHW051219130726
47988CB00001B/137

9 798989 803361